A Private Inquiry

A Private Inquiry

Jessica Mann

CARROLL & GRAF PUBLISHERS, INC.
NEW YORK

First Carroll & Graf edition 2001

Carroll & Graf Publishers, Inc.
A Division of Avalon Publishing Group
19 West 21st Street
New York, NY 10010-6805

Library of Congress Cataloging-in-Publication Data is available.
ISBN: 0-7867-0826-3

Manufactured in the United States of America

PROLOGUE

Recovering from mumps at the age of fifteen, housebound and bored, Fidelis had the idea of making an embroidery in the musical design of a Bach suite, its interwoven multicoloured stitches soaring and swooping as the sound did. The end result was a mess, as though she had been sewing in a blacked-out room, but in the pattern's chaotic curves she could discern a symmetrical shape, of two green threads which emerged from the same hole of the canvas, and ran up and apart, and then downwards, returning gradually towards each other until at the final moment they met sharply together: the shape was that of a heart.

The tune had been a favourite for nearly half a century. Fidelis was humming it now, as she wrote, 'There was no way for either of us to understand what was going on without knowing the other side of the story.'

When Fidelis had planned what to say she worked on the word processor, but these events had not yet fallen into a pattern in her mind, and now her own regular, decisive script mocked her inchoate thoughts. 'Both of us were credulous because we were vulnerable,' she wrote, and crossed the last three words out. We were vulnerable because we were credulous, she thought, and credulous because . . . Because there is a stage in life when believing people is easy and desirable. One is credulous because one wishes to be.

As her own voice, unconsciously vocalised, came to the end of the movement, she drew the remembered heart shape on her page.

She thought, there were two independent stories, which began in the same place, moved at first apart and then on converging lines until in the end they met and locked neatly together, like magnets. Go back, she thought, to the day when the threads of this story were joined and first separated. That's where this story began.

1

'I don't know why they have children in the first place if they can't be bothered to take care of them.' The witness was supposed to address the planning inspector, but her words were aimed at the public gallery and greeted with a murmur of approval. 'Mothers ought to stay at home themselves instead of going out to work, no wonder there's three million unemployed.'

'Miss Bates.' The inspector had stopped writing and was leaning forward across the awkward, sloping desk, only just able to see and be seen in spite of the cushions a clerk had brought in for her before the start of the public inquiry.

'It's unnatural, that's what it is, all these young women taking the men's jobs – '

'Miss Bates.'

'No wonder they turn into juvenile delinquents.'

'I must stop you there, Miss Bates. That's all very interesting but it isn't a material consideration in a planning decision.'

'Well then it bloody well should be. We don't want a lot of noisy brats at the end of our gardens.' The shout came from a grizzled, choleric man at the back of the hall. He stood up holding a banner, white material lettered in uneven spray paint: 'No nursery. Keep the peace.'

Some of his companions were saying 'Quite right,' and 'Nor do we,' and 'Hear hear.' A separate group, younger people, some of them holding children, began to shout back.

Mrs Pomeroy seized the gavel and rapped it on her desk. She called out, 'Quiet please,' but the disturbance, if anything, increased. The lawyers on both sides were watching with interest. She feared they were ready to be contemptuous, poised to say hers wasn't a suitable job for a woman or tell each other it took a man to keep control.

'Ladies and gentlemen,' she called, in too high a tone. She breathed in deeply and said loudly, 'I shall have to ask you to behave properly or to leave.'

'Try to make me,' a girl screamed. Early that morning, the same girl had been waiting outside the council offices with a group of other campaigners holding posters, designed like a child's drawing, and saying 'Crèche? Yes!' The inspector was inconspicuous in her discreet navy blue suit, cream silk shirt and court shoes. Known, so far, only by the name written on the notice of a Public Inquiry, she slipped unnoticed into the building. In the mayor's parlour, her 'retiring room', she used the mayor's telephone to ring home and tell her husband she was terrified.

'Don't worry,' Colin said, 'you've been doing this job for three years; that must be twenty inquiries you've sailed through, or more.'

Twenty-three, actually. But the worst Barbara had faced so far was an arrogant Queen's Counsel who had expected, wrongly, that he would be able to run rings round her.

'You'll be all right,' Colin Pomeroy said. And so, until mid-afternoon, she had been.

Barbara Pomeroy had entered Dorchester's Town Hall at nine fifty-eight, walked briskly on to the dais, opened her notebook, uncapped her pen, looked around the room in a friendly but generalised manner and on the dot of ten o'clock began to read.

'Good morning, ladies and gentlemen. This is an inquiry into an appeal made by Cox Kindergartens under section 78 of the Town and Country Planning Act 1990 against the decision of the Mid Dorset District Council to refuse planning permission for a day nursery or crèche on land at Honeysuckle Lane, Sherbury. I am Mrs B. Pomeroy and I have been appointed by the Secretary of State to determine this appeal. I will now take the names of those who wish to speak at this inquiry.'

Barbara knew many people found the system arcane and inexplicable. Obviously land use could not be uncontrolled – that was axiomatic in all developed countries – but the British system baffled outsiders, with its combination of local control, government regulation and a right of appeal against refusal of permission. Barbara was not a lawyer or a judge, she was a civil servant, but in this job, as a planning inspector, she judged.

Today there was a long list of witnesses, and numerous interested persons as well as lawyers for both sides, and Mrs Pomeroy set a brisk pace for the proceedings, speaking very little, but easily heard when she did, her voice a clear alto with sharply enunciated consonants and rounded vowels. Her creamy, freckled skin, candid blue eyes and bubbles of short auburn hair could have been those of a much younger woman, thought Dr Fidelis Berlin, but nobody much under forty would have been appointed to that powerful position.

Fidelis watched her with interest while the tedious proceedings trundled dutifully on. Evidence in chief, cross-examination, re-examination, the inspector's own questions. And the next witness. And the next.

Fidelis was sitting with the appellant, Neville Cox. At the same table were his barrister, solicitor, planning consultant and architect. Fidelis herself was an 'expert witness', ready to testify about the innocuous effect Cox Kindergartens always had on the surrounding area in other places.

Fidelis believed in 'body language'. She noticed how firmly the inspector's knees, just visible under the table, were crossed, how rigidly the shoulders were held, how tightly the pen; Mrs B. Pomeroy's back would ache later, Fidelis thought, realising the inspector was not as self-assured as she seemed. She was perfectly attentive to each speaker in turn and only indicated that she had heard enough on any point by ceasing to write, or, if that hint were not quickly taken, laying down her pen.

Neville Cox had been jubilant when they found the appeal was to be conducted by a woman. He said, 'That's a stroke of luck if ever there was one. She's got a kid of her own, she'll understand why mothers need kindergartens.'

'I'm not so sure,' Fidelis said. 'Professional women who have reached the top aren't always all that sympathetic to less successful ones.'

'I share Neville's optimism,' his solicitor said. 'I've always found women inspectors more likely to let supermarket developments through, they know exactly how useful they are. Unfortunately for us ninety per cent of planning inspectors are male.'

'I hope you are right,' Fidelis said, keeping up the show of feminine solidarity on principle, though knowing only too well how illusory it was. Fidelis had devoted her working life to understanding women and their children, and trying to make their lives easier, but she knew her most vehement opponents had often been women.

'Any working mother would understand this development's a godsend,' the solicitor said.

'And a gold-mine for us,' Neville said smugly. He was beginning to look, Fidelis thought, like a man who had found almost too much gold, as though he had been rather too well fed for rather too long, like an over-glossy, tightly stuffed soft toy. When they first met she had thought him cuddly, and so he seemed during their brief affair. Now, as so often with her former lovers, she felt a little sisterly, a little proprietary, and highly critical. No lover had ever lived up to her dreams, though it was not until she was over forty, twenty years ago, that she had properly understood why: it was because what she was searching for was not really a husband or a lover, she wanted a father.

Men showed themselves as they really were in bed. No doubt women did too, but Fidelis had been strictly heterosexual. Children, however, she could understand while keeping a proper and professional distance from them, observing and interacting across a desk, on the playing mat, at the zoo. But to know an adult, she had always needed intimacy. Fidelis's sexual life was over now and she was afraid she might have become a bad judge of character as a result.

Fidelis Berlin had identified her own knacks and most of her own needs early on in her career as a psychologist; and even before that. She had grown up watchful, minutely observing the species which controlled her life. Just as a naturalist studies the behaviour of animals and birds, so Fidelis drew conclusions about human beings; first about the foster family which had taken her in at the age of four, and later about her teachers. She had always been wary, careful not to startle people or put them to flight, because subconsciously and irrationally she seemed to believe she had once done just that: the infant Fidelis deduced that she had driven her own parents away.

Most of Fidelis Berlin's published work had been on the subject of mother substitutes. She had studied methods of day-care for infants throughout her working life at the Woburn Clinic. She had spent years preaching to policy makers and politicians. At last at a dinner party to which she had been invited by a new acquaintance called Buffy Cox her well-rehearsed speech had fallen on more receptive ears. Hearing Fidelis's enthusiasm for nursery education

Neville realised there was money in it. That was the moment when he first got the idea of starting a chain of franchised kindergartens.

Fidelis had been officially associated with the business as a non-executive director for some years. Her role was to give advice. Her lucid persuasion helped sell the product to clients and she had appeared several times as an expert witness at inquiries such as this, quoting a long list of degrees, honours and publications to lend authority to her views about the need for the service.

Today she had forced herself to come. Her flat had been burgled earlier in the week and she was suffering, self-diagnosed, from post-trauma shock. She'd come home from lecturing, sweating and tired in London's heat, irritable that there was nowhere to park, dragging herself and two heavy bags up the hill to her own house thinking about iced tea and a cold shower. There was no sign of anything wrong in the shared entrance hall, nor when she turned the two keys in her own scrupulously defended front door. Walking with single-minded thirst towards the kitchen, she took a moment to realise the living-room was not as she had left it. Where was the silver tray presented to her after twenty-five years on a research committee, where were her lustre jugs and enamel snuff boxes?

She dropped her parcels and sank down on the sofa dizzy and panting. My sanctuary, she thought. Someone – who? What have they –? It took a while to summon the strength to look. She sat still, speaking aloud to herself. 'Get up, Fidelis, take a grip. You've had a break-in, that's all. You've got off lightly.' That at least was true. No excrement smeared around, nothing smashed or shattered. Whoever it was had got in through the open window of Fidelis's first-floor flat. Cringing from the idea of what she would find, her fingers sweating with reluctance to touch what nobody else should have touched, Fidelis made herself look everywhere. Her cupboards had been rifled but not much had been taken, as far as she could tell, only small and readily saleable objects, the little real jewellery she possessed, brooches and ear-rings which were token presents from former lovers. For herself, Fidelis bought well-designed modern adornments in cheap materials.

The police were businesslike and, with them, so was Fidelis. She knew and they knew there was nothing to be done. A neighbour had noticed some kids in bikers' gear in the street, unidentified and unidentifiable. 'I shouldn't have left the window open,' Fidelis admitted, but the insurance company would pay. After the officials had gone she collapsed in a heap, trembling. The woman police constable had advised her to stay with a friend.

If I do that I'll never come back to this apartment, Fidelis thought, and told herself, 'Take a grip. Be sensible. You wouldn't mind if the cleaner or a workman had touched your things, why should this be so different?' The one concession she allowed herself was to change the sheets and towels, to wash every dish she possessed, to scrub the bath. She got rid of contamination. And it was not until the next day she realised someone had been into her word processor.

Someone had read her files, all the archive material she kept on disc, her accounts and tax return. The word processing program recorded the date each document was accessed to the screen, and yesterday a stranger had read all about her life.

And never had it felt so empty. I'm nothing but a lonely, wealthy, elderly woman, and they've seen me undisguised, she thought, shaking. She had a temperature. Her limbs ached.

She rang her friend Ruth, who said, 'Honestly, Fidelis, you're the one person who needn't worry about being exposed. If we all got the message that said, "Fly at once, all is discovered," you'd stay put.'

And her other great friend, Tina. 'Fidelis, what is this? Where's your self-confidence, your self-worth? What have you got to be ashamed of?'

Nothing. She knew it. Hers was a successful, useful, happy life. Why shouldn't the whole world know its details?

Physician, heal thyself.

Time heals all wounds.

Fidelis often found clichés and hackneyed quotations useful. She knew the passage of time would numb, dull and eventually deaden her distress. Soon – in a few days, or weeks – she would enter her home without terror of what had happened in her absence; she would write without wondering whether unauthorised eyes had read her words. It was a very busy time for Fidelis, her last term at the university with retirement looming and lists of commitments to finish off, and others to undertake as a freelance later on. One unmissable appointment was the planning inquiry in Sherbury. Obsessively locking every door and window, Fidelis drove down to Dorset in the blazing heat. The clarity of her unease was already blurred, she realised, for when a biker passed at speed she felt a spasm of dislike first, and only afterwards remembered what she had against him. She made a mental note. Perhaps there was a study to be done on the duration of anxiety; a thesis subject for a student? Academic, professional study was always the answer, to put suffering at one remove by rationalising it.

Nevertheless, whenever Fidelis argued for nursery schools it needed only one mother to say she couldn't understand without children of her own, to make her doubt herself. Fidelis knew the children with whom she had been professionally concerned were abnormal by definition, for why else would they have been seeing a child psychologist? Could it be true, after all, that normal children did need their mothers twenty-four hours a day? But this was no moment for the familiar old enemy of self-doubt to show its head over the battlements of Fidelis's professional judgement. She banished the thought when she gave her own evidence after the lunch break, and talked fluently, knowledgeably, persuasively about the value of nursery education, the benefit to the individual parent and child and to society.

The local council, opposing the development, was represented by a young, brash barrister with ferocious acne.

'Have you got children and did you look after them yourself, Dr Berlin?'

'That's not relevant here,' Barbara Pomeroy said. 'You needn't answer, Dr Berlin.'

'I just wanted to establish, madam, whether the witness had personal experience – '

'No. It isn't material to this issue.'

The afternoon dragged itself wearily on. Outside the sun was blazing on to the streets of Dorchester. The archaic council chamber, long since superseded by a modern building but still used as an attraction to tourists on the Thomas Hardy Trail, was put to service for public inquiries. From time to time members of the public, exploring the building in which Tess of the D'Urbervilles was tried, came into the room and immediately retreated in embarrassment at the sight of the formal proceedings, the dark-suited lawyers, the architects and land agents in their tweeds, the rows of observers, the screens to which maps and plans were pinned, the isolated woman on her raised platform on whom all attention was focused. If the planning inspector was not listening, there was no point in anyone else speaking. She alone, unaided by tribunal, advisers or clerk, would decide the issue.

Dust mites whirled in the shafts of sunlight which fell on to scratched old benches and portraits of long-forgotten aldermen. It was a lovely day, Barbara Pomeroy realised. Her back ached. She had drunk too much water at lunch-time and needed to go to the lavatory. Her watch was propped in front of her beside the little board on which she had displayed a plan showing the names of the parties and lawyers in the order in which they were sitting. Getting names right was a potent weapon in a planning inspector's armoury.

That morning she had announced she would rise at five o'clock, a warning, vain in this case, which was supposed to stop people wasting time. We're going to run into another day, she thought, perhaps I'll adjourn early and go and have a look at Hardy's Wessex.

For the umpteenth time Barbara straightened her papers on the archaic desk whose slope and splinters made writing so uncomfortable, and adjusted the pile of cushions she was sitting on. This antique chamber had been designed for men, bulky, burly Dorset farmers and landowners, influential men who ran the district without ever expecting a woman to be involved except when, like poor Tess, she was entirely in their established masculine power.

Barbara looked attentive but let the words slide over her. All these people, she thought, so passionate and committed. Will they shake hands and be friends afterwards, when one has won and the other lost? Not the appellant. Neville Cox looked as though a tough and unforgiving man lived in that hard, broad, expensively dressed body. He'd stand up well to the nakedness test – a trick one of Barbara's colleagues once passed on for keeping awake. Imagine all these people with no clothes on. Fidelis Berlin would be lean and angular, probably rather tanned, and even at her age – fifty-five? sixty? – unashamed. She'd eat men for breakfast, Barbara scribbled, and then cross-hatched the words over until they were unreadable, her pen moving to show she had noted the point made by the chairman of Sherbury Parish Council, who was trying to please everyone by saying such a facility as a kindergarten would be very valuable in the community, but somewhere else, not next door to his own house.

Then a naturalist gave evidence about moths. He stammered, but was understood to say the appeal site was the habitat of a particular weed on which alone a particular moth could feed and both were threatened species.

13

Fidelis Berlin tried to guess what the inspector was thinking. What sort of help did she have back home herself? Would she think about kindergartens in principle or this particular development in practice? Such decisions could not, in the end, be entirely objective. Everybody used supermarkets and garages and the products of factories, they drove on motorways and sent their children to schools or crèches, but they all – we all, Fidelis corrected herself – wanted the facilities to be somewhere else. Not here. Not in my back yard.

Planning committees were lobbied and persuaded, elected members dreaded odium and ducked responsibility. Personalities would be discussed, enemies made and friends lost. Then an appeal against refusal would be lodged.

Inspectors such as Barbara Pomeroy were professional outsiders, unconnected with the locality. They were not exactly anonymous, but no personality or identification was attached to the name. When they wrote an address in hotel registers, it was the planning inspectorate's, an office block in Bristol. The cars they drove were often hired. Mrs B. Pomeroy could live in Brighton or Banff for all anyone here knew. She would make a disinterested, objective decision on the planning merits of the case. The goddess from the machine would pronounce, Fidelis thought.

Her mind had been wandering. Abruptly she realised the atmosphere had changed. A group of people had entered the public seats behind her, noisily, their feet clunking on the wooden planks, their voices unlowered.

A member of the residents' association was saying, 'I'll never understand it, what's wrong with parents nowadays? First they choose to have children and then they hand them over to complete strangers to look after.'

Maintaining the appearance of attention to the evidence Barbara looked and saw there were another four witnesses to go.

Counsel for the appellant was not even pretending to write. He sat back in his pew, legs stretched out, his eyes lazily fixed on the ceiling, and yawned without covering his mouth.

The witness had got on to the good old days now, when families took care of their own children.

How much easier my own life would have been, Barbara thought, if there had been a convenient crèche when Toby was little and I was an assistant planning officer and Colin was still with the bank.

A procession of unsatisfactory child-minders ran across her memory. Life had been one long, frantic rush, too many things to do and no time to do any of them properly.

Barbara said, 'Mrs Gordon, thank you very much for making that point, but I must stop you there.'

As always it was a relief when the witness did what she said. Barristers, solicitors, planning officers, witnesses, general public and all, spoke to Barbara with exaggerated deference, larding their speeches with 'May it please you, madam', and 'With the greatest respect', but she was always afraid her authority might suddenly evaporate.

The next witness made similar points. 'Interested persons may consider that repetition will add to the strength of their case,' inspectors were warned. 'Inspectors must discourage this.'

In a discouraging voice Barbara said, 'I'm not sure that this gets us very much further.'

'I'm sorry, but this is a very important matter. The noise of children, the traffic and disturbance – our peace and quiet is at stake.'

Barbara remembered the firm, exhortatory style of her training. 'The inspector must be seen to be positively in control of the proceedings throughout. He should be authoritative without being domineering . . . it cannot be emphasised too strongly that the atmosphere in which an inquiry is conducted is entirely within the control of the inspector.'

Facial expression must be controlled and impassive if inspectors are to retain their position and respect, Barbara quoted to herself. Inspectors must not make a crisis out of minor interruptions. She said, 'Yes, I have taken a detailed note. Do you have anything to add which has not been said already?'

'Well, not really, but – '

'Then we'll get on. Miss Bates, you have asked to be heard, but if your point is the same as the previous witness's you may assume I understand it already.'

But Miss Bates was determined to have her public say about modern mothers, the good old days and the country going to the dogs. When her supporters joined in, to an immediate response by their opponents, Barbara realised this was the inspector's nightmare scenario, one rehearsed during training sessions and spoken of in planning folklore. 'Stamp on any incipient disturbance immediately,' she had been instructed. She had a brief, surrealist vision

15

of her huge booted foot, like something out of *Monty Python's Flying Circus*, coming down on all the little people as they gestured and shouted. They were not even doing it to impress her; it was a private fight, locals against locals, no longer accepting her as umpire. The solitary reporter present was scribbling furiously.

Barbara could feel herself flushing and sweating. What shall I do? she wondered. Suppose I just leave. I could go home, give up, chuck the job, get back to my own kitchen because I can't stand the heat of this one.

Two council officials had gone to the back of the room and were failing to soothe the electors. The appellant's lawyer flicked his eyes from the public to the inspector, a sardonic audience. The expert witness beside him, Dr Berlin, looked sorry for Barbara and flashed her an encouraging smile.

Barbara thought desperately, I'll never be allowed to hear the last of this, I'll always be known as the one who lost control.

She beckoned the lawyers forward to her table and managed to make them hear her say, 'I'll adjourn until tomorrow morning.'

'I've sent someone for security, madam,' the local authority's barrister shouted.

'It's too late.' With sudden, self-protective inspiration, she added clearly, 'I have noted the council's failure to ensure a police presence or give warning this appeal was likely to be contentious. You must have been aware of it, but none of the papers supplied to me make it apparent.'

Now that she was on the point of leaving the noise was dying down. She announced, 'This inquiry stands adjourned until ten o'clock tomorrow morning,' and with tattered dignity, swept out of the room.

2

The appellants and their companions waited in the council chamber until the inspector, the council representatives and most members of the public had gone. A reporter asked some questions: what did Neville Cox himself, or his advisers, think of their chances?

No comment, no comment. The inquiry was not *sub judice*, not being a proper court of law, but it would be counter-productive, the barrister warned, to give quotes that might annoy the inspector. They all knew she was supposed to consider nothing but objective planning criteria, but she was only human.

'Very human, in fact,' the solicitor said. 'Quite a looker, didn't you think? Don't write that down,' he added.

The reporter went off to try for a good quote from the protesters. Neville Cox turned to his advisers and said with a grin, 'Quite high on the Richter scale this time.'

'I always forget how experienced you are,' his solicitor said, and turning to the barrister added, 'Neville's won more planning appeals than most of us have had hot dinners.'

'Though I say it who shouldn't, I have had an almost unbroken record of success,' Neville agreed.

The barrister was busy putting yellow post-it markers in his notebook. Without looking up he said, 'I didn't realise you had quite so many of these kindergartens.'

'I've got a finger in many more pies than that,' Neville said. He opened his mouth, perhaps to list his other interests, but was interrupted by his solicitor, who said smoothly, 'Let's just say, a variety of property developments, right, Neville?'

A young woman, who had been sitting at the side of the public benches, uninvolved with the disturbance, came towards them, her heavy boots clattering on the bare floorboards. She was tall and dark, and in spite of the black shadows under her eyes, looked sharp and athletic. Fidelis Berlin made a quick, automatic assessment, a bet she often had with herself on her own judgement of character.

Clever, middle-class, vegetarian, or even vegan, she thought; keen on some semi-mystical exercise – yoga or t'ai chi; in reaction against a conventional background.

'Dr Berlin, could I speak to you for a moment?' The voice was warm and low, posh with an overlay of democratisation.

'Of course.'

'I'm Sophie Teague. I'm a psychology student, I'm doing my dissertation on methods of child care.'

'Do join us then. Let me introduce – '

The lawyers and planning professionals were already going through the door. One of the council officials stopped and called back, 'Hey, it's Sophie Teague! Remember Bullwood Hall? This is the last place I'd have expected to see you!'

'I didn't recognise you.'

'You'll never change, girl. See you.'

'That's someone I met when I was on a work placement,' Sophie explained to Fidelis, who said, 'Neville, this is Sophie – sorry, I didn't catch – '

'Teague. Sophie Teague.'

Neville Cox took the thin, brown hand, with its clutter of silver rings and slightly dirty fingernails, in his own manicured, soft palm. He was not much taller than the girl, but his blockish shoulders in a light grey suit were twice as wide, and beside her sallow complexion his face looked very pink, the eyes, with their brilliantly clear whites, as blue as his expensive, striped shirt. Neville's hair had become uniformly silver, but his eyebrows were still bushy and black. Even after this long, hot and exhausting day, he smelt agreeably of some spicy cologne.

'Nice to meet you, Sophie,' he said. 'Specially after an exhibition like that one.'

'I've never been to a planning inquiry before. Are they always like that?'

'Sometimes people get very worked up. You said you were a psychologist –'

'Only a student.'

'Well then, you know how territorial the human animal can be. Hell knows no fury like a member of a local conservation society threatened with a development they don't want.'

'Even when it's something like a nursery! How selfish.'

'For real drama, see what happens if one suggests a caravan site or a rubbish tip,' Neville said.

'Do you ever – ?'

'Oh, no, no. But Cox Kindergartens aren't my only interest by any manner of means. I'm what you might call an all-purpose entrepreneur.'

He was using on Sophie Teague all the mannerisms and wiles he had directed at Fidelis a few years before, emitting waves of pure animal magnetism, but Sophie Teague seemed unresponsive. Turning to Fidelis, she said, 'Dr Berlin, I wonder whether I might just speak to you a moment? If Mr Cox will excuse me, I don't want to interrupt if you –'

'Don't worry,' Neville said. 'I'll go back to the hotel. See you in the bar, Fidelis. And you, Sophie, if you'd like to join us.'

18

The two women went out into Dorchester High Street. It was full of jostling shoppers and tourists, their bare, reddened skin sweating under the unaccustomed sun. A man in a panama hat was telling a cluster of people about Thomas Hardy's use of the setting in his novels.

'I wonder where Mrs Pomeroy's gone,' Sophie said. 'Into hiding, d'you think? Stressful sort of job, what sort of person would choose it, I wonder.'

'It's an interesting question, I agree,' Fidelis replied, looking with pleasure at the bright, young face. I was like that myself, she thought: ambitious, urgent, perpetually curious. 'I'd guess planning is a rather dry and impersonal profession, nobody who wanted to deal with people would choose it.'

'But people use the environment.'

'At a remove from the planners, though.'

'She did seem remote, sitting there,' Sophie said thoughtfully.

'That would be a control mechanism to some extent of course, a way of enforcing her authority, but I would also suppose her own interpersonal relationships are tightly focused, emotions directed towards those closest to her and others viewed quite intellectually.'

'To tell you the truth I don't know the first thing about planning permissions and appeals. I came because my dissertation's about the public perception of child care. I got lots of good quotes today, but I didn't really understand what was going on.'

'It was all because you can't build anything without planning permission from a local council. They refused, so we appealed to the Minister – the Secretary of State for the Environment, actually.'

'So that woman is just a civil servant advising the Minister?'

'Sometimes. But in most cases, she's the one who grants the permission after all, or finally refuses it.'

'All alone, without a jury or anything?'

'As far as I know.'

'Gosh, she could make a fortune.'

'What do you mean?'

'Well, what's to stop her selling planning permissions? Who would ever know?'

Fidelis looked curiously at the young woman and said drily, 'That's not the first possibility which leapt to my mind, I must say. In fact it never occurred to me at all – I'm rather shocked. That's not how things work in this country.'

Sophie Teague laughed. 'Of course not, I wasn't serious. My brother's a lawyer, so I hear quite a bit about the seamy, criminal side of life, that's all. Actually, I think it's one of the reasons I first wanted to study psychology, to see what makes villains tick. And then I got hooked on the psychology of child care.'

'Walk with me to my car,' Fidelis said. 'Tell me what I can do for you.'

Sophie Teague wanted to work with Fidelis, or for her, while she completed her degree course. She had read every word Fidelis had written. 'I'll do anything. Secretarial, admin, domestic – Jill of all trades. But I'd most like to help with your research.'

'I haven't the funds for an assistant, now that I'm retiring,' Fidelis said.

'I don't need much, honestly, just a part-time job while I write my dissertation next year.'

'Have you approached anyone else?'

'I've got a list, if I need to. But you're the top of it. Look.'

Recognising the blatant flattery, Fidelis was pleased by it all the same. 'I couldn't do anything for months, I'll be in the States later on this year.'

'When you come back?' Sophie pleaded.

'I'll give it careful thought, I promise you. Write and tell me all about yourself. Can I give you a lift anywhere just now?'

'I came down on the bike, but I'd love to follow you, perhaps I can have a word with Mr Cox if he's got time, about the economic basis of private nursery provision.'

A powerful Yamaha was parked near Fidelis's sober little car.

'What a huge machine.'

'She goes really well,' Sophie said.

Fidelis did a lightning reassessment. Sophie might want to work for Fidelis but it could hardly be just for the money if she could afford a bike like this. But Fidelis had a proud and exact knowledge of her own consequence. A young graduate with a recommendation from Fidelis Berlin had a head start over rivals for good jobs.

'It must be fun,' Fidelis said enviously. 'Pity I'm too old to have a go.'

'You're not – come on, d'you want to? Here.' But Fidelis did not take the key from Sophie's hand.

'No, thanks, really I'd better not. One just has to admit one's past some things and riding a powerful bike for the first time is one of them.'

20

Concealed under leathers and helmet, Sophie followed Fidelis's car to the country hotel where the party from Cox Kindergartens was staying.

They joined Neville in a rose-filled garden, with iced drinks and the tick-tock sound of other guests playing croquet. They sat beside the herbaceous border, which was, perhaps for no longer than this one glorious day, at its beautiful best, in full, multicoloured, heavily scented glory. In the mellow sunlight of late afternoon the lawn was as green and smooth as a billiard table, the water glinted in the pool as clearly as glass.

If I swim now, Fidelis thought, I might have it to myself.

She left Sophie asking Neville questions and listening to fluent answers, the impersonal statements and figures incongruously delivered in a tone which implied something more intimate and quite different.

3

At the end of the day Barbara spoke to head office in Bristol to say the inquiry would overrun – and why. Her immediate superior was sympathetic but later that evening she was rung back by a more senior official whose superficial concern made a thin wrapping round a reprimand for failing to keep control. A black mark on her record. A public laughing stock. Jokes behind colleagues' hands at the annual general meeting. Three hundred men, all knowing and many gleeful that Mrs Pomeroy had messed up.

Ringing off, she said aloud, 'Keep a sense of proportion, Barbara, it's not the end of the world.' She dialled her home number, and Toby answered, panting.

'Where have you been, darling?' she asked.

'I was just helping Auntie Clarissa unpack her stuff.'

'Auntie who?'

'You know, she was in the holiday let downstairs. She's really ace, Mum. She was in a car crash, she had two black eyes! She's all better now. I'm helping her get settled.'

Barbara heard Colin telling Toby to go and have his bath. 'Hullo, Barbara, how did it go in the end?'

21

Telling him, rehearsing the story as she would have to tell it again, later, in self-defence, and the sound of his warm, reassuring reply, made her feel better. Don't forget, he said, how she had sailed through the probationary period, how seldom her decisions were queried, how her conduct of public hearings and inquiries had been praised in her last annual report. 'Mrs Pomeroy has natural authority,' the assessor had written.

'Nil carborundum,' Colin said. 'Don't let the buggers get you down.'

'But you know what a black mark it will be. They'll think it was my fault I lost control, even though I can't think what else I could have done.'

'Barbara, it's one little set-back, that's all. Remember what things were like this time last year. Think of Toby.'

Think of Toby. Of course Barbara already, always did; but how quickly she and Colin had come to take him for granted. It was not even three years since Toby had received the transplant which had literally transformed him from a frail, patient, docile invalid into a perfectly normal boy, who went to school like other children, played football, swam, argued, gobbled his meals and disobeyed his parents. Every time he was naughty it was a perverse delight. It was Toby's eleventh birthday next week, coinciding with the last day of the summer term, and he was going to get his own proper surf board and wet suit.

Toby's kidneys had begun to fail when he was seven. His parents had watched him suffering, growing ever weaker, less able to live normally until it really seemed as though he would not live at all. And then – a miracle. To keep a sense of proportion Barbara need only remember the preceding few years, which had been a nightmare unrelieved, it seemed at the time, by even momentary waking up.

At the time they lived in Leicester. Colin worked for one of the big clearing banks, Barbara in the local authority's planning department. When Toby was first diagnosed as having a complaint for which there was no quick and easy cure, Barbara gave up her job to stay at home and look after him. Six months later Colin was made redundant. That seemed utterly unimportant compared with Toby's illness. But mortgage payments have to be kept up even when there is mortal illness in the home. Special, expensive, tempting food has to be bought, the rooms need to be kept warm,

22

washing is done in unprecedented quantities. Money soon became as inescapable an anxiety as Toby himself.

When Barbara saw the advertisement for new planning inspectors, she had applied, at once with reluctance and pessimism. Colin said, 'All they can do is say no,' and spent an evening rewriting her curriculum vitae.

The job was regarded as the final career boost for senior town and country planners, and used to be Barbara's ultimate ambition. Now it simply represented a way of earning some money while being able to do most of her work in her own home. Perhaps she impressed the interviewers precisely because she seemed indifferent to their reactions since nothing really mattered at the time except Toby. Perhaps they had simply been told to recruit more women. Whatever the reason, she got the job.

It had been an exhausting struggle at first. 'I can't go through with this,' she would say, and Colin would reply, 'Don't then. You don't have to.' But she did have to. One of them must earn a living.

Barbara would travel all over the country to visit sites or listen to the parties' arguments in public. She was away from home one or two days a week, or more if an inquiry ran on longer than scheduled. The rest of her working life was spent in her office at home, with rare meetings at headquarters in Bristol. She grew used to evenings and nights in anonymous hotels, obedient to the inspectorate's prohibitions.

'Never get talking to anyone in a bar or dining-room, you might find he's involved in the appeal.' The advice was always couched in the masculine, whether it concerned the parties or the inspectors. 'Never be alone at any time with anyone involved for fear of being accused of improper bias. Not even in the car-park or lavatory. Don't give anyone a pretext for saying you've been got at.'

It was a lonely life that first year, clouded by incessant anxiety about Toby. Barbara would return home to a cauldron of complicated emotions – love, terror, solicitude and a seasoning of disgust and boredom. And somehow she had to prepare her files beforehand and write her decisions afterwards, long, carefully phrased quasi-judicial letters, every word, every reference number, every detail of which would be weighed and measured on the chance of finding grounds for appeal.

It had been almost impossible to concentrate in the study while Toby suffered upstairs and Colin went to him when he called – yes, quite impossible. But somehow Barbara did it. In retrospect, she really couldn't think how.

Then Toby had the operation, and it was a success. He was recovering, he was much better, and at last, for all intents and purposes, and crossing fingers and touching wood and not saying it too loud for fear of the jealous fates hearing, he was cured.

The Pomeroys decided to make a new start.

Colin was nearly sixty. There seemed no point in his even trying to find another job. He would paint full time. Barbara would remain the family breadwinner, but she had a job which could be based anywhere in the country; at least one planning inspector for England lived in Edinburgh. So the Pomeroys would move to live where nobody remembered Toby as a pitiful invalid, where it was not thought peculiar for Colin to be an artist, where Barbara would find sanctuary when she came home exhausted by contention and aggravation.

'I mean, there's no reason why we shouldn't even live in Cornwall,' Colin said, almost as a joke. But the fantasy quickly became a reality, when they saw the perfect property advertised in the batch of estate agents' leaflets.

Two adjoining flats overlooking a beach in St Ives, in a block originally designed for holiday letting. Each flat had been designed to provide two bedrooms and a large living-room whose plate glass windows opened on to a balcony overhanging the sand and sea. With a door knocked between the two, they had a studio for Colin and an office for Barbara, two bathrooms, enough bedrooms, a sun trap three floors above the ocean. It meant Barbara had to spend many hours driving every week, but they agreed it was a price worth paying. They had been there nearly a year and Colin had already exhibited his work in two local galleries. Toby went to school in Penzance and had made lots of friends, none of whom behaved as though he was fragile.

Last New Year's Eve they had taken stock. An unseasonably warm and clear night, stars and a misty moon over the burnished sea, the soft rippling of breakers below; Colin and Barbara stood on the balcony without coats, holding glasses of pink Spanish champagne and waiting to hear the church bells and ships' sirens at the stroke of midnight.

'We're so lucky,' Barbara sighed. 'It's all turned out so well. If only I believed in God I'd be thanking him.'

'I know. I go round in a kind of haze of unfocused gratitude too. Look, there he is.' A group of children had gathered round a bonfire on the beach below. A few of them were dancing on the hard sand below the high tide mark, to the sound of a portable player. Some girls were crouched at the flames, holding out food to grill on sticks. The smell of sausages and burnt potatoes wafted upwards. Toby and another boy were playing with a boomerang, just visible in the faint light. They threw and retrieved it, competing, running with careless grace. Two dogs followed them with leaps and yaps.

'Did we send Christmas cards to the doctors in Leicester?'

'Of course, and the transplant service.'

'Do you know,' Barbara said, 'I think it's time for me to write to the parents.'

'Who?'

'The donor's family. Just so they know it worked, that something good came out of it all for someone.'

'I don't know whether that's such a good idea.'

'Oh Colin, suppose it had been Toby, wouldn't we want to feel someone else had got their child back even if we had lost ours?'

'I think it might be rubbing salt in the wound. They might not want to be reminded.'

'Oh, I would, after all this time, I'd feel it had made some sense of something senseless. Just to be thanked and know it had worked and the recipients hadn't forgotten what they owed to my son.'

'We don't even know who they were.'

'I shall write care of the British Organ Donor Society. I'm going to do it now.'

She had gone in and composed a letter immediately. She headed it New Year's Eve, 1992, and then when she heard the sound of bells and cheering, and car horns, and ships' hooters, loudly from the harbour in St Ives and just faintly, across the peninsula, from Penzance and Newlyn, crossed it out and wrote New Year's Day, 1993.

Now, six months later, Barbara sat on the bed in her hotel room and counted her blessings. Under her breath she repeated to herself the words she had written in that heartfelt letter of gratitude. 'Your child gave my son life.' She must never forget her good fortune. So what if she made a mess of the job or even lost it? Balanced against Toby's well-being, against the integrity of their impregnable family unit, nothing else mattered. Nothing else mattered at all.

4

Fewer people attended the resumed inquiry, and there was no disturbance during the rest of the proceedings, which were declared closed by lunch-time on the next day. The inspector and both parties to the action arranged to meet after a lunch break to inspect the appeal site, and Sophie Teague found herself leaving the council chamber beside the owner of the face from her past.

Dermot Brown said he was now working for the West Dorset council. He was gangling, forty years old, and had black greasy hair in which a twiddling finger was almost permanently embedded. He wore a hairy tweed coat over a shirt one collar size too small. Sophie had always realised he fancied her, but she had found him physically repulsive, and now there didn't seem to be any reason why she should hide it any more. But she had forgotten his ability to ignore signs of other people's irritation or dislike. Dermot would still blandly persevere, smiling with invincible benevolence. Short of the kind of rudeness not usable in public, it was virtually inevitable that Sophie should find herself sitting on a slippery banquette facing Dermot Brown across a red formica table and stirring her spoon round and round in a thick white cup of orange tea.

'If you say "quite like old times" I'll kick you,' she warned, but all Dermot did was repeat how thrilled he was to see her again.

'Have you heard how the others are getting on, all the old crowd from – '

Sophie said sharply, 'I don't want to talk about them, Dermot, I've moved on.'

'What are you doing now then?'

When Sophie told him, Dermot exclaimed, 'Oh Sophie, now that really is great news, I always said you had it in you. Didn't I tell you colleges were keen to take mature students? Which one are you at?'

Sophie was at a university in outer London which had been an institute of higher education until two years previously; her degree subject was psychology and social studies. 'There were vacancies in that department, that's why.'

'Very sensible choice,' he said approvingly. 'It leads to steady careers. Will you go in for some kind of social work?'

'No way, I've had quite long enough at the bottom of the heap. I want something with status and a decent income, like Dr Berlin, you've no idea what a lot people like her make a year.'

'This the first time you've met her?'

'Mmm. Do you know her?'

'Only by sight but I think she's bloody terrifying.'

'Men like you always say dynamic women are terrifying. It's your way of putting them down.'

Dermot was impossible to discompose. He said mildly, 'I suppose I might seem a bit prejudiced. Could it be your role to turn me into a properly reconstructed man after all?'

'Not a hope. But tell me what you've heard about Dr B.'

'Well, you know all about her being an authority on her subject.'

'Yeah yeah, I don't mean that. What's she like in private?'

'I only know what I've heard. People say she used to be a real goer.'

'Gay?'

'Don't think so. She has a reputation for swallowing men whole, chewing them up and spitting them out again.'

'Isn't she a bit old for that?'

'It's probably just what they said when she was younger, but I was asking the director of social services about her, they used to work together, and he says she's the original Snow Queen – incapable of real emotion, runs away from love, splinter of ice in the heart and all that. Never been married, no children, she's not really the best model for a girl like you, Sophie,' he added with apparent concern.

'Not that it's any of your business, but I'm going to work with her next year.' She looked at Dermot's gormless and harmless face and said more gently, 'She's a leading authority in her field and she'll give me references and I'll be able to get a decent job and make a proper living. I'll be able to afford decent clothes and all that stuff. And a fast car.'

'You always liked speed. Do you remember Jed's machine? You heard what happened to him, Sophie, he – '

'Got to go, Dermot.'

'You will go carefully, Sophie, after everything that – '

'Shut up, Dermot. Look, I'm doing OK, right? You should be pleased for me.'

He said sincerely but sadly, 'I am pleased for you, Sophie. Don't I look it?'

She stared with unconcealed distaste at the coil of hair his restless finger had woven and the egg stain on his tie. 'Not very,' she said. 'I think you liked it when you were Mr Big who knew it all and I was young and powerless. But things have changed, now I'm in control.'

Outside in the hot street traffic was backed up to the top of the hill. As she paused to say goodbye to Dermot, Sophie's eye was caught by exactly the car she was going to get herself one day; long, low, egg yellow. As her eyes caressed the curved bonnet, its roof whirred smoothly back. The driver was Neville Cox, enclosed by the blond leather seat as though it were moulded to his powerful body. He fiddled with the stereo and lit a long, thin cigar before looking up and noticing Sophie.

'What a lovely car,' she said and he leant across to the handle of the passenger door.

'Nice, isn't it? D'you want a lift? Why don't you come along and see the site we've been arguing about? Here, get in, you can come along with me.'

5

Barbara paused on her way into St Ives, as she often did, to pay her respects to the view, a wide sweep of sea, bounded on the landward side by a hemisphere of pale sand until, on the far side, a green headland pointed out towards a pair of rocky islands on one of which the white finger of a lighthouse stood sentinel over the bay. Its beam was beginning to blaze out in the summer dusk; the sun had just slid behind a reddened sea, leaving streaks of colour in the darkening sky.

On down the hill into the town centre. It was not yet the high holiday season, but there were already a good many tourists around. They wandered along the narrow streets where most of the shops had stayed open in the evening as though this were a Mediterranean resort, with bright coloured racks of clothes or toys hanging at right angles to the frontage, or blackboards propped outside with menus chalked on them.

Barbara manoeuvred her car cautiously past couples walking hand in hand and jostling family parties. Nearly everybody was eating, and the crowd had reached the stage of being large enough to make drivers afraid of pedestrians, rather than the other way round. People stepped out without looking, and made angry gestures at the moving vehicle.

'No place to bring a bloody motor,' one man shouted, banging his fist on the roof.

'But I live here,' Barbara protested, whispering so that he should not hear her defiance. Women drivers had been dragged out of their seats and beaten up for less. She bared her teeth in the primate's gesture of submission, and edged very slowly along the harbour front, and up and round through lanes hardly wider than the car, into the private parking area on the landward side of Barnaloft. Colin must have come down to open the garage doors for her. She backed the car in, gathered her overnight case and the much heavier paraphernalia of files and maps, with the bag containing what she called her 'inquiry kit', and climbed the three flights of stone stairs wearily but eagerly, looking forward to the welcome Colin and Toby would give her.

Actually she felt too tired to eat; but it would never do to show it. Since they came to Cornwall Colin had become a meticulous and energetic cook, making dishes Barbara herself would never even have thought of trying, and sometimes travelling the twenty-five miles to Truro for the sake of a single exotic ingredient. His feelings would be hurt if she were not immediately enthusiastic.

Colin was waiting at the door to take her bags from her and put a glass of pink liquid into her hand. 'Kir,' he said. 'And I've got crab for supper.'

'Lovely,' Barbara said. 'Just let me – '

'No, you're not to do a thing. Look, I'll dump this lot in your office. You just freshen up and then come and sit down.'

The table was laid by the open doors of the balcony. The afterglow of the setting sun still coloured the sky and the smooth sea with a vestigial rosy glow. Colin had lit candles, shielded by tall glass holders, and had set out three bowls of pale green soup, with ice cubes, cream and chives floating on the surface.

'Where's Toby?'

'He'll be right back. D'you want to change first? I thought we might look in at the opening at Gil's gallery afterwards.'

'You go. I'm too tired.' Barbara needed to feel on good form to go out with Colin. He had rapidly become part of the local scene and seemed to know everybody, the painters, the collectors, the gallery owners. He was always careful to include her in conversations. 'Do you know my wife, Barbara?' and after all this time many of them replied, 'Yes, of course, how nice to see you again,' politely welcoming but, she always felt, without the taking-for-granted intimacy which Colin had achieved. A few people remembered what her job was, and would tell her about their planning problems, minor, when permission was delayed for a new roof, or major, if they were part of the action group trying to protect the town from the destruction which was part of a massive sewage scheme. Barbara would have preferred to talk about the pictures. She would have felt less of an outsider.

'Do come. It's paintings by Alfred Wallis, you like those.'

'I think I'd rather look in at the weekend.'

'I'll just – oh, there's Toby now.'

The quick, bouncing thump of training shoes as Toby ran full tilt up the stairs and into the house could still give Barbara a frisson of delight.

'Hi, Mum.'

'Hullo, darling.' She refrained from hugging him, merely ruffling his orange curls and touching the back of her fingers to his healthily pink cheeks. 'Where have you been?'

'Auntie Clarissa was showing me her Meccano.'

'I can't think how Toby's acquired a new auntie I've never even met,' Barbara said crossly.

Colin said, 'Didn't you meet her in the spring? She was here on holiday in the Bartletts' flat and liked it so much she's rented the studio on the top floor of the Piazza for a year. You know, the one that's been on the market for such a long time?'

'I know the studio,' Barbara said. 'But not Clarissa – what did you say her name is?'

'Clarissa Trelawny.'

'Sounds like someone out of a romantic novel. Who is she, anyway?'

'Well, she's very nice. A bit older than you, I'd say, but quite good-looking. And she's taken a terrific fancy to Toby.'

'She took me to the Bird Paradise at Hayle on Tuesday, when Dad was at his life-class,' Toby said. 'Yuk, what's this?'

'Iced cucumber soup.'

'Ugh. I thought it was pudding.'

'It's delicious,' Barbara said, forcing herself to scrape the plate.

'Good. And here's the crab. I made aioli to have with it instead of mayonnaise, I'm not sure you'd like it, Tobe.'

'I'm not hungry, actually. I had a hot dog with Auntie Clarissa. Can I go back? She's got Roskilly's ice cream. Strawberry and chocolate!'

'Not for long then. Bed in half an hour, OK?'

The crab was fresh and sweet, the garlic mayonnaise unctuous and savoury; and Barbara would have liked a boiled egg on a tray. She swallowed with every indication of appreciation, before saying, 'Who is this Clarissa Trelawny, anyway? She doesn't sound like the sort of person Toby usually wants to spend his time with.'

'You'll recognise her when you see her, I'm sure, she's been around since the last long weekend. About your height, blonde hair, always looks nicely turned out.'

'Is she on her own?'

'Seems to be. No sign of family that I've noticed. She wears a wedding ring though.'

'No children?'

'She hasn't mentioned any.'

'Oh well, it's nice of her to bother with Toby, I suppose. I'd better call at the weekend.'

Toby came in virtuously on time and went to bed, followed quite soon by his parents. They stood at the open door of his bedroom listening to his quiet breathing, looking at the chaos he chose to live in, which was a sign of health in itself, Barbara thought. Then they went to bed too.

Colin and Barbara shared the double bed. They still kissed and embraced. But it was three years since they had made love. Barbara could date it exactly, to the day Toby's kidney failure was diagnosed. She had turned to Colin that night for comfort, to drown the silence from their son's empty bedroom in the warmth of momentary passion. Colin had kissed her briefly on the forehead and turned away. 'I couldn't,' he said, his words half muffled in the pillow. 'I just can't. Not with Toby . . .'

And he never had again. Unwillingness, impotence, boredom? Barbara had thought of all possible explanations. He loved her as much as he always had as far as she could tell, looking after and cherishing her, always considerate and concerned, but he had simply lost interest in her as a sexual being. He had *gone off sex*. There was not the slightest indication – and goodness knows she'd looked for them – that he was seeing anyone else. As long as Toby was so ill they simply did not talk about it; they lay in bed clutched together for consolation, but when Barbara touched his penis it stayed soft and unaroused. He would politely, gently, lift her hand away.

When Toby was better Barbara had tried to have it out with Colin. 'It's not as though you're old . . . and anyway, what about me?'

Sixty years old, an ex-army officer, he was not of a type or generation to talk about sex in any other than barrack room terms, to barrack room boys.

'Am I supposed to do without it too? For ever?'

Colin was so pitifully embarrassed and sorry, that whenever Barbara raised the subject she felt forced to change it. Once he muttered that he'd simply grown out of it. He was sorry. He was too old for her. Past it.

'Perhaps you should see a doctor, or a psychiatrist or a sex therapist or someone.'

'Please don't say that again.' He used the tone of voice she had hardly ever heard, that note of command which must have been part of his professional skill when he was in the army. Barbara suddenly understood he might actually be relieved all passion was spent. But she was only just forty, too young to welcome release from the bondage of physical desire.

What was she supposed to do for the rest of her life – use a dildo? Get a vibrator? She took to buying explicit women's magazines and read other women's open confessions of their needs and what they did to satisfy them. They always made it sound so easy. You want sex? Get a lover.

Barbara had taken no interest in other men since she met Colin, a widower of forty-eight, handsome, authoritative, capable

32

and charming and charmed by her. He'd been wonderful in bed. Inventive, considerate, persevering, enduring.

Barbara lay in the bath for a long time listening to Classic FM and leafing without concentration through a Dick Francis thriller she had read before. Later she put on long-sleeved, long-legged silk pyjamas, and got into bed beside Colin, kissing him briefly on the cheek. As usual she sensed a frisson of nervousness, as though he still feared she might make advances to him.

If only he would talk about it. But Colin had grown up in a world, at a time, without words he found acceptable to use with his wife. Tarts. Intercourse. Nice girls, bad girls. But the fact was, Barbara thought, the silence at the heart of her relationship with Colin, the physical distance, affected everything else in their lives. She had conversations with him silently in her head.

'I can manage without making love with you, that's the least of it, if only we weren't starting to lose the out-of-bed intimacy too. I don't know what you're doing all the time when I'm away, or what you're thinking, or whether you really care for me at all any more.'

After that dreadful time with Toby Barbara would have thought she and Colin should have been closer than ever. That's what it did feel like at first, but recently . . . 'You treat me like a flat-mate, or as though I were your sister. Marriage doesn't only mean the matrimonial bed, does it?'

He doesn't give a damn who I sleep with so long as I leave him alone, she thought.

Colin had fallen asleep, his quiet, steady breath just out of time with the gentle breakers on the beach below.

Barbara began to caress herself; but physical release did not bring the pleasure she needed from a man's body. Any man? No, she thought, I'd rather have this man.

Colin looked very much as he had when they first met, as straight as an animated ironing board, with a small, round head, obedient, smooth hair, and, since they had lived by the sea, always tanned like weathered wood. The very image of a retired soldier, he was often addressed by strangers in pubs as 'Major'.

He's a good man. Kind. Protective. Honourable. Gentle. Reliable. But Barbara needed more than that.

The idea that a mother of forty-one should require or desire a sex life would have seemed utterly bizarre before the second half of the twentieth century. Barbara lay panting beside her sleeping husband, not expecting to sleep herself. I've got everything, she thought. Touch wood.

6

When the daylight shortened, Barbara would leave home the day before her hearing or inquiry, so this October evening she drove off in a fog, which the TV weathergirl had promised was only localised, to stay in a hotel in Bristol. Toby and Colin, who had carried her bags down to the car, waved her goodbye.

'Drive carefully,' Colin said, the words part of their ritual. Then he said Toby could go out to play for half an hour. 'Synchronise watches. Be back at nineteen hundred hours precisely.' Then he went upstairs to tidy up.

Colin enjoyed the work of a house-husband, making, mending, cleaning, arranging. He wondered why so many women complained about it. Barbara, of course, had never needed to; housekeeping had never played a large part in her life since she had worked without a moment's unemployment between her graduation at twenty-one and Toby becoming ill.

Colin's first wife, Rosemary, had devoted herself, from choice but with constant complaints, to domesticity. She had been a perfect 'army wife' and full-time mother. Their daughter Clare followed her mother's pattern and had ceased to work when she got married. She had gone to live in Hong Kong with her banker husband and spent her time playing tennis and buying clothes. Whenever Colin remembered Clare's incautious decision to rely on Brian for a lifetime's support, he felt anxious about her. It was not every husband who would remain as willing to accept responsibility as he had for Rosemary until she died, aged forty-three, of breast cancer.

Colin decided not to vacuum Barbara's office now, but he emptied the waste-paper basket and wiped over the furniture and computer with a damp cloth. She always left her files and plans in an order only she understood, so he was careful not to muddle them, but he glanced at the work in progress, leafing through the typed draft of her decision and the green notebooks in which she wrote down, in longhand, almost every word said in evidence at the inquiry.

She was back on the kindergarten case from Dorset which had given her a good deal of trouble.

'Always know what your decision will be before leaving the area,' instructions said, but Barbara had still been unsure after leaving Sherbury, and even after an extra look at the site fitted in when she was on her way to Winchester three weeks later. She had changed her mind twice even while she was drafting her decision. Then her initial letter had been sent back twice for technical amendments suggested by the legal department. This must be the final version, designed to be proof against any challenge in the High Court, to which, though only on a point of law, an appeal might be made.

'From my inspection of the appeal site and its surroundings and from the representations made to me in writing and at the inquiry I consider the main issues in this case are . . .' Lists of material authorities. Consideration of possible harm arising from the proposed development: noise, disturbance, failure to conform with the development plan, unnacceptable effects on amenities . . .

With an experienced eye Colin skipped the formalities and four pages of argument to find the decision. 'For the above reasons and in exercise of the powers transferred to me I hereby grant this appeal, subject to the following conditions . . .' Plenty of them. She had tied it all up as tightly as possible. 'I am, gentlemen, your obedient servant . . .'

Barbara was conducting a running battle with her employers about the form of words. She wished to address appellants or their agents as 'ladies and gentlemen'. How was she to know what sex initials and surnames represented? She knew women solicitors or estate agents who were offended by the masculine appellation. None of the standard feminist arguments swayed her bosses. Clerks at the head office still whited out the offending words when she used them.

Colin admired his wife's gutsiness. It was what enabled her to do the job at all, to find the courage to go back next day after a riot, such as she had described at the kindergarten appeal, and control the unruly roomful. He thought she would have made a good officer but an insubordinate other rank.

It was that combative sharpness which had attracted him to her when they first met in the De Montfort Halls in Leicester, at a concert jointly sponsored by the local authority and Colin's bank. The programme of early music played on authentic instruments did not appeal to the senior staff of either. Tickets had been handed out around both offices. Colin and Barbara, shifting restlessly about in their seats during the first half, looked at each other with rueful smiles when the interval came. It was Barbara who spoke first.

'I'm not enjoying this much, are you? No? Well look, let's escape and have a drink instead. My name's Dutton. Barbara Dutton.'

She had bushy red curls like the model for a pre-Raphaelite painting, with very clear eyes and freckled skin. He noticed a clean, citron scent and that she was not wearing a wedding ring. Colin towered above her when they stood up. They went to a small Italian restaurant together and ended the evening in Barbara's bed. It was not Colin's first adventure since Rosemary died, or indeed, before, but it was by far the best. She was imaginative, enthusiastic, athletic. They made love and talked all night.

An unprofitable line of thought. Colin shook his head, stacked the papers beside the word processor and shut the window against an increasing wind. Then he went into the kitchen intending to cook Toby real fish and chips, the fish dipped in batter flavoured with mustard and dill, the chips hand cut, the fat real lard mixed with the best oil.

'Dad.' Toby came pounding up the stairs just as Colin had tied the striped apron round his thin hips. 'Dad. Auntie Clarissa says can we both go to supper with her, she's got a roast on and it's too much for her alone. Can we? Please, Dad.'

The Pomeroys ate very little poultry and no red meat. Toby hankered for beef, white bread and sugar, and Colin knew that Clarissa had got into the habit of getting hamburgers in buns when she had Toby to tea. Colin said, 'I don't know, Tobe, it's – '

'Come on, Dad, it smells scrumptious. Please.'

'All right then. It's very kind of Clarissa. Go and say I'll be there in a minute.'

Colin had become friendly with Clarissa Trelawny over the last few months. She was obviously glad of the contact. She had got talking to Toby on the beach and he had introduced her to his father. She explained she had no previous acquaintance with Cornwall but had fallen in love with St Ives when she came down on holiday at the end of May.

'I looked out of the window and thought I'd come to heaven. Straight out on to the beach, that soft sand, and then the sea, different every day, so beautiful . . . so I thought I'd just stay.'

Colin had asked her where her home was, and she answered with a vague wave of the wrist. 'All over the place. London mostly. But London's never really *home*, is it? Not like Cornwall. I really like it here, it's on such a human scale and everyone is so friendly. I was wondering whether to take up painting.'

'I'm a painter.'

'Really? Do you show your work?'

'There's one in that gallery in Fore Street. A little semi-abstract one of this very view.'

'Not – I don't believe it, how extraordinary! Is it signed CP? I bought it today, come and see where I've put it.'

'This deserves a celebration,' Colin said. He ran up to fetch a bottle of his best claret. Clarissa showed him into her flat, a lobby leading to a galley kitchen and small bathroom, and one very large, high room, with a half-gallery on which he could see a bed. One wall of the room was glass and faced directly west over the sand and out to sea. The other three walls were plain white, Colin's the only painting visible. The furniture, presumably belonging to a landlord, was unremarkable pine and wickerwork, but the effect was softened by some silk cushions in fondant colours, a large, fine Persian carpet and a cashmere rug in brilliant daffodil yellow thrown over the sofa. A page torn from a glossy magazine was lying on the table; the photograph showed a living-room, decorated with similar cushions and an identical rug though the model sofa did not also have a baseball cap on it. 'Oh, there's Toby's cap,' Clarissa said. 'He was up here earlier with his project about fishermen, I was showing him the knitting patterns in their smocks. I do hope you don't mind.'

'Don't let him be a nuisance.'

'Nuisance? Certainly not. I love having him around. He's a delightful child. He's welcome any time.'

A half-finished woolwork embroidery of flowers lay on the low glass table beside a pile of glossy hardback books. 'You've got the new Patrick O'Brian!' Colin exclaimed.

'Oh, do you like him too?'

'Certainly do, I've got all the earlier ones.'

'I think they are wonderful. Do borrow it if you like, I've finished it.'

'If you're sure, thank you very much, I'd like nothing better.'

'And do lend it to your wife too, if she'd like to . . .'

'Barbara isn't much of a novel reader, thanks all the same. I'm the fiction addict in the family.'

'Do you like this one? He's one of my favourites.' Clarissa held up the latest novel by Naguib Mahfouz.

'Oh, yes indeed, I always get them the moment they come out, he's one of the greats. I discovered him when I was military attaché in Cairo. We share the same tastes, it seems.'

'I certainly share your taste in wine,' Clarissa said. 'This is perfectly delicious.'

'I'm glad you like it, because I brought it to drink to your purchase. You're the first person to buy one of my paintings.'

'No, I can't believe – it's so good! My eyes went straight to it in the gallery, it's brilliant, the way you've caught the movement of the waves, and the sand gleaming through the shallow water at the tideline – you can't be a beginner, surely.'

'I always used to dabble a bit in the army and then when I was living in the Midlands, but I never really had time to get going properly until we moved here. I'm going to classes three times a week, one learns such a lot, and it's a good way to meet people too.'

Clarissa sat holding her glass, listening with wide-eyed attention as Colin talked about himself. She was a charming woman; so responsive and understanding, and made intelligent comments which showed she understood exactly what he meant when he talked about his work. She realised it was not simply a hobby or a way of passing the time, but a passion, a profession or career, deferred but embarked upon not too late for success to come. She said she fully expected to find she had made a brilliant investment by buying his work before its value was well known. 'I'll live to see you hanging in the Tate,' she said, gesturing roughly in the direction of the art gallery. 'I'll be in there saying I knew it all along!'

She was a woman of undeniable middle age, with a network of fine lines on her forehead and around her lips and eyes; but her medium-length hair, by nature or art, was a waving, shining silver gilt, her complexion rosy and white, her eyelids delicately gleaming. Always as smell-conscious as a tracker dog, Colin noticed her scent with pleasure. It was sweet but spicy, warm, ultra feminine. He was rather sorry that Barbara would never use anything like it.

Clarissa had very white hands with almond-shaped nails the

colour of pink pearls and kept them clasped in her lap as Colin spoke. She was wearing something loose and draped and of a smoky blue material. Suddenly Colin said, 'I'd love to paint you, Clarissa, sitting there in that dress against that yellow cloth.'

'Do you paint portraits?'

'Not yet, but I'd like to try. Those colours look wonderful together.'

That had been in July. Now, three months later, the picture was nearly finished. Colin had painted it in Clarissa's own flat, which had in fact been designed, twenty-five years earlier, as a studio and for a long time used as such by one of the famous St Ives painters. 'It will bring you luck, to work where he did,' Clarissa said, showing Colin a conveniently empty cupboard where he could store the work in progress between sittings.

He had posed her on the sofa, against the yellow wool rug, with the gleaming sea-filled window behind her, not wearing the blue dress, but another, the colour of blackcurrant jam. Colin always admired Clarissa's clothes, most of them made of soft, glowing materials which hung in sculptural folds. He had never thought he was at all interested in such things before, and could not for the life of him remember anything Rosemary had ever worn except her long, white wedding dress. Barbara had two uniforms: suits to confront the world of work, jeans, fishermen's sweaters and track suits for home. When she dressed up to go to parties or out to dinner he always said she looked lovely. But Barbara often remarked that if she put her hand over Colin's eyes and asked what colour she was wearing, he would not be able to answer.

The portrait went slowly. He felt his way, redoing and rethinking all the time. Clarissa was patience itself, sitting for hours at a time, and as he painted they chatted idly about St Ives, Toby, other people's pictures, music – they both had a passion for Wagner, and would joke about running away together to Bayreuth – and books; they had read many of the same books and she said his opinions gave her new ideas and insights about them.

Now, nine weeks since he began the portrait, Colin had not done anything to it for ten days running, because Barbara had had a period of working at home to catch up with paperwork. When she was there Colin went out to the painting club, as much to chat and have a glass with his friends, or stayed in and got on with his painting in his own studio, a smaller space than Clarissa's room, but with the same brilliant light reflected off the sea outside. He planned to create a series of studies showing the relationship of the waterside buildings, such as Barnaloft itself, with the sand and water beside them. He wanted to say something about the contrast, the juxtaposition of man-made materials, of artificiality, with the elemental, eternal shore.

It should have been a useful period of work; by early October there were not so many visitors in St Ives, so there was less distraction from the beach, to which, that summer, his attention had often wandered as surfers, team games players, entertainers and noisy family parties wove their intricate, colourful dances three storeys below his window. Toby had been away for five days on a school trip and the Pomeroys did not yet have enough friends in Cornwall to be distracted by much socialising. They went to an opening of a new exhibition at the Penwith Gallery, at which Barbara remarked in surprise on the number of people Colin now knew to say hullo to, and for a drink with a local solicitor called Robert Stanley, who was another member of the painting club.

But for some reason the pictures didn't seem to be going anywhere. He needed . . . what? An impulse? Encouragement? Someone to discuss them with? But Barbara was preoccupied by a difficult decision letter, and, he thought, had been irritable and dissatisfied.

She had made advances to him in bed, pressing herself against him, stroking and touching. When she felt his soft penis he lifted her hand away.

'I don't arouse a flicker of interest, do I?' she said.

He apologised as he had so many times, embarrassed, ashamed, wishing she would leave the subject alone, buried. 'I just can't help it, Barbara, it's no good. It's the price you pay for marrying someone twenty years your senior. Can't you just accept that I'm past it?' He was sorry for her, sorry and guilty and regretful.

But he had come to realise, if he was honest with at least himself, that it had been a relief, this last year, to be in the calm water of sexual abstinence, to see women without visualising them in bed, to have no desires which took will-power and determination to quell, no itches to scratch or urges to satisfy. It was what one of the experts he had consulted said might happen. He had been to doctors, who found nothing physically wrong and said he could not expect to be thinking of sex when his son was so ill, and just

40

wait, it would come back on its own. But he had been referred, at his own request, to an expert in sexual problems, an elderly woman with a central European accent. She established that nothing aroused him any more. Not young girls, not sexy underwear, no smells or sights or sensations. His libido was defunct. 'Perhaps you should be glad of it,' she suggested. 'After the storms, the calm. Think of the time and trouble you save by not thinking about sex.'

That's not the advice I'm paying through the nose for, he had thought with some indignation. But now, two years later, he wondered whether she had, after all, been right.

He rolled further apart from his wife and tried to think about other things: Toby, his shoreline series, the portrait. Thinking of Clarissa, so very womanly, so understanding and undemanding, he momentarily felt stirrings of a long-lost impulse. Then Barbara said softly, 'Come closer. Let's just try . . .'

It had gone again. Now she would be considerate, undemanding, pliable. And nothing would happen. He would disappoint her again.

'I'm terribly tired,' he said. 'And I've got a splitting headache. It's the oil paints in that little room. When the wind's off the sea I can't open the windows enough, I'm going to see whether some kind of ventilator – '

Barbara turned abruptly away, taking much of the duvet with her, hunching herself into a foetal position with her back to her husband and her hands over her ears. Neither had referred to the episode next day; and now Barbara had gone away, so Colin could sit on Clarissa's sofa listening to a Mahler symphony and watching her move quietly between the white, galley-style kitchen and a round table which she was laying with a red cloth and flowered plates. She set out horseradish sauce and mustard in silver pots and then repolished the two wineglasses, holding them up to the light before placing them exactly parallel. She had on a red dress he had admired when she wore it before, with pearls, shining, light coloured stockings and high-heeled shoes. She looked entirely domesticated, and immensely feminine.

'Clarissa.'

She did not reply until Colin repeated her name, and then she said, 'Oh, sorry, I wasn't listening.'

'Come and sit down here.'

'Of course.' She moved across the room, but changed her mind

41

when she heard footsteps outside. 'There's Toby just coming up the stairs. Well timed, Toby! Come in, get yourself some Coke, you know where it is. Colin, you like your beef rare, don't you? Toby, I remember you like cauliflower so just decide for me. Shall we have it plain or with a cheese sauce? You can choose.'

7

Time, time, there was never enough time. Life consisted of rushing from Newcastle to Dover, Birmingham to Blackpool, writing and reading in hot stuffy hotel rooms, waking to work out where she was and which case she was doing. There was certainly no time to find a new lover. I'd do it like a shot, Barbara thought, it would be no skin off Colin's nose, but where, how, who . . .? She'd listened to a radio discussion on the way up to Bristol this time. It was a repeat from the previous September.

Turning on mid-programme Barbara had not realised why the deep, warm voice was familiar. After an advertisement break the presenter mentioned Dr Fidelis Berlin's name again, and her image flashed into Barbara's memory, the expert witness at an inquiry back in the summer. She was talking about confidence. Believe in yourself and others will believe in you – yes, she insisted, men too. Think yourself attractive and sexy and they will think so too.

All very well, Barbara thought, if you ever meet any. It was on her list of things to do. Find a lover. When there's time, when there aren't five decisions waiting to be written and dentists and new shoes for Toby to be fitted in, and suits to be collected from the cleaners and shirts to be ironed . . . Men with wives have time for mistresses.

Before setting off on the long drive home Barbara had time to go down to the Broadmead shopping centre, where she had promised to find Toby a particular football strip. Clarissa Trelawny had given him boots for Christmas and taken him to a match in Southampton. Now he wanted the full gear. Eventually Barbara tracked nearly all the kit down in John Lewis's just before closing time. Then it took nearly an hour to stop and start her way out of Bristol and on to the motorway. There was a torrential downpour on Dartmoor and thick fog crossing Bodmin Moor. Altogether the journey took over four hours.

Toby was not in bed when Barbara came in. He was waiting for his mother at the top of the steps, sheltered from the rain by the canopy, but without a coat in the chill night air. Barbara's first reaction, automatic since his illness, was to tell him to go into the warm. Her second was one of dismay. He was wearing the full team rig, even with the cap which Barbara had not been able to find. She let the carrier bag drop on to the floor.

'Where did you get that?'

'Isn't it magic? Auntie Clarissa got it for me, she went to Plymouth specially.' He bounced the ball up and down like a spring. 'Harry and Crispin will be sick.'

Colin called, 'Is that Mum at last? Come in, you must be exhausted. I've got your meal in the oven.'

'Look, Mum, Auntie Clarissa got me this too.' A further expensive refinement, a nylon bag in the team colours, and in it a matching, striped towel.

Colin came into the hall. 'I did tell Clarissa she shouldn't have bothered.'

'Isn't it nice of her?' Toby's open, clear face, beaming in uncomplicated pride, was like a pain in Barbara's heart.

'It's lovely, darling,' she said.

'I knew you'd like it. Dad said I could wait up to show you.'

Barbara picked up the carrier bag containing her own, inferior offering and put it, with her briefcase and overnight bag, into her office. She said, 'Now I've seen it you go and have your bath. I'm just going to go across and thank Clarissa myself.'

'Can I come?' Toby said.

'What about your supper?' Colin said.

'I'm not really hungry. I'll just go round alone, I think, Toby, it's long past your bedtime.'

She pattered down the steps in her high-heeled work shoes, and across the dimly lit courtyard. The Piazza, where Clarissa Trelawny was living, was a development of flats and studios next door to the similar but not identical Barnaloft. Not many of the apartments were occupied at this time of the year, a large proportion of them being used for second homes and holiday lets, so the place seemed deserted, and, in the low light, a little creepy. In the courtyard of the Piazza stood a large abstract sculpture in granite by Barbara

Hepworth, who had owned an apartment there herself, impressive always and cheerful on a sunny day, but now seeming indefinably threatening.

Clarissa's studio, on a corner and on the top floor, was approached, like the Pomeroys' flat, by an outside staircase. Barbara ran up them without pausing for breath, as though she were fuelled by fury. How dare this stranger usurp Barbara's role, provide Toby with treats and presents which were his mother's prerogative? Just because I have to work, she thought, it doesn't mean I can't look after my own son. I know what he wants better than anyone else. I can provide it.

He's seeing too much of her, Barbara thought. It's not healthy for a boy of eleven to spend his time with a woman of her age. How do I know what goes on between them? We don't know anything about her. It simply won't do, I'm going to put a stop to it. She came to a halt outside Clarissa's door, hearing voices. The door between the hallway and living-room must be open, because Clarissa's voice was clearly audible. She was on the telephone.

'How on earth did you track me down here? . . . What? No, I shan't. I'm settled here for the time being, it's a lovely place . . . I'm perfectly well now . . . Yes, really . . . No, not a lot so far, but I have met a few nice people . . . No. Are they in Cornwall? I didn't know . . . I might go over sometime . . . People called Pomeroy . . . Yes, Barbara and Colin Pomeroy. He's retired and she's away a lot, she's a civil servant, something to do with town and country planning, and they've got a son, a lovely child, I'm getting to know him very well, I feel he's partly my own, in a very special way, I'm going to make sure he gets everything, all my – What? No, not yet. But I'm going to, I've decided . . . No, you can't. Certainly not . . . It's all different now . . . Yes, I have changed. Are you surprised? . . . Well, I might think about it. But don't ring again . . . Who? . . . No. I mean it. Just don't . . . Goodbye.'

The emphasis on the last word implied the receiver had been slammed down after it. Barbara raised her hand to knock but changed her mind. Perhaps, she thought, I did over-react. If Clarissa's just a lonely woman who has been ill, it can't really do any harm to let Toby . . . After all, he is my son, not hers. Nothing can change that.

I'm the one, she thought on her way to bed, who picks his clothes up off the floor and tucks him back into his duvet at midnight. I shall make him a dentist's appointment tomorrow and go to a parents' evening on Friday. It is I who have the right and the chance to stroke his warm, jelly-smooth cheeks with the back of my fingers as he sleeps, who in this sleeping pre-adolescent can see the baby and toddler he once was. The wind had dropped so Barbara opened the window a little to let the smell of schoolboy dissipate in the night air.

Colin was already in bed when Barbara got in beside him. She picked up her book, a biography of Octavia Hill, but he could never sleep with the light on and said in a disappointed tone, 'Oh, aren't you tired?' so she closed the book and lay down.

Colin was quickly asleep, his breathing deep and regular. He lay neatly on his back, his arms at his side in what she once called his effigy position. He emitted a little snort, not quite a snore, at the end of each in-drawn breath. The window was tilted open at top and bottom and Barbara could hear a moderate surf breaking below, and, further away, some sexually rampant cats. They should be spayed and so should I, she thought.

Trying to move under the duvet without disturbing it, she tossed and turned. She ran her mind over the get-to-sleep topics which were her personal substitute for counting sheep. Usually she visualised a house she had been to, and how she would alter and arrange it. Half-heartedly she recreated in her memory the rambling farmhouse where Toby's friend Crispin lived in a valley between St Ives and Penzance.

Replace the PVC windows with white-painted wood, reinsert the glazing bars, put back a panelled front door, retile the roof . . . One could turn that big room downstairs into a studio for Colin – No. This was no good. Barbara felt as far from sleep as ever she had. Using the torch which she kept on her bedside table she found some clothes in the wardrobe and took them, with her running shoes, out to the bathroom where she could turn the light on and get dressed again.

Never a heavy sleeper, Barbara had become a confirmed insomniac when Toby was ill. Indeed, at that time sleep had been unwelcome, because such nightmares galloped in with it. In those days Barbara would get up in her dressing-gown and sit by the sleeping child's bed. Since they came to St Ives she had taken to going outside when it was mild enough, to walk or jog along the beach or through the silent lanes and alleys of the little town. Now, as so often before, she went softly out of the flat and down the stairs, through the paved tunnel under the building and out on to the soft, silent sand.

8

Fidelis Berlin spent a long, lazy summer. It was not only a deferred period of convalescence from an operation after which she had had to go back to work too soon, but also the first period of complete freedom she could remember, for she had retired from her university post. So she went to stay with friends in a gîte in Provence and then, in almost unbearable heat, with others in a villa in Umbria from whose shelter they ventured only at the beginning and end of each day.

New York that September was just as hot and much more humid. Fidelis had come to do some work, but was her own mistress, so she went off on a series of intensely sociable visits in Maine. She felt renewed after the weeks of rest. 'But not rejuvenated,' she told her third host, an old friend called Lionel. 'I can't tell you what fun I'm finding it to be my age.'

'Forty-two?'

'Don't be silly. Sixty last birthday and looking it.'

'Not if you wear – '

'But you don't understand, Lionel, every party I've been to since getting here, I'm the only woman not pretending to be younger than she is. I'm like a lamb among lions, the only non-predatory female there.'

'And every man makes a beeline for you.'

'Because I'm so restful and unthreatening.'

'Until you drop the disguise.'

'It isn't a disguise, Lionel, it's the real new me. I don't suppose I've looked at a man without wondering what he'd be like in bed since I was thirteen. Now I'm developing a whole new way of looking at life – at my age. It may sound perverse but I feel rejuvenated. It's all so interesting – you should try it sometime.' She caught sight of the horrified expression which flashed across Lionel's taut tanned face. They were sitting in the long kitchen of his summer house, a light, cheerful room which always looked as though it had just been arranged for a publicity photograph, with green-stained Shaker furniture and cream draperies.

'Fidelis.' He stretched his manicured hand across the heap of vegetables he was meticulously cutting into matchsticks. 'Is this the woman who once described herself as a man-eater?'

'I know other people said so.'

'You did too. Remember that British self-deprecation?'

'I think of myself as strictly truthful.'

'No. Modest, funny, courageous – you've always been a feisty lady, Fidelis.'

She didn't feel it; just interested in a new way of living, though after she returned to New York she was so busy there was little time to think about her own feelings.

She had been lent an apartment in the West Village, and got back there in mid-October in time to have her best friend from London, Tina Svenson, to stay for a fortnight. The two women gossiped and giggled, went to midnight movies, biked in the park, ate hot dogs and french fries out of paper cones as they walked along the street, took in experimental and traditional theatre and three poetry readings and spent money on unnecessary clothes, buying hand-painted silk shirts for Fidelis to wear with her Joseph jackets, designer jeans for Tina; they rootled through the racks at department stores or thrift shops with whoops of derision or glee. They even experimented with one another's cosmetics.

'You do realise we've been behaving like teenagers rather than grandmothers,' Tina said.

'That's OK, I'm not a grandmother anyway.'

'Well, I am,' Tina said tartly. She had three children who had four children and a variety of stepchildren between them. 'And you can jolly well come and help me buy presents for the lot of them, do you realise I've got to go home tomorrow? Work on Monday, oh God.'

Tina was an academic publisher and loved it, so Fidelis ignored the ritual moan and said, 'One of the things about not having had children – '

'Another thing? Surely you've published the last word on that subject by now?'

'I can't remember. Did I ever say it means one never grows up?'

'Yes, Fidelis, I think you might have said that,' Tina said affectionately. The two women had been friends since Tina met her first husband just after his affair with Fidelis had come to a mutually satisfactory end. Frank Svenson had been as little suited to family life as Fidelis had guessed he would be, and quite soon left Tina and their two children. Fidelis felt a little responsible at the time. Should she have warned Tina? But all that was many years ago. Tina had been married twice more since then, and the two women had been intimate for thirty years.

On Tina's last morning, as she was trying to pack everything she had bought, Fidelis opened a document, more a rambling autobiographical essay than a letter, of self-recommendation sent by Sophie Teague, and read it aloud as Tina struggled. It was written over half a dozen large pages of thin paper in a round, schoolgirlish handwriting.

Sophie had listed all her own defects and disasters, which included four failed subjects out of seven at GCSE when she was sixteen, retakes and two failed A levels.

'I call that disarmingly candid,' Tina said.

Fidelis read on. 'She says, "Here comes my alibi." ' Sophie had appended confessional explanations. She had 'got into the wrong set'. She had made friends with the wildest kids at school, the ones who were familiar with all aspects of social workers and juvenile courts, supervision orders and police cautions. In her teens Sophie thought them all unspeakably glamorous.

' "My poor mother was in despair. All she'd ever wanted was a pretty daughter with shiny hair who loved her pony, but I was always a bit of a rebel. In retrospect I realise it must have been because my father left home when I was four. He was a civil engineer and moved around the world a lot, so my mum was left with us and Dad had three more wives. I hardly ever saw him because he didn't really approve of me and there was always a row whenever we did meet. Just before he died I went to stay at his place in Sheffield with my father and his fourth wife and her three kids, the whole thing was a complete disaster but he was killed the very day I left when his car's brakes failed and he went off the road. He left my brother and me two thousand pounds each, so I spent the lot on a motor bike and Dominic invested his in unit trusts." '

'Humph,' said Tina.

'What does that mean?'

'Doth the lady protest too much? What's she making excuses for?'

'You're too cynical.'

'No, I'm not, I'm a mother of daughters, that's all.'

Fidelis continued. ' "I bummed around for a few years after leaving school but my mother kept saying I needed a qualification and went on about how different her own life would have been if she'd been able to get a proper job. She never had a chance to learn anything else after Dad left, because she had to work all the time to support me and Dominic, as secretary at the primary school we went to in our village and she's still there. Anyway, I eventually came to realise she was right about getting a proper education, though I've picked up lots of skills along the way which is why I'm sure I could be useful to you, Dr Berlin. I can fix a car and word process and do things like washing your porcelain or polish copper ornaments." '

'How does she know you've got them anyway?' Tina said.

'Most people have ornaments, don't they? Listen, she says, "Unlike the others at college who are the usual age, I really do know how lucky I am to be doing the course, because being a mature student they let me off the strict entry requirements. I think it's been a good thing to wait and study psychology when one has seen a bit more of the world." '

'Sounds as though she's quoting you on that subject, Fidelis.'

'I don't see why, it's true anyway.'

'I'm getting interested in this young woman. What does she tell you next?'

Sophie wrote she'd had more than one boyfriend but nobody really serious. Fidelis paused over the bland statement, wondering whether the girl thought it might influence an older, single woman in her favour, and said, 'D'you suppose she thinks I'm gay?'

'Could be. She's obviously weighed every word.'

Fidelis recognised that the whole document had been written carefully, probably copied out several times, and purposefully slanted to say what might be supposed to appeal to its recipient. Or was that unfair? Probably she should take this as nothing more than the curriculum of a young life, artlessly expanded at the request of someone who had asked not for a CV but a letter.

Fidelis read on. ' "I expect what you really want to know is why I chose to study psychology. I think it's partly because of my dad." '

'There, that's the lot,' Tina said, plumping her weight down on the suitcase lid. 'Tell you what, Fidelis, that girl knows you didn't have a father or mother.'

49

'Maybe. She says, "I've realised a lot that's happened to me has been directly on account of growing up in a single parent family and it's made me wonder about other people in that situation, I'd like to understand how they cope and get through life, what effect does it have, and – this is why your own specialism interests me so much – would things have been different if they'd had access to better crèches or nurseries?" '

'Is there a lot more of this? I want to go to MoMA again.'

'A bit,' Fidelis said, but read no more aloud. She found the naïve splurge of self-exposure endearing and innocent. It was, in a way, a case study for the very problem the girl was interested in.

'You're always such a soft touch for young people, I'd think twice if I were you,' Tina said, but she had spent thirty years telling Fidelis to be more careful than she ever thought necessary. Fidelis wrote to Sophie at the college's address which was the only one given on the letter, to say she would employ her on a part-time basis when she got back to London in the early spring.

9

It was a sick coincidence, Barbara later realised, that the seminar at headquarters was the very day before the Reading appeal. She was having lunch in the canteen with some colleagues when one produced a cutting from the *Sunday Telegraph*. The article was by a journalist who had made it his personal crusade to hold back the interference of what he called power-mad bureaucrats. One, described as 'a junior civil servant from the planning inspectorate in Bristol', was vilified for giving permission for the garden of a village rectory to be used for low cost housing.

'The only thing to be said for this junk is that he hasn't accused us of corruption,' one man said.

'Funny, when you think how much easier it would be to bribe one of us than a whole planning committee,' another agreed.

'I was offered a bribe once,' said one of the oldest people present. He told his awed colleagues about the episode: a hot night in the middle of an interminable inquiry. 'I'm drowning my sorrows on the hotel terrace when this bloke joins me, the waiter brings another drink I never ordered, and we get chatting. And then he says it, bold as brass. Fifty thousand smackers in a numbered account on the day they get their permission, what did I say?'

'What did you say?' the others chorused.

'Told him to get lost, what d'you think? Told the boss, told the police, inquiry aborted . . .'

'So what happened?'

'Nothing much. The chap I'd spoken to couldn't be found – the police thought it might have been someone with no connection hired for the purpose – and the next inspector gave permission anyway, on the merits.'

'Just as well this journalist never heard that story.'

A mild-mannered former architect said, 'He'd have sung a different tune if he'd wanted to build something in his very own back garden. Then it would all have been, What's it coming to when an Englishman's home isn't his castle any more?'

A former county planning officer said, 'Next thing, he'll be saying we're all bribed, or bought off, or even freemasons giving each other permissions.'

'That lets Barbara out then. Or are you part of some feminist secret society?'

Shaking her head she wondered whether it would be naïve to say the idea of corruption had never so much as crossed her mind before. But one of the others said it for her.

'Not Barbara, she's sea-green incorruptible, I remember that from training,' said the water engineer. 'Starry-eyed about this being the fairest system for environmental protection ever devised, weren't you, girl?'

'I don't know about starry-eyed,' Barbara said. 'But I'd point out what happens when you don't have planners.'

'London Docklands!' her companions chorused. That was the classic example, now used in textbooks all over the world, of the mess which had resulted from the developmental free-for-all of the 1980s. Office blocks had been built without car-parking, before there was public transport for their workforce, homes were out of reach of any shops, the uncontrolled diversity of architectural styles detracted from the appearance of each individual part.

'Enough said.' They all nodded, reminded of the value of their own profession.

Barbara left early to get to Reading before it was very late; even before dark there was freezing fog and the motorway was night-marish. She checked into the hotel with relief. Travelling from Newcastle to Dover, from Birmingham to Blackpool, it could become hard to keep her bearings, and Barbara often woke not knowing where she was. But on days like this she found comfort in the impersonal familiarity of the hot, stuffy room, its thick net curtains covering the rectangle of sealed glass which, as usual, overlooked a busy road. She ordered an omelette from room service, spoke to Colin and Toby, prepared her notes for the next day and watched an emotional documentary about a man who had abducted and murdered seven small girls, before sleeping un-usually soundly and well.

The next day's appeal was routine; a property company proposed to demolish a large suburban house in Chambers Grove and build a cluster of cheap little houses on the site. It was a one-day inquiry, but the wintry weather was persisting so Barbara decided not to drive back to Cornwall until the next morning. She made her formal visit to the site, where she solemnly looked at the house and its surroundings, walking up and down the street between the rival parties and followed by anxious neighbours. Though she had been there on her own before the inquiry opened, she forced herself to do it slowly so nobody could later accuse her of basing her decision on inadequate information, before, at last, thank goodness, being able to get into her car and turn the heater on full blast.

Another lonely evening, another documentary, this time about social security fraud. Barbara watched the late headlines on *Newsnight*, with pictures of impassable roads and isolated villages, and was taking off her dressing-gown to get into bed when the telephone rang.

'Hullo.' A silence. 'Colin, is that you?'

'Mrs Pomeroy?'

'Yes, speaking. Who's that?'

'Don't ask questions. Just listen. You'd better give permission for Chambers Grove.'

'I can't talk about that – who the hell is this? You know perfectly well there's no – '

'You've got a handsome little boy at home, haven't you?'

'What?'

'Toby. Nice name. Nice kid, I dare say. Needs a lot of looking after. You take good care of him, you and Colin, don't you?'

'What – who – has something happened to Toby?'

'Not yet. And it won't if you do what I say.' It seemed to be a female voice, husky as though there were a cloth muffling the telephone, with a slightly cockney accent.

'You must be – '

'Listen, missis. Listen good. You don't want a nasty accident to happen to the kid. Just write out the planning permission and he'll be all fine and dandy.'

'But – '

'And don't think you can get out of it by resigning from the case. That would do his health a bit of no good and no mistake. Make your decision and make it right. Make sure we get that permission and you can all live happy ever after, get it? And don't kid yourself I don't mean it 'cos I do. No backing out of the decision, no making the wrong one. Otherwise . . . hit and run . . . acid in his little eyes . . . an accidental drowning . . . it doesn't bear thinking of, really, does it? Not when it's so easy to keep him safe.'

She rang off and Barbara held the receiver, paralysed by horror. Then she frantically jiggled the button and dialled home, making a mistake with the numbers in her haste, tears springing from her eyes as twice she had to redial, and the telephone rang five times unanswered. And then at last there was Colin.

'Barbara? It's a bit late, I was asleep.'

'Colin – Toby. Is he all right?'

'Yes, of course, he's fast asleep. What's the matter?'

'Go and look, make sure – now, please.'

'All right, if it will make you happy.'

She waited in anguish until Colin came back and said impatiently, 'All present and correct and fast asleep. What's this about? Did you have a bad dream?'

'No, I . . .' She stopped. If she told Colin, if she told anyone else, she would be forced to withdraw from the case, like the inspector who had been offered a bribe. There would be a police investigation and a new public inquiry and the woman who had threatened her would take her revenge. On Toby. One couldn't protect him all the time. There's nothing so vulnerable as a little boy. But Colin – he'd see that, he'd understand . . . No. He might not. Suppose he behaved like an honourable soldier, suppose he said one must never give in to threats any more than to blackmail or bribery, he had often talked about it when such cases hit the headlines. She

53

knew exactly what he thought, what he had been trained in the army to think, about terrorism and hostage taking.

Never pay, never bargain, he might say, even with Toby's safety at stake.

Slowly Barbara said, 'Yes, it was another dream. I'm sorry for waking you.'

And now, no doubt, he would go back to easy sleep.

Barbara sat in the livid illumination of street lights and neon signs wondering whether she would ever rest again. The same thoughts came in sequence, joining up into a closed circle within which she was imprisoned.

How did they know where to find her? Not difficult. She would never have noticed if her car was trailed from the site visit to the hotel.

How did they know about Toby and Colin? Not that difficult to find out, once they knew who would be conducting the inquiry. Her name had been posted for all to see on the notice at least a month in advance.

But even then . . . how many Mrs Pomeroys must there be in the country? Actually, with the letters which denoted her membership of the Royal Town Planning Institute following the name, very few. Probably only one. Although the planning inspectorate's office in Bristol was the address now beside her name in membership lists, earlier editions had her home address in Leicester, and in Morpeth where she had been working when she joined. It would not be difficult to find where she had moved to. And a single visit to her present home would have shown all anyone wanted to know about her family circumstances.

Toby. Colin.

She knew what she ought to do. Tell Colin, tell her boss, tell the police. There would be a trial at which she would be a witness. Today's inquiry would be void.

But the woman had threatened Toby if Barbara even withdrew from the case.

They couldn't mean it. What would be the point?

Future intimidation. Maybe of her, maybe of others. 'Inspector Smith, you have two pretty daughters, how would you like acid thrown in their faces? Inspector Jones, what would you do to keep your son safe? Remember what happened to the Pomeroys.'

But if they found who'd made the threat, surely that would stop it from being carried out?

It might be too late. And Barbara would never feel safe again, not for the rest of her career, not for the rest of her life.

Several times round that mirthless merry-go-round and Barbara put on the light and switched on the electric kettle. Sachets of instant coffee and powdered milk, chocolate drink, shortbread biscuits. She couldn't swallow any of it.

The files: evidence taken at the inquiry, written down by her in longhand; proofs of evidence; photocopies of precedents, maps and plans, copies of government guidance and regulations. The original appeal form. Reading District Council against Allday Property Developments. The appellants had been represented by a firm of chartered surveyors, the council by a barrister, a snooty young man who spoke to Barbara as though she might not understand. What would he say if he knew what had happened? What would the High Court say in an appeal? But there was no appeal against the granting of planning permission, only against its refusal, unless the inspector made some major blunder about law or procedure.

Was that the way out? Grant permission in such a way it could be overturned, commit a major breach of the laws of natural justice, fail to take into account something that should have been considered, do something blatantly unfair which the High Court would castigate?

But then they might take it out on her all the same.

Not on her. On Toby.

Round and round. She opened the thin curtains and looked out on to falling snowflakes coloured pink by the reflection of the hotel sign. There must be two inches of snow. Some cars were still moving along the road below, their roofs burdened by the snow, their tracks curving as they slid and skidded. How would she ever get home tomorrow? Just as well, perhaps, if she couldn't. If I never went home again, she thought, if I just kept away from Toby . . . but that wouldn't keep him safe. They'd still know she cared about him. She could still suffer through his suffering. As though he hadn't already had to endure enough for a whole lifetime.

What if she did back out, what if she gave up this inquiry and the job itself, resigned altogether, then they might not . . .

But you couldn't be sure. They still might do it. Just out of spite, out of wickedness.

They. Who? Somebody who stood to make a lot of money out of this appeal. Funny, she used to think, that one of her own decisions, so often finely balanced, could enrich or impoverish people. Land value could multiply a hundred times if it had the benefit of planning permission. These applicants . . . Allday Properties.

I've come across that name, she thought, Allday. It rings a bell. Where have I seen it or heard it? It won't come, but never mind, what does it matter? Whoever it is, if I don't tell the authorities and back out of the case and start the full procedure of detection and retribution, it doesn't make any difference who has made this threat.

I'll do it, she told herself, I'll give permission, I might have done in any case. It won't do all that much harm.

No. If I give permission it'll be because I've been blackmailed into it, that's the only reason, to keep Toby safe.

And then what?

Barbara wondered whether she could carry on, knowing herself to be corruptible, corrupt, no longer impartial, just, balanced.

She was proud of her work, proud of herself for doing it. She had job satisfaction.

Had had. She thought, I'll never enjoy it again if I carry on.

The sound of a tune through the wall and then the unmistakable intonation of a news reader's voice interrupted the treadmill of her thoughts. It was morning, another day, time to get herself going. Get dressed. Eat, or at least drink something. Pack. Load the car. Go home.

10

Early in the New Year Neville Cox passed through New York on his way to a business meeting further south and arranged to join Fidelis for a drink. He brought good news of the kindergartens – new building and bulging waiting lists. Seeing him reminded her she had a separate life to go home to in England, away from the absorbing, time-consuming bustle of an over-full lecture programme and the exhausting adulation of students wanting to follow in her footsteps and to be told how to do it, what to read, what to write, how to think, even what label was inside Fidelis's beautiful clothes. She had never previously been made so aware that she was a role model for these younger women. It flattered but frightened her.

Unlike some British friends who seemed diminished and out of place when she met them on the other side of the Atlantic, Neville's accent and manners fitted in well. She knew he bought his clothes and shoes in America, and he took care of himself in a way less usual in London than New York. He had tanned skin, glossed hair, bright eyes with very clear whites. His muscles were hard and stomach flat, and he talked about skiing and water skiing, golf and a rowing machine. He had recently been to Hawaii and Tenerife, and while he was here was going to take a quick trip over to Aspen.

'Lovely to see you, Fidelis, how are you doing?'

'I'm having a marvellous time, actually, Neville, there's so much going on over here.' But she let her voice tail off without telling him about her fascinating days and stimulating evenings. He wouldn't really be interested. They were in a bar whose walls were lined with mirrors. Seeing their reflections side by side would once have made a bitter pill for Fidelis to force down. She sat there swirling the ice round in her glass, smiling, tilting her head to attend to Neville's account of the deal he was fixing up in South Carolina; and at the back of her mind was a pleased, almost smug realisation that it didn't worry her to know she was too old and past it while he was still an attractive, potent man.

Neville's and Fidelis's affair had been short and not so much sweet as savoury – an experience to savour. Though selfish, he made a remarkably good lover. He only did what he wanted to do, all his motions made for his own pleasure, but what Neville took pleasure in was the sensual side of life. He was a very physical man, enjoying good food, wine, clothes, fabrics – and women. He liked the feel of women, he touched and tasted for his own sake not hers, but the effect was as good as, perhaps better than, with a man who more anxiously considered her reactions.

Something of her thoughts must have showed in her expression, for Neville leant forward and said intimately, 'We had fun, didn't we?' The grey-haired, lined woman in the pinkish mirror nodded and smiled her lop-sided smile, and he added, 'It's not too late. Don't forget, it was you finished it, not me.'

It had been ten years ago. Fidelis summoned her memories of Neville's lack of education, his intellectual vacancy, the blankness

57

with which he always received any mention of books or art. She reminded herself of the episode which broke up their affair; a disagreement – she couldn't even remember what it had been about – which ended with him grasping her arm painfully tight and threatening her with his other hand on her throat. In her long list of lovers, none had ever been violent or used force. She managed to struggle free, stamping on his instep and jabbing her elbow into his chest. He'd been ready for bed again after that. But Fidelis wasn't, then or later. She would never go to bed with a man who hit her. Never. Not even if – when – she was desperate. She looked at her watch, a plain silver disc by Jensen.

'Nice watch. Replacement on the robbery insurance?' Neville said.

'I didn't know you knew about it. No, I gave it to myself, an impulse buy in Barney's. I can't stay long, Neville, I'm due at a concert.'

'I should have remembered how busy you always are but I hoped I might persuade you to come to a club with me.'

'Thanks but no thanks.' Gambling and girls would never at any time have been Fidelis's idea of fun. 'What a horrible shock you'd have got if I'd agreed.'

'No fear of that, is there? You and your old music. I never could understand what you see in it.'

'Have you ever been to a classical concert in your life?'

'I had to once at school, that was more than enough for me.'

Neville, she knew, had been to what was then still called a council school, and left at fourteen to become a clerk in the City. There he had watched, observed, recognised what he wanted for himself, and worked out how to get it. The original self-made man, he'd once boasted to her. A go-getter. A man, she'd concluded, without scruples.

'How's Buffy?' she asked.

'Oh, much the same I think.'

'You think?'

'I've been away from home a good bit recently.'

Fidelis translated his words in her mind: I'm spending my free time with another woman. Who am I to disapprove? she wondered, but said, 'Things are difficult for her.'

'She doesn't seem able to get over Andy dying.'

'I don't suppose you can either.'

'Actually I hardly think of him any more, but these things are always easier for men.'

'Do you really think so?'

'Nothing to be done but pick oneself up and carry on.'

Three years before, Andrew Cox, then in his mid-twenties, was dreadfully injured in a car accident. At the time Buffy was in New Zealand staying with her sister, who had emigrated twenty years before and kept in very intermittent contact with her family. It was her and Buffy's first meeting in fifteen years and the two women had gone to a holiday resort somewhere on the North Island. Buffy was contacted with the bad news, flown to Christchurch and squeezed on to a full flight. She was thousands of feet above south-east Asia at the moment Andrew was certified brain dead.

Fidelis seemed to be in the position of 'best friend' if only because there was nobody else. She had been waiting in the house when Neville and Buffy got back from the airport, had gone with her to the morgue to see the body, had received the neighbours' offerings of cakes and casseroles, had listened, for hours at a time, to Buffy's outpourings of rage and grief. Who better than a professional psychiatrist to know exactly what Buffy was feeling?

Know was the operative word. Fidelis knew what mothers felt about their children because she had made it her study. Not being a mother, not having been a mother's beloved child, she had no memory, in her own experience, of the emotion. Indeed, self-analysis had made her realise that she had chosen her professional path precisely because she had not had the experience. Of course one could sympathise – a word derived from the Greek meaning, literally, to suffer *with* someone. But she had made herself an expert because she could not empathise – suffer *inside* them. Always the outsider, always the recorder or observer of human emotion, she sometimes accused herself of having spent her life trying to reduce maternal love to a formula simply in order to learn it for herself. And when Buffy accused her of never being able to understand, Fidelis was sadly afraid it was true.

'I should have gone up to see Buffy before I came away, but I was so busy sorting everything out . . .'

'I know, it's much too far. Inconvenient. I wanted to move further in before Andy died, but there's no point in trying to discuss that kind of thing these days and to tell you the truth I stay up in town a lot of the time.' He smiled at her with friendly, familiar complicity. 'You know me,' he said.

11

She had three weeks. Three weeks before anyone noticed she'd missed the deadline. Three weeks to decide.

Barbara knew what Colin would say and her colleagues would insist. Giving in to threats would seem no less reprehensible than exposing herself to blackmail or taking bribes.

Sleeping on it – or, mostly, failing to sleep – was no help at all. Not the faintest glimmer of a solution came to her. And meanwhile everything else went to pot.

Colin, who seldom complained, did complain of Barbara's short temper. She snapped at him on no provocation, shouted at Toby, had silent spells which were interpreted as sulking.

Random checks routinely made on inspectors' decision letters began to turn up errors in Barbara's – most of them simple typing mistakes such as a wrong figure in the reference number but some serious enough to matter, as in one case where Barbara granted planning permission to the wrong address, and another in which she omitted essential conditions. She was summoned to head office, where she spoke of family problems and promised to be more careful in future. What would they live on if she lost this job?

Ten days after the first call, Barbara was rung at home.

'Mrs Pomeroy?'

She would have slammed it down if she had thought to do so in time, instead of saying, 'Yes, speaking.'

'Just thought I'd remind you.' The voice was not muffled or husky this time; low, clear, feminine, with south-east English vowels. 'Don't forget now, will you, about reaching the right decision in the Reading case?'

She gripped the receiver, unable to speak. 'Nice little chap, that kid of yours, shame if anything happened to him. But you won't let that happen, will you, Mrs Pomeroy? Look forward to hearing from you.' Click. And she hadn't even pressed the record button on the answering machine. 'Oh, God, what shall I do?'

If only there were someone she could talk to. If only she had anyone to rely on except Colin.

It was a long time since Barbara had regretted having no relations; indeed there had been periods when she thought herself lucky, when friends complained about their own demanding parents or jealous siblings. But now was the time when she could have done with a mother's shoulder to weep on. A mother. Some ideal mother. Not her own mother.

Barbara had grown up in what was not, in her childhood, called 'a single parent family'. She was Katie Dutton's by-blow, little mistake, bastard, or at best, illegitimate child. Katie Dutton used the words herself.

Katie was thrown out by her family when she got pregnant. She never tried to hide her own shame, but nobody could have regretted her sin more than she did, and she became a walking penitence, her daughter's existence the visible penance. Katie stayed in her home town, Sheffield, and worked as a charwoman to support herself and Barbara, who spent her days with a child-minder until she was old enough for school. Then she became a latch-key kid. Katie never mentioned Barbara's father, whoever he had been. Barbara was brought up from day one to know she had been a mistake and that she had better not make a similar blunder when her time came. Barbara's earliest, consuming, changeless ambition was to get away from home and her mother. She hated her cheerless home and was unhappy at school, where many of the girls copied their own families in despising the Duttons.

Barbara realised very early on that education would be the key of her release. She would rely on her own abilities. She worked obsessively to get through all the necessary exams and escaped to Oxford Polytechnic on a full student grant when she was just eighteen. Katie died the following year. Barbara never missed her mother, only the imagined, perfect parents and other relations she always wished she had had.

No father. No mother. Not even a mother-in-law, since Colin's mother died the year after they were married. No sister, no brother, no friend with whom she could share this dilemma. Should she ring the Samaritans? Go to her doctor? Encounter, for the first time in her adult life, a priest or minister?

Night after night, tossing, shifting, agonising.

61

On the first day of March, a Tuesday, a postcard addressed to Mrs B. Pomeroy came in the morning delivery. It was a picture of the Queen, an elderly woman in fancy dress sitting on a horse and saluting. The typed message was brief. It read, 'Don't forget to take good care of Toby.' Neither Toby nor Colin had seen the card and Barbara tore it across and across again, before putting the pieces into a plastic bag of vegetable peelings and pressing them down into the bucket under the sink.

Toby was due for a check-up at the hospital in Plymouth; his appointment had already been postponed once when one of Barbara's cases ran on for an extra day. The evening before, the clerk rang from Bristol to say Barbara was needed urgently in the office.

'I'm afraid they say it's vital,' he said.

'Well look, I'll ring back. Give me a couple of minutes.' She rang off and asked Colin whether he thought the appointment could be rearranged.

'Not again,' he said. 'But look, don't worry, you don't have to be there.'

'Of course I do, it's important!'

'I can manage on my own.'

Toby said brightly, 'I know, Dad, let's get Auntie Clarissa to come. Then we can go to the dry ski slope on the way home, she promised to take me there. Crispin says it's *wicked*.'

'That's a good idea, Tobe, we could do that. Clarissa's the ideal person to go with,' he said reassuringly to Barbara. 'Very sensible and unfussed.'

'And I really like her, Mum. She's great when you're away, she cooks us meat and stuff. You go to Bristol, honestly, we don't need you.'

He meant it well. That was the awful thing. Toby did not realise his unkindness. He loved his mother, but he'd got used to her absences. When he was in trouble he had learnt to turn to someone else because Barbara was not there.

Colin said, 'That's fine, it means you can take the car to Bristol and we can go with Clarissa's driver – '

'Driver?'

'She hires a car when she needs one, with a chauffeur.'

'Last time it was wicked, Mum, we went in a Jaguar, it can do a hundred and thirty.'

Toby's face was brilliant in its uncomplicated pleasure.

Barbara said in a low, controlled voice, 'Clarissa's become quite a little mother substitute, hasn't she?'

'Don't take it like that,' Colin said soothingly.

'Hasn't she got a family of her own?'

'She hasn't mentioned anyone. I think she's divorced.'

'Of course you'd never ask!' Barbara was well aware of Colin's unwillingness to ask personal questions. She interpreted it as a lack of interest in other people. After two weeks in an office, she, like most other women, knew the family circumstances of every single one of her colleagues. It's not nosiness, she used to insist, she really cared.

Colin said, 'Clarissa's just a neighbour, a kind, helpful woman with time to spare.'

'And you and Toby fill her time nicely, I suppose.'

'We don't,' Toby said. 'I haven't seen her for ages. Dad says I'm not allowed to go and pester her so I only ever see her if we meet on the beach or she comes round here.'

'Which she does whenever I'm away, presumably.'

'No . . .'

'And I've been here since last week so Clarissa Trelawny has kept clear. Right?'

'You're reading too much into this, Barbara, I assure you. You can't grudge her a bit of company, it must be lonely for her on her own and she's taken a fancy to Toby, that's all.'

'And to you, Dad,' Toby said eagerly. 'I told you, Mum, we all went to the fair and she and Dad went in a bumper car together for hours.'

'You told me you went to the fair. I didn't know Clarissa Trelawny had gone with you.'

'We just happened to meet her there,' Colin said.

'But Dad . . .' Toby's voice died away as he noticed his father shaking his head in warning at him; but Barbara noticed it too. She felt a lump in her chest, as though there were a round, sizeable ball of something light inside her, something rising to the surface just as a ball would in a pond, until it burst into the open and she cried out in release of the emotion it enclosed, her voice raucous, screeching, like – she realised it even as she shouted – like her own mother's angry voice, years before.

'I don't want to know about bloody Clarissa Trelawny. Who does she think she is, taking my son out, buying my son presents, cooking red meat in my kitchen? I'm Toby's mother, this is my house, I'm the one slaving away to earn enough to keep it all going, if anyone takes him to the renal clinic it will be me, do you understand?' She stopped. Toby had started to cry and Colin looked disgusted, his mouth screwed up in an expression of distaste and disdain. The unaccustomed yelling had hurt her throat. She took some deep breaths and then said quietly, 'I'm sorry I lost my temper. It's OK, Toby, it's not your fault, you know I'm never really cross with you, I'm tired, that's all, and I'm worried about something at work. I didn't mean it, stop crying. But you'd like it to be me that takes you really, wouldn't you? To the hospital, I mean, you know how you've always . . .'

He was embarrassed by tears, brushing his cheeks with his hands. He stood very close to his father and whispered, 'Yes, please, Mummy.'

Barbara told an embarrassed male clerk at the inspectorate that she had an unalterable hospital appointment of her own on account of 'something feminine'. She cooked chicken and roast potatoes for supper herself. She played Monopoly with Toby and told Colin they should have a dinner party and invite Clarissa to meet some of the friends they had made in St Ives. She would have done some long overdue mending of Toby's and Colin's clothes if the basket had not been empty and the clothes, beautifully darned, with all their buttons back in place, clean and ironed in their drawers. She did not ask who had done it.

Colin took longer than usual to fall asleep, sighing for a while before the familiar even breaths took over. Barbara realised it would be a sleeping pill for her, or long hours of wakefulness. But all sedatives made her feel dreadful throughout the following day, as though there were a layer of padding between her brain and her skull. It was a cool but clear night, so she put on her dark blue track suit and training shoes and went out.

Across the road and down through the shuttered craft market, where cats were loudly squabbling, across the empty car-park, up along Fore Street, looking into the windows of all the shops and art galleries as she passed. Since the Tate St Ives had opened its doors last summer the private galleries had been booming. Visitors who came to the town were in the mood for buying art and here were pictures and crafts of every kind to tempt them; conventional paintings of marine and rural scenes, geometric abstracts, fully, semi and only slightly representational art, useful and useless pottery and ceramics, photographs and lithographs, metalwork, jewellery, woodwork, sculpture. Barbara's taste in art and interior decoration was rather different from Colin's. She would have liked to decorate their home with simple post-war fabrics and furniture instead of the antiques he brought from his first marriage, and instead of hanging the good nineteenth-century oils of animals and fields, she hankered for a very few, very strongly coloured abstract paintings.

There was little traffic, only a couple of cars and one motor bike which passed her at speed, its leather-clad, helmeted rider horizontal over the handle bars. Nights were silent here.

She stood for a moment looking at the seductive display in the New Craftsman, and then pressed her nose against the window of the Wills Lane Gallery round the corner to see a joyful sunburst by Terry Frost. On down towards the harbour; this gallery's work was post-war representational and not usually to Barbara's liking, but it was here that Colin's pictures had first been shown in a mixed exhibition last year, and they still kept a few of them on show. He had sold one or two, but the gallery owner said he believed Colin's style would prove to be 'commercial' in the long run. Now, in the dim light, Barbara could just see a painting he had finished last month, a long low oil on board, of stones and shells with an impression of shallow, clear water washing over them.

Art. It's supposed to be a comfort and inspiration, she thought. Much good it's doing me now. It just reminds me that Colin's at home with Toby and I'm not. I leave to do my job and that's why our son's in danger.

It's all my fault, I shouldn't have been away so much.

It's not my fault. Why should it make a difference if the child's looked after by his father rather than me, he's got two parents which is more than I had.

But I should have been there. Then he wouldn't prefer a stranger to me. Clarissa Trelawny wouldn't have had the chance to worm her way in.

She walked round the harbour front, past the old and the new lifeboat houses, the closed apartments, most of them unused at this time of year, past the shuttered shops which would open again in the tourist season, and out along the wide outer wall of the harbour. The fishing boats would already have put out to sea. A few cars were parked here, but there did not seem to be anyone else around.

One of us has to earn a living, she thought.

Sitting with her legs dangling over the harbour wall, Barbara watched the rhythmic flashes from the lighthouse on the far side of the bay. The sea was quite still, a metallic, shining darkness, and the beams of light were reflected on to it.

Be honest. You always wanted to work, you wanted to have a career and a husband and a child. You wanted it all.

The tide was rising. Behind Barbara, in the sheltered horseshoe of the harbour, the moored boats were rocking on the moving water. She listened to the splashes of sea, the flapping of rope and line.

I had it all, she thought. Toby was well again, Colin was happy and busy, the job was exactly what I'd aimed for. I've been happy and fulfilled, travelling round to see so many new places, a different county every week, slums, suburbs, muddy farmyards, windswept moors. I loved deciding on permissible development, protecting the look of the place, making sure people wouldn't suffer from what went on next door, or letting people do things when prejudiced local councillors wouldn't. Why am I using the past tense? It *is* useful work, it's constructive, a good way to spend a life. Why shouldn't I have it all?

'Everything OK, is it, mate?'

Barbara looked up to see a police constable standing above her, his jacket glistening with moisture. She had not noticed it had begun to rain.

'Oh, sorry, miss, I thought you were . . .'

'That's all right.'

'You've got a place to go, have you, miss?'

'Yes, don't worry about me, I just couldn't sleep. I live at Barnaloft.'

'Oh right, I've seen you around. You're the lady with the black Golf, aren't you? I see you leaving early some mornings.'

'That's right.'

He fell into step beside her and they walked together back along the wide wall. She thought, He wants to make sure I don't jump over.

'Work up country, do you then?'

'I move around. I'm a planning inspector.'

'Ah, planning,' he said wisely. 'Now when I wanted permission to convert the attic . . .' He told her his story. Like doctors or law-yers, planning inspectors often provoked new acquaintances into relating their own problems with the profession. Finishing his com-plicated saga, he asked, 'How d'you get into that business then?'

'I'd been in a planning department. Local government, you know.'

'I wouldn't have thought . . .' He stopped, but Barbara knew what he was going to say because she had heard the words so often. Funny sort of job for a pretty girl to choose. 'Sort of thing you can drift into, I suppose,' he said wisely.

'As a matter of fact it was what I always wanted.'

'Why was that then?'

'Oh, it started when they built a factory on the park I played on as a kid. I thought it shouldn't be allowed and my teacher said I'd better become a planner and stop it happening anywhere else. The idea stuck.'

'Would you have given permission to all this then?' he said as they approached the entrance to Barnaloft. 'My dad said it used to be a fish cellar.'

'A very good example of post-war design,' she said briskly. 'Thank you for walking back with me, officer.'

He waited until she had reached the top of the outside staircase and gone along the walkway and in at her own front door. No suicides on his patch, she thought. No suicides and no abductions or – or anything else, unnameable, which could happen to a vulner-able small boy.

Barbara went upstairs and into her study, and composed her decision on the Reading appeal. To stop herself changing her mind, she went out to post it before going to bed and to sleep.

12

Colin Pomeroy, like many soldiers, was a mild, pacific man, but his patience was sorely tried when Toby lost his expensive, uninsured wet suit, or, to be more accurate, left it lying around somewhere it could be stolen. There had been a spate of thefts of wet suits, and Colin had specifically warned Toby to be careful of his. Wanton waste and carelessness, Colin often told him, was the one thing he could not abide. And Barbara was not herself. Colin was both irritated and mystified. Was it trouble with her work? Unlikely, because she'd have told him. Worry about Toby? Surely not. The hospital visit a month before had confirmed what they hoped, that he was all right now and there was no reason he shouldn't stay well; there would be no need to dread the check-up visit this time next year. Toby was a slow developer, probably because of the prolonged illness, but it was a good thing in many ways, delaying the transformation into a hostile adolescent with acne.

Or was she taking it out on Colin because of his – even in his thoughts, his mind skidded away from using the word *impotence*. Colin realised he and Barbara had not made love for almost four years. He had not given her any sign that his physical winter seemed to be beginning to recede, as though, he thought, uncharacteristically fanciful, there had been a snowstorm in August followed by better weather, not actually hot, but mellow and sunny. Clarissa was a very attractive woman; lonely, too. True, she was older than Barbara and kept herself less fit, she didn't rush around working all week or jogging. When he embraced her – only, so far, as a friend – she felt soft and enfolding rather than lithe and muscular. Clarissa deferred to him. If she were the one sharing his bed . . .

Colin did not finish that thought. Instead he reminded himself how fully he performed his side of the unspoken bargain between him and Barbara. He gave her all the help and encouragement Rosemary had once provided for him. A man or woman doing a full-time job needed support services, as he had sometimes had occasion to tell his own staff at the bank and his juniors in the army; no time for fusses on the home front when you're busy at work.

Colin carried out his side of the bargain, though many men would find it boring and limiting to be stuck here in this little town while Barbara travelled the country. Barbara really ought to be pleased Toby and he had found a good friend. If only she'd make the effort to be more outgoing he was sure the two women would get on extremely well and find they had a lot in common.

All the same, until Barbara went off on a round of site visits in the Midlands the following week, the occasion to ring or call on Clarissa did not seem to arise, and Colin realised that, oddly enough, neither he nor Toby had run into her, as they usually did, on the beach. On the way to school on Monday Colin asked Toby casually whether he'd seen Clarissa over the weekend.

'I think she's gone to get the puppy,' Toby said with a note of joyous confidence in his voice. When he explained to Clarissa that Barbara felt she couldn't cope with a dog, Clarissa had said she was planning to get one, and asked Toby whether he would walk it for her. Colin, who had heard the conversation, watched his son's face light up.

'A puppy,' he had breathed longingly. He had always wanted one. Clarissa said she'd be glad of his help and wondered what breed he thought would be best. They had discussed it for a long time, considering such details as long or short hair, hunting or retrieving tendencies, loyalty quotient and loudness of bark. In the end they had agreed a spaniel would be the best and Clarissa said she would find out about breeders and kennels. 'I may regret it,' she said, laughing. 'You've got to promise to help me with the house-training, Toby. Why don't you start thinking about a good name.'

On Tuesday Barbara drove off, still in a state of unexplained tension. Colin was sorry to realise he was relieved to see her go. She was getting to be so touchy these days! He rang Clarissa's number without getting a reply, both in the morning and just before he set off to fetch Toby.

'You're sure Clarissa said she was going away, Tobe, are you?' he asked in the car.

'She didn't say, actually. I just thought she probably did, 'cos of getting the puppy. Is she back? Has she got it? What's it like? Is it black?'

'No, I left a message on her machine, but why don't we go round and see if she's back?'

She did not come to the door, and Toby, peering through the kitchen window which gave out on to the walkway, said, 'The doors are all closed, Dad, I don't think she's there.'

She was not there the next day either, or the next. Ashamed of his curiosity, Colin peered through the kitchen window and letter box. She had been away for a while, he could see from the pile of what looked like junk mail on the mat.

Funny she hadn't mentioned going away to him. She must have been called away suddenly.

He knew nothing about Clarissa's family or previous life. She wore a wedding ring, she was called Mrs, but she had never mentioned a husband or children. Colin had assumed she was a childless widow or divorcee but he would never have dreamt of showing any inquisitive interest in her private affairs.

He paused, uncharacteristically irresolute, at the bottom of the stairs.

What if she'd had an accident in her flat? Would anyone have heard her call? Most of the apartments in both Barnaloft and the Piazza were empty at this time of year since so few people lived in them all the year round. Did he have any right to ask neighbours if they knew where she was? Should he go to the estate agent who handled her lease, a firm in Penzance, and inquire whether they had a key to her flat? Better not, he realised; it would seem an entirely unwarranted interference.

Colin walked along the beach, and paused when he came level with Clarissa's flat. He stood squinting up towards it, a stick-like figure in his spare uprightness, lightly balanced in his conker-bright shoes.

Was that Clarissa's light hair at the tightly closed window? No. It was the reflection of a cloud. The plate glass, without a light inside, showed nothing except external reflections.

A tall man in a wet suit, carrying his surf board towards the sea, paused and asked, 'All right, mate?'

Colin started and said, 'Oh, yes, yes, thanks.'

'Locked yourself out, have you? Bad luck.' He went on to join the others in the sea. They were taking advantage of the strong offshore wind which whipped the breakers on Porthmeor Beach up into a roller-coaster of spray and water. Agile and graceful as they twisted and balanced, they looked like a new form of life, not humans nor seals but some amphibian hybrid. He could paint that, the shining figures against the elemental waves. He saw the picture in his mind, an almost abstract arrangement of dark forms.

I'll give it another day, he thought, and then I'll get in there, interfering or not. Better to intrude on a friend's privacy than pass by on the other side if she's in some sort of need.

Colin went home and dialled Clarissa's number. After the answering machine's bleep, he said, 'Clarissa, this is Colin Pomeroy. It's noon on Thursday. I'm getting a bit worried about you. If I haven't heard anything by tomorrow I'm going to get into your flat, so give me a call to say you're in good form, will you?'

But it was the police, not Colin, who forced the door open. Colin was seen by a neighbour, the short-term tenant of the flat next door, who dialled the emergency number at the sight of Colin with his credit card and pickaxe.

Colin had just realised the credit card trick, apparently so simple when used on the screen, did not work, and was about to break the kitchen window with the axe handle. At that point he heard a police car siren. Two uniformed police officers, a man and a pretty, very young woman, came running up towards him.

It took every form of identification he had on him and back in his own flat before they believed him. Then he and the neighbour watched as the police forced Clarissa's front door.

'It wasn't double-locked or bolted,' one of the constables said. 'Stand back, sir, please.' He stepped over the substantial pile of mail and opened the door into the big living-room.

The smell of putrefaction, instantly recognised by Colin, if not by his companions, surged towards them.

'Oh my God,' the young policewoman exclaimed. She clapped her hand over her mouth and nose. He heard her running away down the stairs, and, before she reached the bottom, stopping to retch and heave.

Colin straightened his back and marched across the little lobby.

'You can't come in here, sir.' The constable, ghastly pale, stepped towards him. 'Outside. Out of here.'

'She's dead.' A statement, not a question.

'Yes, sir. Are you all right?'

'Fine, fine. Carry on.' Major Pomeroy's automatic reassurance; but Colin's voice betrayed the desolation he felt. He had seen into that room, once a warm and welcoming refuge, hideously changed into a charnel house in which Clarissa's body, battered and bloody, must have lain putrefying in the warm sunlight for several days.

13

After six months lecturing in the United States Fidelis Berlin felt out of touch with her English life. She was pleased to get home and relieved to find that the agency had kept the flat clean and unharmed during her absence, but the sight of the hall table, its surface invisible under a burden of mail, and the atmosphere of airless disuse were lowering to the spirits of a woman of nearly sixty-one who had spent the night upright between elbowing teenagers.

She had been looking forward to the peace of her quiet, light, high rooms after the peripatetic months abroad, to pleasing only herself after making the necessary efforts to entertain a variety of hosts. She had especially longed to get back to her own music centre. Fidelis had been to some wonderful concerts in America and paid for excess baggage to bring back dozens of compact discs which she wanted to hear in privacy and at leisure on her own state-of-the-art equipment.

She even looked forward to her correspondence. What invitations, what news of old friends, what fascinating offprints would be waiting? But now the envelopes were in front of her the idea of opening them seemed unenticing. So did the thought of unpacking and making her bed, or compiling a casualty list of the plants which filled the bay window in the hall.

Turn on water heater and telephone answering machine. Open windows. Straighten into casualness the cushions which the contract cleaners were trained to balance formally on their corners. Coffee. Try to ring best friends Ruth and Tina, to hear that one was away on a Nile cruise, the other in attendance at a grandchild's birth. Write a note to tell the neighbours the footsteps were her own and not an intruder's. Take a taxi to the garage where her car had been stored and drive home again cautiously in the temporarily unfamiliar traffic. Stop to buy eggs and milk, fruit and flowers. Note that the parking permit had expired and decide to risk it in a residents' bay all the same. Back into the flat. Greet the retired doctor who lived in the ground-floor front without giving him time to start a conversation.

Fidelis lived on the upstairs drawing-room floor of a large house in a tree-lined side street in Hampstead, into which fitted two double bedrooms, a sizeable living-room, a bathroom and kitchen. The five-storey house had been built for a Jewish immigrant whose fortune was founded on importing nuts and fruit from North Africa. The architect who designed the house in the 1880s made tactful references to the business. A lemon tree in azulejo tiles decorated the stone frontage. Pineapples and bananas were carved on to the front door and window surrounds. Fidelis's balcony, from which she could almost touch the branches of some overgrown

lime trees, was enclosed by a wrought-iron balustrade in the shape
of a vine arbour and her fireplaces were surrounded by brightly
coloured tiles embossed with a cornucopia of fruit. She had
retained the theme, choosing decorations in lemon yellow, her
furniture made of wood stained a misty green like unripe grapes.
Cherries on a blue plate, an early Perdita Whitchurch picked up
before her prices rocketed, gleamed in a gilt frame. The grateful
mother of a patient had given Fidelis an artificial orange tree,
convincing from a distance, and much as she disliked things which
were pretending to be other things, she had felt obliged to keep it
in a corner of the hall.

With daffodils and pink tulips in the living-room and edible fruit
in the wooden bowl, the place felt more homely. Fidelis unpacked
her clothes in the bedroom which had once been a piano-room. She
pulled out the flat drawers designed for sheet music in which her
own underwear, shirts and scarves were stacked. Some seemed as
unfamiliar and desirable as a new season's stock in her favourite
shops, others were old, neglected friends. With slow, sensuous
pleasure she laid out silk and cashmere; pleasing, ghostly aromas
rose from the fabrics. In the bathroom Fidelis arrayed new bottles
from the duty-free shops beside atomisers she had begun to use in
America. Expensive scents were one of Fidelis's major extravag-
ances, worn to suit her mood.

By this time the water was hot, so she had a shower in the
mirror-less bathroom. Fidelis had recovered well from the double
mastectomy two years before and there were even moments when
she could actually believe what she told herself, that it was convenient to be without the wobbling weight of her once beautiful
breasts. But she could not bear the sight of herself, or bear to let
anyone else see her. 'Counselling' had not been pressed upon her,
being, as it were, in the trade herself, but she knew what a counsel-
lor would have said: she was not hideous, not unsexed; she was still
desirable. She could not tell herself anything of the kind. She felt
deformed. Her sex life was over. It was very seldom, now, that she
wished it were not so.

Fidelis washed her hair, and at last felt strong enough to settle
down at her desk with Alexandre Brussilovsky playing Brahms
sonatas on the turntable and the letters and a rubbish bag on the
floor beside her. The greater part was inevitably junk mail to be
discarded unopened, or notification of debits to her bank account.

Astonishing, she thought, how many bills had to be paid in half a year. There were invitations to launch books which were probably out of print already, and to private views of terminated exhibitions. There were requests to lecture on dates long gone, to join the choir in concerts long since performed. Above all there were Christmas cards, dozens of them from acquaintances Fidelis had not warned she would be abroad. She forced herself to open them all, ignoring the gust of depression their anachronism blew over her; this was an intimation of celebrations past, chances missed. But some contained personal notes, circular family letters, changes of address – one could not throw them away unopened. Eventually she reduced the mail to a bulging black plastic bag and a basket full of things to deal with, not this week, for which engagements had been made months before, but soon.

It's ridiculous, Fidelis thought, that I'm busier now I've retired than I was before. Mercifully Sophie Teague was to start work next week. Her title, research assistant, obscured the role she was to fill. Fidelis rang the department where Sophie was based, and in which Fidelis herself had lectured. It was a university in name but bore small resemblance to traditional places of higher education. Every autumn it had to advertise unfilled places on courses staffed by lecturers who would prefer to work elsewhere. But the telephone was answered by a familiar, deep voice, and Marlene recognised Fidelis at once.

'Dr Berlin. Oh yes, we all know about you and Sophie, she's been telling everyone. She's not here just now. No, sorry, I don't have her number, she's moved to stay in a friend's flat. She should be in later though.'

'Oh well, just say I rang and I'm back,' Fidelis said, and Marlene ambiguously replied, 'And very welcome too, I'm sure.'

As it turned out Fidelis was very glad she had made the arrangement; there would be more than enough for Sophie to do. Most ex-academics lecture, attend conferences, write articles and review books. Fidelis, in addition, had started a major research project funded by the Leverhulme Trust and was involved in making a television programme based on the work.

The topic arose out of the subject, child care systems, which had filled her working life. Fidelis wanted to study a large sample of mothers of adult children to find out what they thought about their own ways of dealing with the problem now it was long since solved. Did those who had used nannies and child-minders wish they hadn't? Did full-time mothers who never worked outside the home still feel the results justified their choices, were their children noticeably more secure or happier grown-ups than those who had received less of their mothers' attention? She was never convinced the end result justified sacrificing a mother's happiness to her small child's. Were those first years of life in fact the most important? For, Fidelis told her friend Ruth, we don't have children to have children, we have children to have people. Or to abandon them, the silent voice in her brain said in its regular, secret and silent refrain.

'You don't have either,' Ruth had said crossly, thinking of the obtrusive cuckoos deposited in her nest (a pretty Regency cottage beside the Thames) by a second marriage to a man with a large family.

'I know. It's all theoretical.'

Ruth, impelled by the need for an excuse to get out of the house as much as possible, had stopped being a television script writer and become a producer with a small independent company. She said, 'It might make a good programme though.'

Other people thought so too; money had been forthcoming up-front and Fidelis was committed to producing enough material for the team to work on by midsummer. There was to be a meeting of the production team next week. Before then she must check through her notes, recall the work she had done before leaving England the previous summer, revive her own enthusiasm for the project.

As though that was not enough to be going on with, she would have to go to a meeting at the day centre of which she was a trustee tomorrow, speak at a fund-raising event for Newnham College on Saturday and go to a board meeting of Cox Kindergartens on Monday morning. Exhausted at the very sight of her own engagement diary, Fidelis told herself firmly it was midnight as far as her own metabolism was concerned even if the clock said it was early evening. She went to bed and lay sleepless for hours, willing herself to be still.

Fidelis forced herself to carry on despite feeling, for several days, as though she had flu. Jet lag took longer to recover from now she was getting older, and it had an embarrassingly ghastly effect on her skin and hair.

Fidelis had always taken a good deal of trouble over her appearance, spending more than she could afford on interesting, unconventional clothes and using expensive cosmetics with well-taught skill, paying, every few years, for a 'make-up lesson' at a salon in Knightsbridge.

Her thick, straight hair, now a soft grey improved and polished with vegetable dye, was cut into a geometrical bob. She had a long face with regular, angular features and heavy-lidded brown eyes. She kept herself thin by eating little. Periodically shamed into exercise, she always found it made her feel *much worse*: swimming gave her cramp in the legs, jogging bruised her feet and at her second yoga class she had snapped an Achilles tendon, an injury which was dreadfully painful and slow to heal, and after which she swore she would never do any equivalent of physical jerks again so long as she lived. She enjoyed walking in towns, not for the sake of the actual walking – hikes across muddy fields, even in childhood when they were inevitable, had always been her idea of hell – but to see things which interested her: people and how they interacted, shops full of things people wanted to own, or not, as the case might be, buildings designed for people to use. People-watching; observing human beings and their works. That was what Fidelis liked. Tina had once remarked that Fidelis was like an eternal child with its nose pressed to a window.

The board meeting of Cox Kindergartens was in its office in Docklands. By Monday Fidelis had recovered and was able to enjoy the journey above scenic slums in the Light Railway and her walk through the marble halls of Canary Wharf.

Passed through the barrier of security, she took the lift to a high floor, where, as always, she paused to admire the panorama of London below before going into the office of Cox Kindergartens. Belying the grandeur of the approach to it, the office consisted of a small room in which a series of disaffected temporary secretaries whiled away the hours in captivity, and an inner room now containing Neville Cox and his sleeping partner, a little sharp man with little sharp eyes and an old school tie.

This, the annual meeting of Cox Kindergartens, was a formality. Neville had the ideas and did the work. Brian Day lent his name, that of a once well-known construction firm, now subsumed into a much larger one. Fidelis confined her input to the kindergartens themselves, although using the business's name Neville had diversified during the 1980s into up-market caravan sites and long-stay convalescent homes.

Plans and photographs showing work in progress were passed round. There were several proposals now awaiting various authorisations, Neville explained, but the Sherbury development already showed six-foot walls in their sea of mud, for the builders had begun work the day permission came through and were now well ahead of schedule. Fidelis leafed through the folder in which the photographs were stuck, along with five pages of discussion arising from the planning appeal, at which Fidelis had given evidence last summer.

'Government guidance on development plans requires planning authorities to have regard to social considerations in preparing their general policies . . . I consider the need to protect residents from undue disturbance and noise is outweighed by benefit to the area of much-needed facility . . . the effect of increased traffic on the local highways . . . public amenity space . . . I have carefully considered all the other representations made but have found nothing of such significance as to alter my conclusion . . . in exercise of powers transferred to me I hereby grant planning permission. I am, gentlemen, your obedient servant B. Pomeroy BA, MRTPI.'

Good for B. Pomeroy, Fidelis thought, remembering the cool, distant woman sitting like an icon on her pedestal. I knew she'd empathise with the need for child care.

'Is it going to be a success, can we tell?' Fidelis asked.

'There's a waiting list already. The manager tells me they could fill every place three times over.'

'That's good news.'

'Yes, to balance a slightly less cheerful picture elsewhere. The cash flow is getting backed up in the pipes, in some areas.'

'Profits?' Brian Day barked, and Neville said, 'Yes, of course, Brian, you've seen the balance sheet. If you turn to page three . . .'

Fidelis never listened to money-talk. She got up from the small table and walked to the window, fumbling for her distance-spectacles. A thin fog was rising from the river, tendrils of obscurity over the City. From the other window she could look eastwards, over the desolate mud fields which were supposed to become the booming, bustling heart of late twentieth-century regeneration.

One could come to believe oneself important up here, Fidelis thought, as though by overlooking those minified buildings one could exert control over the little people in them.

'Well, if there's nothing else . . .' Neville said.

'There's more to discuss,' Brian Day said. 'Not all to do with the matter in hand, and I'm on my way to the airport. Paris for luncheon. I'll get my girl to make an appointment.'

He was already half-way to the door. He led a busy public life as one of the Great and the Good. On first meeting him Fidelis had checked in *Who's Who* and been more amused than impressed by the diversity of his occupations, which ranged from chairing hospital trusts, television companies, and his county Conservative party, to directing a publishing company, and the Royal Opera. Under hobbies, he had admitted to music and golf. Neville had described him to Fidelis as a safe pair of hands.

As Brian Day bustled out, Fidelis changed gear, becoming 'friend' rather than 'colleague'.

'Neville, how's Buffy? I've been away, as you know, so I'm out of touch.' And come to think of it, she suddenly realised, there hadn't been anything from the Coxes among the Christmas cards. 'Is everything all right?'

Neville looked momentarily irresolute. Then he said, 'To tell you the honest truth I'm a bit worried. Well, very worried really.'

'Why, what's happened?'

'Well, it's . . . look, let me give you lunch, it's a long story.'

'That would be nice. I'll just ring my research assistant and tell her where to meet me later.'

They went by taxi back to the City.

'You still hum,' Neville said.

'What?'

'You don't even notice yourself doing it.'

'Oh Lord, I'm sorry. I know it's a maddening habit.'

'I always liked it,' he said with a reminder of old intimacy. They drove on westwards to the Savoy, where Neville, evidently well known, was given a table in the Grill Room.

'This is nice. Like old times,' he said.

'I don't remember going to the Savoy in those days.'

'Oh, didn't we? I could have sworn . . . You have such an exciting life, Fidelis, you've forgotten.' But it was he who had forgotten. The Savoy must have played a part in a different adventure. Fidelis had never had any illusions about Neville, either as a lover or a colleague. She felt like the handler of a tricky animal, knowing its faults and propensities and being able to cope with them.

He plied her with delicacies. She thought, He's softening me up,

I wonder why? They spoke about trivialities until Fidelis had been served with Chablis, bass and various adornments and vegetables. Neville ordered, as he always did, a large, rare steak and claret. He'd decided long ago that it was the only food for a real man.

Fidelis said, 'Right then, spit it out. What's the problem?'

'It's a bit awkward.'

'So I assumed from the build-up. Is it Buffy? When we met in New York you seemed worried about her.' She expected him to say it was and would have laid bets on exactly what was to follow, a confession that he had found someone else, a younger woman who wanted to marry him and have another family. Fidelis could see it would be difficult to tell Buffy that. She was so dependent on him, in every way.

Neville was uncharacteristically tongue-tied and made a great business of tasting the wine and carving his slab of meat. Fidelis said, 'Go on, tell me. I suppose you're leaving her.'

'No, it's not that as a matter of fact.' He sounded almost surprised himself. 'No, the fact is, I don't know where she is.'

'What d'you mean? Has she gone away without leaving the freezer full for you or something?'

'It's more serious than that.' He put down his knife and fork. 'Literally. I don't know what's happened to her. I'm worried about her.'

'Buffy's a grown woman, Neville, she doesn't need your permission to leave home.'

'But she would have told me.'

'I don't expect you were listening.' Fidelis had seen enough of the Coxes' home life to have a very fair idea of what it was like. Buffy would speak without being heard, while Neville's every word was answered, every request meticulously fulfilled.

'Oh don't be silly, Fidelis,' he snapped. 'I'm serious. Buffy hasn't been at home for God knows how long and I've no idea what's happened to her.'

'God may not but I'm sure you do know how long. Two days? Two weeks? Two months?'

'More,' he said with a hangdog expression.

It was Fidelis's turn to put down her knife and fork. 'Are you seriously telling me that Buffy disappeared months ago? When, exactly? She must have been at home for Christmas!'

'But she wasn't.'

'What? She's been gone since last year and you haven't done – *have* you done anything about it?'

'I haven't been sure what to do. You know how peculiar she's been since Andrew died.'

'But you must have asked the police – the hospitals – '

'I did that, yes. No sign at any hospitals, and the police said it wasn't their business if a healthy grown-up woman chose to walk out on her husband. They thought it was a joke, really.'

'Let me get this straight. Just when did you last see Buffy?'

'You remember when we went to that planning appeal in Sherbury last June?'

'Yes.'

'She'd gone by then.'

'But you never said anything then about it, or when we met in New York.'

'It didn't seem important, I thought she'd be back. As you said, she's an adult, free, white and twenty-one, she doesn't need permission from me to go away. It was sometime in May, I got back from a trip – I can't even remember where to – and she wasn't at the house when I got back. I thought she'd gone to – oh, I don't know, a health farm or on some cultural outing to art galleries in Italy with her friends, they are always doing that kind of thing. She might even have gone to see her sister again.'

'Surely she'd have told you.'

'Not necessarily. We haven't been communicating much since Andrew died. You know how it hit her, the whole thing. She seemed to blame me.'

'A natural reaction,' Fidelis said briskly in her psychiatrist's voice.

'So you said at the time.'

'Have I got this right? You're telling me that you last saw Buffy in May last year? But why didn't you say anything before? Why did you make so light of it in New York? All you said was that she was away, not that she'd been away for literally months!'

'I don't know. I suppose I was embarrassed.'

'You? Embarrassed? Did you tell anyone at all?'

'I spoke to Sally, that's Buffy's sister, in New Zealand, that must have been around Christmas time, and she hadn't heard from Buffy for months, but then they never did correspond anyway so she wouldn't have expected to. They were never very close. But you don't know what to say, in circumstances like that. I couldn't very well ask the neighbours when did they last see my wife and what did she tell them when they did, specially as I've been away from the house so much myself. I did ring some of Buffy's girlfriends, but she's been keeping people at a distance since Andrew died.'

'I know. I told her it was quite natural if she couldn't bear to see other people who still had their children safe,' Fidelis said. 'And of course it was even worse once grandchildren started arriving.'

'I kept thinking she'd turn up, one day I'd walk in and she'd be there.'

'What do you want me to do?' Fidelis knew Neville wanted something out of her, since otherwise he would have told her about Buffy in some less expensive place than the Savoy. Fidelis had noticed the celebrities at other tables, smiled at a conductor she knew slightly and surreptitiously stared at an actress she admired, while Neville, who had always been interested in fame and famous people, had not interrupted his concentration on Fidelis. He was trying to win her over, but to what?

She ordered the most expensive pudding. 'Perhaps you should put a private detective on to it if the police aren't interested.'

'It may come to that, I suppose,' Neville said. He too ordered a pudding, less expensive but more fattening. He had put on weight since last year, free, Fidelis realised, from Buffy's scrupulous attention to what he ate when she provided it. He was still well groomed. She thought it must have done him good to have to take his own clothes to the cleaners during these last months having had a body-servant to wait on him all these years. If Buffy had come to no harm, this story might have a happy ending.

Fidelis accepted the suggestion of a glass of 'pudding wine' and said, 'Come on then, Neville, out with it. What do you want me to do?'

He briefly assumed an injured expression before saying, 'I wondered if you could go to the house and have a look round? The point is, I've turned things over a bit, tried to find a hint of what Buffy might be up to. You might see something in her desk and all that, but I don't know how to tell if there's any sign . . . I mean, I've no idea whether any clothes have been packed or make-up. You know how undomesticated I am.'

'Buffy told me she always left the freezer full of labelled meals for you when she went away. Did she do that?'

'I think there were some . . . I don't know. It's months ago, you can't expect me to remember what I ate last summer.'

Curious, Fidelis asked, 'Who's cleaned the house since then?' and Neville assumed a note of conscious virtue:

'I didn't want Buffy to come home to a complete tip so I got a firm of contract cleaners to come in a couple of times. I found the name in our address book.'

Fidelis had given that name to Buffy. She had tried to convince her Neville could afford someone else to scrub floors. Buffy had written the address down, but said she had no excuse for not doing her own housework, because she hadn't anything better to do herself. 'Blame my mother,' Buffy said with a grimace.

Fidelis knew the story of Buffy's background: father prematurely retired from the Indian Civil Service in 1948, to live in Cheltenham on a small pension with his wife and two daughters, who, he never let them forget, were degraded by having to attend the local state school. He could not afford the boarding school to which, as the children of a colonial administrator, they would have been sent at government expense. Their mother made a martyr of herself in the house, ensuring her family understood how far beneath her dignity the menial work was for someone who was accustomed to a large staff of 'natives'. After much ostentatious scrimping and saving, enough money was found to send Buffy to secretarial college, where she learnt shorthand and typing, but she never needed to use it because she met Neville when she was nineteen and married him. She had never told Fidelis so but working out the dates made it obvious that, to use a phrase of the period, 'they had to get married' seven months before Andrew was born.

Fidelis said, 'I can't imagine what you think I could do.'

Neville paused while he glanced down the items on his bill, and then chose a plastic card from a wallet bulging with them. Then he used a wheedling tone to say, 'You are much more sensitive and observant than me, you might notice something which has passed me by. Please, Fidelis, I'm begging you.'

'Well, I suppose . . . I'm very tied up this week.'

'I've got to go to the States. I'm following up a joint financing deal for a development I'm concerned with, I brought you the front door keys on purpose. Here you are. Go anywhere. Look at everything. I was sure you'd agree.'

'I'll fit it in when I can,' she said.

'Whenever suits you. I'm not staying there at the moment, no point in slogging out so far to an empty house. Thank you, Fidelis.'

'I beg your pardon, sir.'

The waiter had brought the plastic card back and spoke in a low voice. Neville's fair, smoothly shaved skin flared scarlet and Fidelis tactfully looked away, fixing her gaze on a telly-don talking to a telly-politician two tables away. Neville wrote a cheque and handed it to the waiter with a different card.

'Ridiculous – computer errors – that could have been very embarrassing.'

'One of the hazards of modern life,' Fidelis agreed, walking beside Neville to the front of the hotel. She had arranged to meet Sophie Teague to go together to a seminar, and could see her through the glass doors, standing under the canopy talking to the uniformed commissionaire.

Neville, looking at his watch, said, 'I'd no idea it was so – Fidelis, I must dash. So sorry. We'll be in touch.' He ran ahead to leap into a taxi and had gone before Fidelis came out through the revolving doors.

14

Buffy and Neville Cox embarked on married life back in 1965 in a one-roomed flat in Hampstead, where the bath, covered with a hinged flap, served as the table and most of the furniture consisted of orange boxes covered with scraps of cloth. When Andrew was born Buffy washed his nappies by hand and dried them on a towel horse in front of a one-bar electric fire. To go out shopping, she lugged him and his pram down three flights of stairs, and she spent sleepless nights walking round with the baby in her arms because whenever she put him down he screamed and disturbed the neighbours. Their diet was starchy and low in fat, at a period when it was thought healthy (and was therefore expensive) to live on first-class protein anointed with butter and cream. Fish and chips from the corner shop were the weekly treat, because they could not afford a baby-sitter while they went to the pictures. Buffy's own parents did not help out, disapproving too much of her social descent ('Clogs to clogs in three generations!' her father accused). Neville's mother had never gone up in the world in the first place. Decrepit at fifty, she could not be trusted with Buffy's baby.

How things had changed by the time Fidelis met the Coxes. They had just moved into their fourth house, adding a room with each improvement. It was a gleaming white, two-storey house overlooking a golf course in the northern outskirts of Greater London. Painted gleaming white, with the twin eaves and leaded windows outlined in black, this house was the outward and visible expression of success.

With Sophie Teague beside her Fidelis turned into the semicircular drive, gravel scattering beneath the tyres, and parked outside the closed doors of the three car garage.

'Buffy's Peugeot 205 has been in there since last May, Neville told me,' Fidelis remarked.

Sophie read his instructions aloud. 'Turn the three brass keys round in their respective holes, open front door, unlock inner porch door with chrome key, push walnut blanket chest aside to find number pad, quickly, within sixty seconds, press in six figure number. Remember: repeat process in reverse on leaving.'

The two women went in together, Fidelis curiously reluctant, Sophie wide-eyed and interested.

The warm air inside the empty house felt still and lifeless, but in the draught from the open door little swirls of dust rose from the flat surfaces and floated slowly down. Sophie picked up the letters from the mat and handed them to Fidelis. There was not much more than a few days' worth, mostly brown envelopes with computer-generated address labels to Mr and Mrs N. Cox, or to Mrs Elizabeth Cox. There was a spring catalogue from the Save the Children Fund and a holiday brochure in a transparent plastic envelope from the West Penwith Tourist Board. Fidelis put them down on a flimsy half-moon table. She sneezed, and took off her coat and cardigan. Sophie hung her leather bomber jacket and knitted scarf on the newel post.

'This atmosphere is unbearable,' Fidelis said. 'Do you suppose the burglar alarm will go off if I open some windows?'

'I'll go and try,' Sophie said keenly and ran off, her heavy boots silent on the thick pink carpet. Fidelis stood irresolute in the hall. What was she looking for? What could Neville have missed himself, that she could find? Did she really understand things about his wife which he didn't know?

Fidelis had first met Buffy Cox at a painting class. Buffy had been dabbling in water-colours for years. Sitting next to her that first evening Fidelis noticed a sketch book full of muddy landscapes and disproportionate cows. Fidelis herself had not touched a paint brush for years but had been inspired to try again in middle life by an essay written by a retired journalist called Mary Stott, who wrote of the satisfaction in learning to look properly and patiently at what was before one's eyes, the pleasure of meeting others who shared the enthusiasm, of having a sedentary occupation for holidays, above all of finding an occupation to fill future, idle hours.

When she read it Fidelis was just beginning to dread her own retirement. The pastimes other people suggested, such as bridge, golf or bowling, made her think early death preferable, but Mary Stott made painting sound so enjoyable that she decided it was worth trying. In fact it turned out not to be for her. The teacher's encouragement was false and patronising. Fidelis was know-ledgeable about art and was so disgusted by her own primitive attempts that she literally could not bear to look at them. But she had got on well with Buffy Cox and accepted the dinner invitation which resulted in meeting Neville and getting on (for a while) even better with him.

Fidelis had thought Buffy by far the nicer person of the two even while conducting her shortish and wholly physical affair with Neville. After redefining her relationship with him, Fidelis and Buffy became genuine, if unlikely, friends.

Unlikely because Buffy was everything Fidelis was not and had never wanted to be.

Buffy never had or wanted a profession. She never wanted to assert her own self-determination and feminism had passed her completely by. She never resented Neville's automatic assumption of precedence and authority, implicitly believing him to be better than she was, more important and entitled to her deference and care. What was more she was a wholly committed full-time mother. Much as Buffy worshipped Fidelis as a person, as, with some shyness, she did, she could not understand her ambition to en-courage child care. Nothing could be worth taking a mother away from her child.

'I simply don't see how there could have been anything more worthwhile to do with my life than bring up Andy. Of course now he's away at university I can see him in the round, at a distance, and I look at that young man, so caring and concerned, so clever – '

'Good-looking too,' Fidelis had interrupted.

'Yes, he's wonderfully handsome, so like his father, isn't he? You can see why I really swell with pride to think I did it. I made him. That's what working mothers miss when they are so selfishly set on their careers.' Then she added quickly and apologetically, 'I do see it's different for you, Fidelis, you chose to stay single, please don't think I – '

'It's OK. Really.' Fidelis did not take Buffy's speech personally. For one thing it was material for her research, an example of mother love taken to its extreme. But also, she had learnt as a child to blank out personal feelings about other people's motherhood. Fidelis had made the subject strictly academic, the raw material of her research. 'There's no emotion or personal experience involved here,' she sometimes boasted; and an unspoken voice in her head whispered, 'Oh yeah?'

At one time Fidelis was in the habit of dropping in at Knighton Rise quite regularly. She genuinely liked Buffy and enjoyed the unfamiliar contact with individuals who were what she thought of as *real people*. By that she meant the mass of middle-class people in Thatcher's Britain – those who read the *Daily Mail* or *Telegraph*, played golf, went to church and voted Conservative. She found it interesting to talk to them, for none of her other friends were like that. Fidelis's social life was spent with *Guardian*-reading liberals who went on protest marches and had dirty cars and lived in messy, colourful houses full of books.

Standing in the quiet hallway, looking with absent-minded dislike at a set of framed prints of the Cries of London, Fidelis realised that this had actually been the only house she knew of its kind, in which the monochrome, unsullied surfaces of carpets and tables were cleaned every single day; where no messy reading matter was left lying round, lace mats stood under elaborate flower arrangements on highly polished surfaces and other lace mats protected upholstery from hair and hands.

Only here had Fidelis ever joined the life portrayed in the magazines she read for research, in which finger buffets and afternoon teas, fork luncheons and coffee mornings played a regular part. Fidelis sometimes looked in at Buffy's all-women entertainments, 'girls' lunches' or coffee mornings. She remembered one to which she had come by accident, arriving to deliver some statistics for Neville at exactly the moment when other women were driving up in their four-wheel-drives and GTis.

'What good timing, come and join us,' Buffy cried. 'This is Penny, this is Sue, this is Liggy, this is Di.' All the women had playful nicknames and wore overgrown versions of baby clothes in day-glo colours – mini-skirts, romper suits, leggings or dungarees. But their hair was adult, cushions of brightly coloured curls or waves, and they wore a good deal of gold jewellery. Buffy, unadorned in a flowered, knee-length shirt-waister and a grey perm, did not match. Nor did Fidelis, who had a severe, geometrical haircut at the time, and was wearing very expensive, very plain layers of beige cashmere.

'Buffy's marvellous, isn't she?' said a woman called Sam. 'I never know how she does it all.'

'I'd never have the patience,' Wendy agreed. She was holding a gold-rimmed platter and a blunt-sided fork, but she made no attempt to eat the rich cake.

'Oh you would, Wendy, you always make those delectable coffee truffles, mmmmm.' Sam moved her features into a simulation of ecstasy. 'They're to die for.' But Sam was not eating her meringue either. Did they put them down the loo, Fidelis wondered, or wrap them in those pink paper napkins and pocket them? She ate heartily herself, unaccustomed both to mid-morning snacks and to sweet cakes.

'Yes, but Buffy puts me to shame. And she's such a wonderful mother – when I think how my lot drive me round the twist.'

'Of course' – a lower, confidential voice – 'it's not as though she has much else to do.'

The other women, it appeared, had jobs. Sue arranged flowers, Liggy had a share in a lingerie shop, Di's husband had just picked up the end of a lease of a dear little gallery in the shopping parade where she was going to sell painted Spanish pottery. They watched their hostess manipulating plates of food and a silver coffee pot.

Di said, 'Buffy just lives for that boy – and Neville, of course. Though I'm not sure he deserves it, he can be quite – '

'Sssh.' The women's eyes met in a complicitous amusement.

'Did I tell you about that new caddy at the golf club?' The two women moved away, talking confidentially, and Fidelis watched as Sam's cheeks grew pink, her breath quickened. Wendy put on an 'Ooh, you didn't!' expression.

It was after that occasion that Fidelis began to see more of Buffy. She liked her and was sorry for a woman who seemed like an outsider among her own friends. It had seemed, that morning, as though the other women were speaking to Buffy with kindness rather than intimacy, as though she belonged to their circle only because she lived where she did, their husbands were mates, their sons all at the same fee-paying day school; but Buffy had never managed to put on the local uniform or learn the language. Fidelis would have liked to know whether she had tried. Had there been a time when Buffy ran along behind the pack, desperately trying to keep up with their fads and fashions? Or was there a steely centre under Buffy's soft exterior, which made her remain the self she had originally chosen to be?

Had Neville asked those women whether Buffy had told them she was going away?

Sophie came down the stairs, hooking her straight black hair behind her ears in a gesture she made perfectly unconsciously every few minutes. She said, 'Done it. But I mustn't forget to shut them again before we go.'

'The windows?'

'You did want me to open them, didn't you?'

'Yes, thank you, Sophie.' Fidelis hoped the girl would soon feel confident that her job was secure; then she could stop showing quite such demonstrative willingness.

'Where do we start then, Fidelis?'

'I wish I knew.' Reluctant to begin exploring the house, Fidelis took the notebook which lay beside the telephone on a small table and leafed through the handwritten pages. Probably every number in it should be tried with the same question, but Neville should do that. Perhaps he already had. Fidelis would ring only . . . yes, here was Wendy McCormick.

No answer.

'I'll try one more,' she said. Sophie sat on the bottom step, her pointed chin in her hands, her clear eyes interested and intelligent. 'I'm glad you're here, Sophie. It would be rather creepy doing this alone. God knows what Neville thought I could . . .' She dialled the number of Sue Smythe, who, surprisingly, was there to answer her telephone.

88

'I don't suppose you remember me, Fidelis Berlin, but we met some years ago at Buffy Cox's.'

'Oh yes, I think so, Buffy often spoke about you, you're a doctor, aren't you?'

'A psychiatrist. I'm so sorry to bother you after all this time but I wondered whether you'd seen anything of Buffy recently? I've been ringing her house for a while and there never seems to be anyone there, would you know if she's moved or something?'

'How funny you should ask that. I was only saying yesterday, to Sam Pollock – you've met her too, haven't you? – we were saying neither of us had run into Buffy for ages. Everything was so difficult after that dreadful business with their son, Buffy never really forgave Neville, she held it all against him. She withdrew into herself if you know what I mean. Now I come to work it out I honestly don't think . . . you know, it must be more than a year since I saw Buffy, isn't that awful. I must confess I've been a bad friend, but simply nothing cheers her up, one sort of gave up trying, do you know what I mean? And then things pile up, everything's always so hectic, the number of weddings I've got to do this month you wouldn't believe – '

'I know what it's like.'

'We saw her at the Christmas do at the golf club, it must have been . . . no, she wasn't there last year, I remember because Neville was with the girl who – but that's not the point. It must have been the year before, Christmas '92. Buffy was there, I'm sure she was. I could check with the girls . . .'

'Oh, please don't bother. I just wondered whether you have any idea where she might be now?'

'Well, if she's not at home . . . are you sure she isn't? She does sometimes leave the phone to ring, I know that because my husband had some business with Neville and it was dreadfully inconvenient. I could go round and see, if you like, not today though, now let me see . . .'

'Oh, please don't bother on my account,' Fidelis said quickly. 'It doesn't matter, really. I just thought I'd ask . . .' Pleasantries continued for a few minutes and Fidelis was relieved to learn that Sue would not be coming right round to Buffy's place because she was about to go up to Harrods with Penny for cruise clothes.

She would have told me rather than those women if she was going away, Fidelis thought, recognising that Neville had some justification for asking her help. Fidelis had picked up some pieces after Andrew died and Buffy grew dependent on her. Too dependent, it seemed at the time. Fidelis had made a professional decision to cool it. Now, standing in the arid, empty hallway, a feeling of shame for her own lack of feeling washed over Fidelis. Buffy needed me then and I failed her, she thought.

All right. So the least I can do now is what Neville asked. Not skimp it, not whizz round giggling with Sophie about the tasteless decorations, but look properly, use our joint psychological expertise and feminine antennae to see if there's some indication of what has happened to Buffy Cox.

Was there any need to look in the obvious places, given that Neville must have done so himself?

Yes. You might as well make up your mind to it, my girl, you're staying here till you've done the job properly. Inside out and top to bottom. 'Get going.' She said the last words aloud, and Sophie leapt to her feet and acted spitting on her hands and rubbing them together.

The task was less arduous than it would have been in the homes of any other of Fidelis's friends. Searching would be difficult if not impossible in houses full of books and ornaments, hobbies and dirt, mantelpieces piled with memorabilia, study floors heaped with offprints and notes, bedrooms where plastic sacks waiting to be taken to the charity shop vied for space with new carrier bags and unironed clothes. But in Knighton Rise the bedrooms were as tidy and blank as hotel rooms.

'We'd never find anything here without tearing the mattresses apart or wrenching the radiators from the walls, the way they do in cop movies,' Sophie said, lifting the cistern lid in the bathroom and peering inside.

'It would help if we knew what we were looking for.'

'You're tired, Fidelis, can't I – ?'

'No, I'll have to do it myself, just in case I recognise something. Thanks anyway.'

Andrew's bedroom had never been emptied or changed since his death, but by that time he had long since left home and the room, its window overlooking the overgrown garden, had been unused for years. Obsolete posters of forgotten singers were still tacked to the notice-board and some dusty model aeroplanes dangled from cotton attached to ceiling hooks. Otherwise, the mattress was bare, the wash-basin had neither soap nor towel and the cupboards were empty.

With her little finger Sophie set one of the aircraft swinging. 'What a shame,' she said softly. 'That poor young man. His poor mother. If one of us died I think my mother would – I don't think she'd survive it.'

Fidelis had realised that Sophie felt a mixture of irritation and compassion for the mother who had somehow managed to keep the family home going by working as a secretary. Money had obviously been very tight, and Fidelis had soon derived the impression that Sophie had resented it, blaming her unmourned father for the discomforts he had left behind him. Hinted at, and implicit in Sophie's behaviour, was a determination to do a good deal better for herself. She very much wanted to be well off, or even rich.

'Let's go down and make something to drink,' Fidelis said. On the way they looked into the dining-room and drawing-room. Both were as impersonal as the unused bedrooms.

'They could let this house to tenants as it stands, there'd be no need to put anything away. Was it always so tidy when your friend was around?'

'Yes, never anything out of place.'

'Anal retentive,' Sophie said.

Fidelis had never used the flip, popularised jargon of analysis. She said a little repressively, 'Buffy likes things clean and orderly, that's all.'

Fidelis opened the dining-room drawers, which contained neat rows of silver cutlery, matched stacks of starched table mats and napkins.

A quick check round the drawing-room, where photographs framed in tarnished silver stood on the mantelpiece. Sophie picked them up one by one.

'This must be the son,' Sophie said. 'Lots of pictures, what a pity. And this is your friend with him, I suppose, it's the only one of her.' In the picture Buffy was pushing a small child in a swing, with a patterned scarf tied over her hair and under her chin and the sun in her eyes. 'You can't really tell what she looks like from this.'

'Medium height, she's let her figure go, nondescript blue eyes, small mouth, large beaked nose, doesn't go in for much self-adornment – Mrs Average.'

The only cupboard doors in the drawing-room opened on to a huge television screen set above a video recorder and below a mirror-lined drinks cabinet. The overstuffed green velvet sofa and armchairs did not even have cushions to search under. A dead house plant, now shrivelled into brown kindling, drooped in a dirty brass holder.

'I suppose it did always seem terribly tidy, but it wasn't the kind of thing you notice as a visitor,' Fidelis remarked.

'We always have things lying round at home, like you do in your flat. And lots of books.'

'Coffee. Come along. It'll probably have to be black though.'

'I'll do it.'

While Sophie found mugs and a jar of caked instant coffee, Fidelis looked into the empty fridge and the freezer where thick ice disguised everything unrecognisably. I've learnt one thing, she thought: Neville's not spending much time at home. I wonder where he's living – or with whom.

The cupboard doors opened on to the predictable tidiness, but not of the kind which implied someone had cleared up before going away. The canisters were half full, the spices and herbs ready to the cook's hand, the sharp knives waiting in their wooden block. Fidelis opened the washing and drying machines, once having read they were the first place criminals looked for hidden valuables, but found nothing in them.

The telephone was hanging from the wall beside a green baize notice-board, with pink tape criss-crossing it, caught with drawing pins at regular intervals. Cards stuck under the tape advertised jumble sales, bring and buy sales, last year's election. A newer, less yellowed page, with a glossy photograph attached to it, described the facilities of a holiday flat in Cornwall. There was a wall calendar with a month to a page, open at May 1993. The few entries on any page were terse. Dentist, 9. Neville America. Neville back.

Neville had gone away for the Whitsun bank holiday. 'Thursday 27 May, Neville Scotland.' Unusually, the words were underlined with two heavy black lines from one side of the page to the other; and after them, nothing. Neville had not seen Buffy since, but there were no entries saying 'Buffy away'. She had just gone.

'You're putting off looking in the bedroom, aren't you?' Sophie said. 'Can't I do it? It isn't quite so depressing for me.'

'No, I'd better. Come up though, give me moral support.'

'It does feel all wrong, doesn't it? I'd hate to be a detective.'

'Or a burglar.'

The double bed was set between white panelled cupboards built in against the long wall facing the window. It was in a mess; presumably Neville, when he slept at home, never changed the sheets or even straightened the duvet. His wardrobe was half empty, with spaces between the remaining suits and some unused shelves, confirming Fidelis's realisation that he'd moved out.

'This must be your friend's,' Sophie said. 'It's full of Laura Ashley and Jaeger. And I mean full, this doesn't look as though anything's been taken away. Aren't they horrid?'

'They suit Buffy,' Fidelis said mildly.

Buffy's wardrobe contained skirts, dresses and jackets, in flower patterns or navy blue, all hung in order of their length, with piles of folded blouses and jerseys, and rows of polished shoes with medium height heels on a chromium rail. The scent of lavender wafted faintly from the handkerchief drawer. Stockings and tights were rolled into separate pockets of an embroidered bag. Fidelis pushed the long dresses, all hanging in plastic wrappers, aside and looked behind them. Nothing.

'Shall I look up here?' Sophie stood on a chair to see the hats and handbags. 'There's a cardboard crate . . . I can't quite see –'

'Pass it down.'

'Gosh, it weighs a ton. Here.'

Books: Mills and Boon type romantic stories, at least a hundred of them, well-fingered paperbacks with swooning heroines and strong dark heroes on the cover pictures. Fidelis had not thought of them for years, but the image of her foster mother popped into her mind, as clear as it had been during those long, bored afternoons of desperately trying to keep quiet while Auntie Megan read her stories, devouring them like the chocolates she consumed at the same time, one hand holding the book, the other alternately popping sweets into her mouth and turning the pages; and with the image came a wave of nervousness: how cross Auntie Megan would be if Fidelis disturbed her.

Sophie said, 'I had a boyfriend once who kept his porno mags in his wardrobe.'

'I suppose Buffy was ashamed of reading these,' Fidelis replied, and thought, I always knew she was putting it on when we talked about books.

They had never done so until Buffy's first visit to Fidelis's flat, where she had gazed at the overflowing shelves and almost in wonder picked up some of the novels and biographies which lay on every surface except Fidelis's working table. The next time Fidelis went to Knighton Rise, Buffy spoke of the novel by A.S. Byatt she had from the library and asked Fidelis what she thought of the new William Golding and said how much she was enjoying the last Margaret Atwood. Fidelis had recommended other authors, her own current favourite, Robertson Davies, and others she thought Buffy might not have heard of and would enjoy. It was so normal for Fidelis to have conversations of that kind with her friends, that its unreality never struck her until now, seven or eight years later, when she suddenly realised Buffy had wanted to please her by trying or pretending to share her tastes.

' "*Tiger Orchid*, a tale of imperial passion",' she read aloud.

'Lots of people read them, Fidelis. Haven't you ever?'

'No, they aren't to my taste.'

'I went through a phase of loving them. They can be very comforting, you know, they provide escape and fulfilment of fantasies,' Sophie said.

'How like a psychologist you sound.'

'So do you.' The girl was gaining courage, to speak more intimately. 'Have you noticed you never say things *are*? You don't say, that's nasty or he's horrid, those books are crap, that dress is ugly. You say, "I don't like it." You're professionally non-judgemental.'

Fidelis went to glance through the bathroom cabinet and the dressing-table. Both seemed fully stocked and told her nothing other than that Buffy did not go in for much self-adornment.

'We'll just take a quick peek in the study and that's it,' she said. Immediately, with habitual self-scrutiny, she recognised she had become less interested in what had happened to Buffy Cox now that she understood how uninteresting she was as a person. Buffy had no secret life, she thought.

'Do you read much fiction, Sophie?'

'Quite a lot. Martin Amis, Marge Piercy . . .'

'Anita Brookner?'

'No, why?'

'I was remembering telling Buffy once to read one. It's about a woman from youth, marriage, right up until she's the age I am now, and how she never did anything at all. I forget what she was called. I said I didn't believe anyone could have done so little for a whole lifetime, and I wondered whether Buffy agreed with me, but now I think her own life must have been just as empty. Tactless of me.'

They went into the room Buffy called 'the den'. Even it did not show any sign of Neville having been in occupation for a while. Sophie went across to the small glass-fronted bookcase, the only one in the house.

'This is the book you're talking about, isn't it? The Anita Brookner.'

Fidelis looked at the row of pristine dust jackets, all familiar, presumably all of books she had recommended, and wondered whether Buffy ever read more than the blurbs. She felt sorry that the pretence should have seemed necessary, and ashamed that for all her own vaunted psychiatric professionalism she had never realised Buffy was bluffing.

Neville's den was furnished with green leather and modern mahogany of antique design. One panelled cupboard was a filing cabinet in disguise, another a safe. Fidelis said, 'He surely didn't want me to look in his stuff.'

'Are you sure?'

'He did say to go anywhere.'

'Well then.' Sophie pulled open a couple of desk drawers and closed them again at the sight of balance sheets and bank statements.

Fidelis was looking out of the window at the neglected garden. She was humming a song from *Don Giovanni*, but broke off to say, 'Anything interesting there?'

Sophie flipped through the papers on the desk. An insurance renewal form addressed to Buffy, but presumably to be dealt with by Neville, an appeal from the friends of a hospital in Northamptonshire.

'That's where Andrew was taken after the crash,' Fidelis said.

'Oh, Fidelis, these cards are unbelievable,' Sophie exclaimed. 'There's one of the Taj Mahal, it's signed "love from Doug and Liggy", that's all right, but the other – ugh!'

'What is it?'

'A prizewinning bad taste message I should think, how my brother would love it. The picture's a full-size Cornish pasty with a very small pixie eating one corner and on the back there's printed messages for ticking off. Do listen, Fidelis. Having a Wonderful

Time, Having a Horrible Time, The Water's Lovely, The Water's Freezing, The Weather's Fine, It's Raining, Wish You Were Here and Glad You Aren't Here. The last one's got a tick beside it.'

'Can you see who it's from?'

'No, the name and address are typed on one of those sticky labels. The postmark's St Ives.'

'You know, it's odd, we haven't come across any of the things people usually have in their desks. Things like cheque books, or credit card statements,' Fidelis said.

'How do you suppose she managed?' Sophie asked.

'Neville always paid the bills, Buffy told me that once. He had ever since they were first married. He said she didn't need to bother her head with that sort of thing and she didn't understand business, she always thought it very right and proper for a husband to deal with all the admin.'

'If I were stuck with a man who behaved like that I'd have walked out after one year, not nearly thirty,' Sophie said energetically. 'Why ever did she let him get away with it?'

'Girls like Buffy weren't brought up to be independent, Sophie. Things were different in her day.'

'You were.'

'I? Ah, that's quite different. Come along, Sophie, I've had enough of this. We'll go back to Hampstead and have rather a lot to drink and I'll tell you the story of my self-reliant life.'

They were scrupulous about double and triple locking the front door; and neither woman remembered that the windows Sophie had opened were still unsecured when they left.

15

Barbara arrived home late on the Friday evening. It was raining and there had been a pile-up on the motorway the other side of Taunton, but that was not the reason for her tension. She had been paged in her hotel the evening before and found her boss on the telephone. An artificial calm overlaid the anger in his voice. Barbara was the target of an attack in *Private Eye*; and by extension, the whole inspectorate. She had given permission for a property company to build a housing estate in a conservation area near Reading and corruption was alleged. 'Who got at the pretty inspector?' was the headline.

She defended herself and the decision she had made. She justified it on planning grounds. It was in conformity with policy. Yes, it was true that, as the article said, she had decided not to be bound by the published development plan but her reasons were as she had written. The words, though not in front of her on the page, were engraved in her memory so she quoted them, managing to sound authoritative, aggrieved, vindicated.

'Surely', she said, 'you aren't going to worry about what a scandal sheet alleges? Haven't you known me long enough to know better?'

She was under suspicion, but nothing could be proved. The conversation did not reach the stage where Barbara would have had to invoke a lawyer or her union, but she could see it coming.

It was the last straw to turn up from the harbour front and find her access blocked off from the narrow one way street which led to Barnaloft. A policeman said she could not drive through.

'I've got to get through, I live along here,' she protested.

'Sorry, madam, you'll have to park somewhere else and walk down, there's been an incident in the Piazza.' Eventually, an anorak over her shoulders, its hood hooked over her head, her heels turning on the cobblestones and weighted down by her overnight bag, briefcase and an awkwardly shaped cardboard carton full of documents, Barbara staggered back home from the car-park above the Tate Gallery, down the long flight of stone steps and then along the road which ran parallel with the beach. Peering in at the entrance to the Piazza she could see nothing except a jumble of police cars, the voices from their radios echoing in the confined space. A knot of reporters and people with cameras were huddled damply on the other side of the road, but took no notice of her as she hurried past. At Barnaloft she had to identify herself to another policeman before being allowed to approach her own front door.

'What the hell's happening here, Colin? And what's the matter with you? You look awful.'

'Come in quickly. Let me take this.'

'And where's Toby?'

'He's perfectly all right, don't worry, but I asked Crispin's family to fetch him from the school bus and keep him safe in Carbis Bay for the night.'

'Why? What's going on here?'

'You'd better sit down.'

Pausing, her hand stretched out for the steaming cup he had ready for her, Barbara said, 'You look as though you need that more than I do. Are you all right? What's happened?'

'It's Clarissa.'

'Clarissa Trelawny?'

'She's dead.'

'What, in an accident?'

'No. Someone killed her, in her flat. We found her body. It must have been there for days.'

'Oh, Colin.' Barbara put the cup down so as to be able to get close to her husband. 'That's unbelievable. How dreadful . . .' She didn't feel as she ought. She lacked human sympathy, and knew it. Barbara was aware her reaction was not what it should be or what he wanted, not warm, or imaginative or spontaneous enough. Clarissa Trelawny was dead and Barbara cared only in so far as it affected her family. Colin had seen something dreadful, his heart was sore, and she averted her mind with lifelong skill from other people's horrors; and she did not want him to be involved, what right had he to involve himself with anyone but her and Toby? She said, 'Here, in St Ives! It's the last place – but I suppose she disturbed an intruder, a junkie probably, he must have thought the flat was unoccupied, most of them are at this time of year. My dear, this is really awful for you, I know how much you liked her, it must have been a terrible shock.'

'It would be even worse if I hadn't . . . It's not as though it's the first time I've seen . . . I've never talked to you about Korea, have I? But somehow, after all these years, in peacetime too . . . Sorry, Barbara. Must pull myself together.'

'Let me share it with you, tell me properly, Colin.'

Colin stood up, as straight as a walking-stick, drew in a deep breath and gave a terse, lucid situation report, as he had been trained to do long before.

No sign of Clarissa since early in the previous week. Anxious because he wasn't sure she knew anyone else in the neighbourhood. Frightened of seeming nosy. Worried. Wasn't sure what to do, until today decided to risk seeming to interfere.

'You needn't tell me in detail, Colin. Just – are you sure it wasn't an accident?'

He said savagely, 'Nobody's told me anything at all. They don't realise how responsible I feel.'

'What do you mean?' she asked quickly. 'Colin, you didn't have anything to do with – '

'No, of course not. But if I'd got in there sooner . . .'

Barbara was not hungry any more but she felt damp and uncomfortable. She said, 'Let me go to the loo and take this suit off, I've just got time before the local news.' Give him something to do, she thought, stop him sitting here wringing his hands. 'Make me a sandwich, would you please? I haven't had time for anything since breakfast.'

Alone in the bathroom she thought, That bloody woman, nothing but trouble, before immediately correcting her own improper thought to Poor thing.

The last gruesome shots in a cop drama, so much more vivid and less affecting than what was going on outside this very door. A trailer for a discussion programme on the role of the police. The weather forecast and advertisements.

'Here it is.'

Colin crouched close to the screen to watch a pretty, vapid young woman read aloud from a teleprompter as though she didn't understand a single word.

It was the lead story. Mrs Clarissa Trelawny was described as a middle-aged recluse. Her body, in an advanced state of decomposition, had been found in her locked flat. It was supposed she must have opened the door to admit her murderer.

'Colin, she never gave you a set of her keys, did she?' Barbara said urgently.

'Of course not. I could have got in without breaking the door down if I had them.'

'Oh of course, that's right,' she murmured, relieved. Colin glanced at his wife in irritation and returned his attention to the screen, on which two 'local residents' from central casting, a woman in a shell-suit with a Birmingham accent and an old man in a fisherman's sweater, pipe and peaked yellow cap, said Mrs Trelawny kept herself to herself but always seemed very pleasant. A detective superintendent appealed for anyone who had seen anything suspicious to come forward.

'They don't know anything,' Barbara said. 'None of that's *facts*.'

She had been afraid the *Private Eye* story would be on the news too, but it wasn't, nor did it reach the national screens over the next few days; while the death of Clarissa Trelawny was rapidly demoted to the status of a story with local interest only. The facts, such as were known, seeped out gradually, staying in the regional headlines at first, but quickly relegated to the end of a bulletin and bottom of a page.

Clarissa Trelawny had been beaten to death. If the police knew what instrument had been used they were not saying. It was hard to be precise as to when it had happened, but it must have been sometime during the seven days before her body was found, because of the sell-by date on the perishable food; and it looked as though she had been alive to buy the *Daily Telegraph* and *St Ives Times and Echo* of the previous Thursday, which were found in the flat.

The police interviewed Colin Pomeroy at length and several times. He was virtually the only acquaintance or associate of the victim they knew of. All they had discovered about her so far, it seemed, was that she had come to St Ives for a week in May 1993 as the tenant of a holiday flat and had paid cash for the rent and a deposit against damages in advance. All they knew about her was her name and that she had bruises on her face, which she explained as the result of a car accident.

That week she went to estate agents in St Ives and Penzance, saying she liked staying in the district so much she wanted to find a place she could rent for a long period. On being shown the studio apartment in the Piazza, she said it was just what she wanted and took it for a year. Again, she paid a large deposit and the first two and then every subsequent month's rent in cash. Asked whether he had taken up references, the estate agent said her money had been good enough for him; anyway, she looked too respectable to need them.

St Ives was a small community and information leaked out. It was not long before it was known that Clarissa Trelawny was exactly what the local paper soon called her, a Mystery Woman.

Colin heard more from his friend Robert Stanley who, as a local solicitor, was on the grapevine of inside information and was one of the people who had been asked by the police detectives whether he had had any professional dealings with the dead woman.

'I had, as a matter of fact,' he said, ordering another pint. He and Colin were in the habit of having a drink together after the

Wednesday evening life-classes. Robert was a stout, cheerful man in his mid-thirties, separated from his wife, who lived in Falmouth, but amicably, so that the children not only turned up for their statutory weekends but sometimes came over by train for the odd half-day in their old home. Robert lived in the house which his grandfather had built at the top of the town just after the First World War, later surrounded by a council housing estate but still with the spectacular view of the grey and yellow roofs of the town below, the enclosed harbour and the bay and lighthouse beyond. His bow window had been the setting for many a 'still life with landscape' by three generations of local artists, and for her last birthday Colin had given Barbara a picture of a jug of anemones framed in the red velvet curtains of that very window, with a background of stormy weather outside.

'I suppose you can't say anything about it, if she was your client,' Colin said.

'I told the police more than I can tell you, that's right.'

'And they told you some details too, no doubt. If there's anything you do feel able to tell me . . . I am very concerned. We were good friends, although I know so little about her earlier life.'

Robert finished his packet of crisps and lit a cigarette. He said, 'She really was the woman from nowhere. You wouldn't have thought it was possible in this day and age but so far they haven't been able to trace her back at all.'

'You mean, before she came here?'

'Just about.'

'Oh come on, Robert, that can't be true. She was no mystery woman, she was a perfectly conventional, attractive woman – that must be nonsense.'

'What they are saying is that she opened an account at a bank in Bristol with cash in January 1993 and that's the first trace they have found of Clarissa Trelawny.'

'My dear chap, I can't believe that. You know as well as I do she must have had an address, given references – how could she have got by without some identification?'

'You only need a financial reference for a bank, and hers was from a Swiss bank where she had a numbered account, which means there's no more information to come. The Swiss are clams when it comes to that kind of thing. Her address was a flat in Bath and apparently that was rented for cash too. She must have been an expatriate before that, because she doesn't seem to have had any National Insurance or paid any income tax. She once went as a private patient to a doctor in Penzance and told him she'd been abroad so there were no medical records available, but the police haven't found a passport. It seems incredible but she was entirely outside the system. Roll on compulsory identity cards, I say.'

'Driving licence.'

'Not in that name at least.'

'She certainly didn't drive, as far as I know. I didn't wonder why, but if I had, I suppose I'd have put it down to her having been in a crash.'

'You have told the police everything you can, Colin, I assume?'

'Of course, but it turned out to be pitifully little. She didn't talk about herself and naturally I never asked. It was nothing to do with me.'

'A woman would have known all there was to know about her after a single session together. Your wife certainly would,' Robert said.

'That's as may be, but Barbara's no gossip. She's far too busy. In any case she hardly knew her.'

'I was under the impression *you* knew her quite well.'

Colin stiffened and frowned. 'I don't know what you mean by that, Robert.'

'My dear Colin, nothing at all, I assure you.'

Colin looked at the other man sharply, understanding the implication and not wishing to respond. He had nothing to hide from Robert, the police or anyone else, about his wholly virtuous relationship with Clarissa Trelawny, but it felt as though it would be somehow disloyal to the dead woman if he said so.

'After all, Robert, it can't be necessary to have every detail of the poor woman's past history to track down the tearaway who killed her. I know we get some very peculiar characters down here in the summer, but surely at this time of year someone must have noticed something. I shall never forgive myself for not having done so. Whoever did it must have been covered with blood, for one thing.'

Colin shuddered, remembering what he had seen, the memory already infected and complicated by other memories, other deaths. But those had been in a professional context. One could rise above those, without undue stress, with no need for counselling or compensation. But this was something else. He forced himself to go on in a steady voice. 'It must have been in the course of robbery.'

'All the things you told the police you remembered seeing in the flat were still there. That's not to say she didn't have valuables you'd never seen, but apparently there was no sign of ransacking the place.'

Colin said heavily, 'To do that, just for the contents of her purse. And if the poor woman had been asked to give them away she would probably have done so out of the kindness of her heart. She was generous to a fault, and so sensitive.'

'You seem to be the only person who knew her well.'

'We had a lot in common as it happened, we shared the same taste in reading and music. Toby once said his Auntie Clarissa bought exactly the same CDs and books as I did, it always seemed an amusing coincidence. Amusing! That charming, lively person, murdered for money. It doesn't bear thinking of.'

16

Sam Pollock and Sue Smythe had promised to do sponsored jogs every night for a week, to raise money for floodlights round the tennis courts. Sam wore a pedometer on her ankle and the tennis club secretary, a gruff ex-marine who was an indubitably independent witness, kept a record of the total distance they covered. This was the fourth evening, and both women were getting fed up with pounding along the rough pavements of the outer suburbs, booby-trapped with potholes, dog turds and, most dreaded of all, dogs. Sue had taken to carrying an ultrasonic deterrent device which was supposed to make any animal run a mile, but it had not worked on the Mehtas' Alsatian, and yesterday the mongrel from number seven had followed faithfully to heel however hard they tried to make it go away. Now, grumpy with self-denial, they panted along in the yellow light of early evening, cheeks and noses cold and bodies sweating. Sam wore a black velvet track suit. Sue was in last summer's beach wear. They were both fed up, and each wondered whether it would look awful to write a cheque and forget the painful fund-raising.

When they rounded the corner into Knighton Rise Sue noticed the rear lights of a car turning into the Coxes' drive. 'Neville's back,' she gasped.

Sam paused to pull her socks up and readjust her elastic headband. 'It could be Buffy.'

'God, so it could. D'you know, I took it for granted she was out of the way for good.'

But it was neither Neville nor Buffy Cox. The two women trotted up, close enough to see that the vehicle was a high-sided windowless van, from which two burly, menacing men had just climbed. Sam and Sue looked at each other and, without needing to speak, moved back out of sight by the next house's hedge. Sue unclipped her mobile phone from her belt. She raised her eyebrows in query and Sam nodded vehemently, watching as her friend's fingers tapped out the three figures, 999.

They waited, breathing fast and unconsciously clutching each other tightly. Nothing seemed to be happening. Then another car swept into the street and up to the house. This one was labelled 'Froggett Alarms'.

They all knew Froggett Alarms. The company had a corner in domestic protection in the neighbourhood, after its special offer two years before which included the services of a civilian security patrol. Most of the householders had paid their three-year subscriptions, but the uniformed men were seldom seen after that. Nigel McCormick, who always hung on to everything like a pit-bull terrier, was suing the company for specific performance in the small-claims court.

Letting go of her friend's hand, Sam strode forward, crying out in a bold, high voice, 'Hey, what do you think you're doing? I've called the police.'

She saw that the two men who had arrived first were waiting on the gravel path while the man from Froggett Alarms, quite unabashed and bold as brass, climbed into the house through a window which was open round the side. In a moment he reappeared at the front door, saying loud enough for the women to hear, 'OK, mate, all clear now, I've disarmed it.'

'You can't just go inside like that,' Sam protested. One of the men turned and seemed to see her for the first time. 'Nothing to do with you, lady, you let us get on, all right?'

'I certainly will not, breaking and entering – '

'Nothing broke here, we aren't allowed to break in. The window was open, round the side, see?'

'Who are you?'

If the man was going to reply, which seemed unlikely, he was interrupted by a high-pitched siren-wail and the flashing blue light of a police car. Sam and Sue surged towards it, both speaking at once, but very little notice was taken of them, and they were urged into the background as the three men spoke to the police officers and showed them a piece of paper.

'Officer, what's going on? It was me that called you, we're friends of the owners – '

'Everything seems to be in order here, ladies, nothing to worry about. I suggest you carry on running . . .'

The two women watched the panda car being driven away, and stood irresolute as the three men went into the house again. Then one came out carrying a television set; he was followed by his companion, with the video recorder. They went back in and came out with some furniture and a picture.

'That's Buffy's half-moon table! Stop it, stop at once. That's Mrs Cox's. Where are you taking that?'

'That there table belongs to . . .' He held a sheet of paper as far away as he could from his eyes, and read aloud, 'Mrs Elizabeth Cox, right?'

'It certainly does, we bought it together in Camden Market, years ago – '

'That's all right then, missis, don't need to take her stuff. Put that there table back, Tel, will you?'

'What is this?' Sam snatched the paper from the man's hands, and read, 'Execution order . . . repossession agents and – Sue, look at this! I don't believe it, there must be a mistake. These men are bailiffs!'

'That's right, missis. Impounding the debtor's goods in lieu of payment. We're entitled. Tel,' he called, 'bring out that there music centre, all right?'

The very words, bailiff, execution order, repossession, struck a chill into the two women's hearts. They lived on a knife edge of prosperity, enriched during the 1980s when their husbands' enterprises and their own flourished. They had all taken out huge mortgages in the certainty of a rising house market and inflation-swollen profits to be made on a resale. Now they or their friends sat in a brick-heap of negative equity, their houses and factories and shops worth less than they had paid for them, their incomes stretched to pay the interest on a network of loans, their security increasingly dependent on credit of two kinds, financial and personal. Banks and other lenders were beginning to seem like predators, waiting to pounce on any victim who showed signs of weakness. If people stopped believing them to be well off, they would, as a direct consequence, be bust.

Neville and Buffy Cox had the bailiffs in. It was more shocking than a nest of rent boys or an opium den. It was a dirty word. Their neighbours could literally not afford to be associated with such pariahs. Not meeting one another's eyes, Sam and Sue jogged speechlessly away.

17

On the Monday morning Barbara was asked to come along to the police headquarters in Camborne. Luckily Toby did not see it; he had just left to catch the school bus.

'Can't you speak to my wife here?' Colin protested, but the two constables, a man and a woman, had insisted Barbara should come with them. Colin went to the door and looked down into the courtyard. 'You're not taking her in a marked police car!'

'If you'd come along with us, madam.'

'Are you arresting my wife?'

'No sir, but we'd like her to help us with our inquiries.'

'Right. I'm sure she'll be happy to be of any assistance possible, won't you, Barbara?'

'Yes, but I don't know what – '

'But she'll come in her own car,' Colin said in his commanding-officer voice. He added less sharply, 'One of you can go with her if you prefer.'

They looked at each other, and then the young woman said, 'I expect that would be in order, sir.'

Barbara asked, 'How long will you – do I need to bring anything with me?' and Colin broke in quickly, 'I'm sure that won't be necessary, you'll be back here too soon. I'm going to ring Robert Stanley.'

'Do you really think I need a lawyer, Colin?'

'Just in case.'

Robert Stanley was in court in Truro. Colin could not reach him until lunch-time and he was not free to drive over to Camborne until after the court rose. By that time Barbara had been sitting in the interview room for hours, answering, it seemed, the same questions again and again.

How well had she known Clarissa Trelawny? How well had her husband known Clarissa Trelawny? Did she object? Was she jealous? Had she ever complained about the relationship? Had she ever quarrelled with her husband about the dead woman? Quarrelled with the deceased? Had words? Disagreed? Threatened her?

Barbara had repeated her replies. 'I hardly knew her at all. I am away so often, it was my husband and son who made friends with her. I think they saw her quite often. They were neighbours. As newcomers to St Ives, they were bound to have a lot in common. She was very kind to our son. No, I was glad of it. Grateful. She and my husband shared an interest in painting. I believe they used to meet each other in galleries occasionally. No, I never quarrelled with him about her. I didn't quarrel with her. Of course I didn't threaten her. It's a ridiculous idea. What with, what for?'

'We'll ask the questions, madam, please confine yourself to answering them.' Barbara's lips twisted in sick amusement at the weird contrast between this use of the appellation 'madam' and the way she had grown accustomed to hearing it, from deferential suppliants at planning inquiries.

At least she had also grown accustomed to sitting for hours in some discomfort. The interview room was furnished with three plastic chairs and a scratched wooden table on which were a tape recorder, some cardboard files and some paper cups. The table was screwed to the floor. The room smelt of stale cigarettes and strong disinfectant overlying something even less acceptable. The floor had been swept, but fragments of cigarette ash still lay in the cracks between chipped vinyl tiles. There was a large no-smoking sign and when one of the policemen took out a packet of cigarettes Barbara said, 'I'd much rather you didn't.' He lit up all the same.

Barbara sat facing two officers in plain clothes who told her they were Detective Chief Inspector Berriman and Detective Sergeant Cowley. A young woman in uniform stood behind them, lounging against the grey laminate wall and chewing gum. She watched Barbara almost without blinking, all the time, as they went over the same ground over and over again.

'You say you never had a disagreement with your husband about the deceased.'

'That's right.'

'Do you know he was seeing a lot of her?'

'They saw each other quite often. We lived so close.'

'Every day? Every other day?'

'You'd have to ask him. I wasn't there.'

'But you knew your husband and son were seeing her.'

'Yes.'

'Your son was fond of her.'

'I suppose she was a sort of grandmother substitute for him. Both my husband's and my parents are dead.'

'Do you know how old she was?'

'No, how could I?'

The man licked his finger and leafed through some papers stapled into a brown folder. He read aloud, ' "A very pretty-looking lady, always nicely dressed and had her hair done, my guess would be she was in her late forties." '

'How silly. Who said that?'

'Why silly, Mrs Pomeroy?'

'Because she was obviously much more than that.'

'What makes you so sure?'

'I'm not sure, and I certainly never asked her how old she was. But you could tell.'

'How?'

'Well, she was always beautifully turned out, she wore very tactful make-up, but there must have been layers of it, and she must have gone to a hairdresser to get her roots touched up almost every week. Have you asked the local hairdressers? They always have a very good idea of women's real ages.'

'Her hair and cosmetics. Is that it?'

'I should think she'd had a face-lift. Actually, come to think of it, you could tell, couldn't you – the pathologist would find the scars. Had she had a face-lift?'

They ignored her question and pressed on. 'So you would say she was more than fifty?'

'Yes.'

'Your husband is . . .' More leafing through papers. 'Sixty-two, is that right?'

'What on earth has that got to do with it?'

'You're twenty years his junior.'

'So?'

'Did the deceased seem like an older woman to him?'

'I have no idea.'

'But they knew each other well?' A just perceptible leer crossed the man's sweating face.

The little room, stuffy and smoky, was growing very warm. Barbara shrugged off her jacket and asked, 'What are you saying? That Colin and Toby both liked the company of an *older woman* – is that it?'

'And did they?'

'I don't know! I mean, yes, of course they did – as a friend, that's all. And I mean friend. Nothing more. She had taken a fancy to Toby. She was probably lonely, it can't be much fun coming to a little place like St Ives all on one's own, it isn't specially easy to make friends, or at least we haven't found it a very outgoing or welcoming community ourselves, so I perfectly understood if she liked having Toby running in and out. Surely you can see that's quite understandable, specially if she was missing her own family.'

'Did she have a family?'

'How the hell should I know?' Barbara snapped. Hearing her own voice, recognising the 'witness's panic' she had sometimes observed from her dais, she thought, Calm down, take it slowly. She took a deep breath, and in a quieter tone said, 'Sorry. I'm getting . . . It's very stuffy in here, isn't it?'

'Would you like a glass of water?'

'Yes please. And I'd like to go to the toilet.'

He said, 'Interview suspended at oh one four five,' and switched the tape recorder off. The woman escorted Barbara down intimidating corridors to a door marked 'Women' and stood outside the cubicle door while Barbara went inside. She sat on the lavatory, in semi-privacy, and tried to collect her thoughts.

The police supposed her to be involved in the murder of Clarissa Trelawny. What made them think so? Did they suspect she had battered the woman to death herself? Could a woman have done it? Or would they say she'd hired a hit-man? And anyway, why?

Rubbing her fingertips round and round on her temples, Barbara tried to work out what made them suspect her.

Someone must have heard her shouting at Colin that time, the evening before Toby's hospital appointment. What had she said? Barbara could not remember any of the words, only the sound of her own loud voice, and the soreness of her throat. Colin and I never shout at each other, she thought. What came over me?

That was the night she had met a policeman on the harbour. They would have been told about that, too.

'Are you all right, Mrs Pomeroy?'

'Just coming.' She pulled the plug and came out. She took a long time over washing her hands, examining her face, putting on powder and lipstick, combing her hair.

Back in the interview room, she tried to pull about herself the psychic mantle of authority she wore when it was her role to note down answers and, when she chose, ask the questions. It was important not to become flustered, as some lawyers could make some witnesses. Barbara always intervened when that started. She gave no licence to intellectual bullies or clever dicks at her inquiries. But she had seen them in action unrestrained, back at the time when she was observing other inspectors in action, during her training. She had always remembered as an example of how not to do it, a passive man who presided without interrupting as a barrister tied one witness in knots and reduced another to tears.

'Interview resumed at fourteen hundred hours. Mrs Pomeroy, do you have any pictures of the deceased in your possession?'

'Photographs, do you mean?'

'Yes, photos or paintings.'

'Not that I know of but Colin might have the odd snap.'

'Have you seen any pictures of her?'

'Only the one which was in all the papers. A portrait. It wasn't terribly like her, I thought, it must have been done when she was younger. If it's signed you might be able to find out where she was when it was done, use it to track her . . . sorry. Teaching my grandmother to suck eggs. Of course you have thought of that.'

'So you were not aware the portrait was painted by your husband?'

'By Colin? Are you sure?'

'He didn't tell you he was doing it?'

'No.'

'It was kept secret from you.'

'That's not what I said. If Colin painted that, Clarissa must have

110

sat for him in her own flat, so I wouldn't ever have seen it in his studio, that's all.'

'He didn't mention it at any time?'

'Not that I remember. But don't read anything into that because I wouldn't have minded, you know! All it means is that I don't keep tabs on everything Colin paints. The other day I saw one of his I'd never set eyes on before in a gallery window.'

'Right, Mrs Pomeroy.' More paper shuffling. 'Turning to your own recent whereabouts.'

'I can tell you exactly where I've been. I got back to Cornwall last Friday, the day Clarissa's body was found. I'd been in Essex. I'd left on the Tuesday – a week ago tomorrow.'

'So you were here the previous weekend?'

'Yes.'

'And the previous week?'

'No, I was in Somerset and Avon for a couple of days, the Wednesday and Thursday.'

'Where did you stay?'

'Tuesday and Wednesday nights I was in the motel at the service station near Taunton.'

'A motel. Can anyone confirm you were there?'

'I checked in, obviously.'

'For two nights?'

'Yes, I told you.'

'So you did not have to see anyone there on the second evening.'

'No.'

'And you went directly to your accommodation from your car. There was no need to go past the office.'

'That's true.'

'Did anyone else see you there?'

'How should I know?'

'Where did you have your evening meal?'

'I did what I often do, bought something ready made in Marks and Spencer and ate in my room.'

'How did you spend the evenings?'

'Working. Watching television.'

'What did you see?'

'I haven't any idea, by now. I suppose I watched the news. The fact is, I spend so many nights in hotel rooms they all seem completely indistinguishable.'

'You worked on both days?'

'Yes, and then I came home after the site visits in Avon, and got back to St Ives late on Thursday.'

'Will you tell us what you mean by site visits?'

'It's when I decide the appeal on written evidence without a public inquiry or hearing. I read the papers and visit the site.'

'Alone?'

'Only if the site's completely visible from the public highway. If I go on to private land I have to be accompanied by the appellant and someone from the planning department. There was a whole gang of people at the second one in the Mendips, it looked like the whole village had turned out to watch me walk round a muddy field.'

'And then you stayed at home for four days.'

'Yes.'

'Mrs Pomeroy, have you got a wet suit?'

'No.'

'Do you have access to a wet suit?'

'Well, Toby's got one, we gave it to him for his – why are you asking about wet suits? What's that got to do with – '

'As I've already said, madam, we'll ask the questions.'

Barbara pushed her chair back and stood up. She noticed the three police officers stiffen, as though they thought she was going to attack them, but she simply bent and straightened her back once or twice, and wriggled her shoulders. She said, 'If I knew why you were asking some of these questions I might be able to give you more helpful answers.' She sat down again neatly, pulling her skirt straight over her knees.

'Do you know whether Mrs Trelawny made a will?'

'I haven't the faintest idea.'

'So you'd be surprised to hear she wanted to leave her estate to your son.'

'What?'

'You didn't know that?'

'Certainly not. How on earth should I have known?'

'She didn't say anything to you?'

'Never.'

It was at this point – at long last – that Robert Stanley was shown into the interview room.

He shook hands with Barbara and with the two detectives. He said, 'Half-past two. You've had my client here for six hours.'

112

'She hasn't complained – have you, Mrs Pomeroy?'

'I'm sure Mrs Pomeroy was pleased to help you. But enough's enough. Are you charging her with anything?'

'No.'

'Barbara, are you willing to go on talking to these officers? Because if not, I think we should be on our way.'

'Mrs Pomeroy's free to go,' Inspector Berriman said. 'But you understand, Robert, you're responsible for – '

'Don't worry. She's not going anywhere, are you, Barbara?'

'Of course I'm going somewhere. I've got two site visits in Oxfordshire tomorrow and an informal hearing in Trowbridge the day after. But if you mean, am I planning to leave the country, the answer's no. I haven't even got a valid passport, it's so long since we went abroad.'

Sinking back on the passenger seat of Robert's car, Barbara closed her eyes for a few minutes before saying, 'Thank you very much. I thought they would never be satisfied.'

'They aren't satisfied now. But they can't keep you there without charging you. How much did you say?'

'What do you mean? I told them everything I know – which is damn all. I couldn't understand what they were getting at.'

'It's obvious you never read thrillers,' Robert Stanley said.

Barbara had never very much enjoyed reading fiction or even biography. Her real interests had always been in buildings and landscape, rather than in the people who used and formed them. As a matter of fact she had always thought reading novels rather a waste of time. She said, 'Thrillers? Why ever – ?'

'Because they'd have given you a better idea of what happens in a homicide investigation, that's all I meant.'

'I don't understand anything. Nothing at all. All those questions. Why did they ask me? What do they think I – ?'

'They need to find out what's happened.'

'But I don't know! How could I? I wasn't even here.'

18

Brian Day asked to meet Fidelis Berlin. He sounded surreptitious, and it took him five minutes of mechanically flirtatious banter before he steeled himself to say he didn't want her to mention it to Neville.

'But if we're talking about Cox business doesn't he need to be there?' Fidelis asked.

'I really would like to have a private word with you.'

'Well, all right. But I'm rather tied up this week. Is it urgent?'

After they had eliminated every day and most evenings, Brian Day said, 'I tell you what, you like music, don't you? Be my guest at the Albert Hall on Wednesday, Colin Davis is conducting.'

Surprised, she said, 'I would like that. Thank you.'

'Good. See you there.'

The door of the box on the second tier was labelled 'Mr Day'. A table, covered with pink damask, was laid with champagne and smoked salmon sandwiches. Twelve chairs, arranged in pairs, stood on the three steps, but only three were occupied, by Brian Day, Fidelis and an extraordinarily pretty young woman introduced as Mandy. Mandy wore an exiguous slip of pink satin with shoelace straps, its hem just low enough to cover her pudenda, with glossy white tights, spike-heeled shoes and nothing else at all.

During the Brahms, which was not one of Fidelis's favourite pieces, she observed Mandy fidgeting, crossing and uncrossing her long legs, stroking her own light brown arms, examining her own spiky red nails, pulling them through her glossy hair. Brian Day's eyes darted from the orchestra to the girl and back, a slight, tight smile staying fixed on his sharp face.

Fidelis remembered, as sharply as though she were re-experiencing, the time when she could look at herself, her own thin, tanned limbs, her own well-filled, smooth skin, and at the same time think herself lovely and know the man she was beside would think she was lovely too. How she had revelled in her own animal nature. Now all she could feel was the flatness of her chest under the concealing dress, and a twinge of remembered pain in ghostly, amputated breasts. She looked at her own bony fingers and ankles, and was reminded of the long, knobbly bones and wrinkled, age-spotted flesh beneath her expensive maroon velvet. Most of the time she was resigned, necessarily even reconciled, to her own decay, but she suddenly thought if the devil offered her restored youth for an eternity in hell, she'd take it like a flash.

She visualised Brian Day's wiry body momentarily restored to youth and vigour as it came into contact with Mandy's delectable, yielding warmth, her self-confident, untroubled vanity. But it isn't age in itself which has desiccated me, she thought, I have dried up from lack of physical contact. Creams and potions would do no good. She needed holding, hugging, stroking, sharing . . . Perhaps I'll get an animal, she thought, a cat or a small dog, something warm, breathing, affectionate, alive. An animated teddy bear.

Fidelis jerked her concentration away to the music. It was a romantic programme, Beethoven, Brahms, Tchaikovsky. The acoustics in the Albert Hall were much better than when Fidelis went there to her first classical concert, standing in the topmost gallery in her second term as a student at London University, enraptured by the sound she had never heard before, that of a full orchestra of professional players, giving to her, to Fidelis, a special, personal gift of Haydn and Mozart. In recent years deforming baffles had been set to dangle above the great space, and the old echoes had gone. The players' precise, practised gusto carried both conviction and enchantment. Or rather, they should have. Fidelis, unusually for her, found it hard to concentrate on the music. She looked down on the rows of multicoloured people below, on the blackness of the players' clothes, on the crimson and gold grandeur of the great round hall, which was not quite full at its lower, more expensive levels, but had standing room only in the top balcony.

The orchestra was the Dresden Staatskapelle.

It was from Dresden that Fidelis had been sent to England with a label round her neck on which was written the name she repeated to kind Red Cross ladies in the reception centre at Harwich. At some point during the long journey on a train full of other refugee children she had lost her little suitcase and if there had ever been other markers on her clothes, they had come off. She was Fidelis Berlin, that was all.

Her foster parents said her family would find her after the war.

'Never you worry, Fiddle dearie, your real mum and dad will come for you.'

Fidelis's foster parents lived in South Wales. They were Fabians and Christians, and were doing their bit by the war effort in taking in a little refugee, because Poppa was disabled and couldn't fight. Poppa kept the village ironmongery store. Auntie Megan looked after him and Fiddle and read romantic novels. Fiddle went to the local school and when she was eleven got a scholarship to the girls' grammar which became her passport to a wider world, but her own mum and dad never did come and find her; nor could they ever be found.

They had been called Berlin. They came from somewhere in the region of Dresden.

One of those players, perhaps the handsome horn player with grey hair and a regular profile, perhaps the pretty blonde playing a violin, might be her relation. She looked for the names of the members of the orchestra in the programme. None was called Berlin.

Beethoven's Sixth Symphony; the Pastoral. Fidelis tried to give herself up to its delights, to let the familiar sounds carry her into the musical realm where intellect and emotion met in perfect balance. But she was not in the right mood for this expressive reminder of country life; the sounds should have evoked well-being and happy memories but Fidelis had never much liked the countryside. When she followed the other children out of the lane and into the fields after school, she was always teased and terrified, ill at ease with the ominous black and white cows or the fierce collie-crosses the farmers in South Wales kept in those days. As an adult she had come to recognise her own preference for nature tamed. When the music spoke of happy and thankful feelings after the thunderstorm, Fidelis was always reminded of her own thankfulness for being able to live in a town.

In the interval Brian Day told the girl to give him and Fidelis a moment.

'I'll be back in time,' Mandy said, waving her fingers and blowing him a kiss over her shoulder.

'She will too,' Brian told Fidelis. 'You wouldn't think it to look at her but she once played second viola in the National Youth Orchestra. Champagne? Sandwich?'

'Thank you.'

'She's my stepdaughter.'

'Oh, really?' Fidelis could not stop herself sounding surprised.

'Pretty creature, isn't she?'

'Very pretty.'

He looked at her as though measuring, assessing, and for a tiny moment she was automatically interested, before remembering her age and abdication.

'Why did you want to see me, Brian? I assume it's something to do with Cox properties.'

'Yes. I'm concerned about the business. In fact I'm extremely worried. Very anxious indeed.'

'I thought it all seemed to be going on very well.'

'Mmm, the accounts looked all right, that's true, and there's a big new development just got the go-ahead, but it doesn't smell right.' He looked momentarily fierce, his lip drawn up over his top teeth like a predatory little animal, before resuming the bland mask of civility. 'I'm getting the impression Neville's juggling trick might collapse. The balls will fall to the ground and roll away out of control, if you take my meaning. And I can't afford to be associated with the business when that happens. My good name's all-important.'

'Yes, of course, but I don't understand what you're trying to say. What's the problem?'

'Have another sandwich.' Brian poured champagne carefully down the side of the glass, estimating the level with care. 'You're by way of being friendly with Buffy.'

'Yes.'

'Funny woman.'

'Why do you say that?'

'My wife used to see quite a lot of her when we were living in Harrow. They both helped out at a charity shop. Allie – my wife that is, Alice – she used to tell me about Buffy Cox. Odd stories, really.'

'What sort of thing?'

'Oh well, there was one time they went to collect a load of stuff from some old lady's house and Allie noticed a very good Persian rug among the junk in a box Buffy was packing up, which she thought would fetch a good bit of money. But the rug never reached the shop, Allie saw it next on the floor in Buffy's house. And she hadn't paid the charity for it because Allie was the treasurer and she'd have known. That kind of peculiar behaviour, just little unconnected things.'

'How extraordinary, I'd never have thought Buffy would ... it must have been a one-off. An aberration.'

'I don't believe it was. The fact is, Allie thought Neville was keeping Buffy short, not giving her enough spending money so she had to resort to that kind of peccadillo. Apparently there were others like it.'

'Did your wife not say anything?'

'No, she never did, because she'd only just made up her mind

117

she'd have to when that poor boy was killed and then it would have been too cruel – quite apart from the fact that Buffy never came back to the shop again afterwards, or anywhere else for that matter. I don't think Allie's set eyes on her for years. Which is why I thought it would be better to have a crafty word with you. You're more likely to have a chance to find out what's going on.'

'Going on?'

'The question is, what's happened to Buffy?'

'She's gone away, I believe. But I don't see why it should affect the business.'

'Oh dear. How to explain . . . There's Neville going round with that beanpole girlfriend – '

'Has he got a girlfriend? Who is she?'

'He calls her Titchy,' Brian said in a tone of extreme gloom.

'He never mentioned her.'

'Well, he wouldn't, would he, not to a friend of Buffy's.'

'Anyway, is it relevant to the business?'

'You don't seem to understand about business, Fidelis, not meaning to be rude. The thing is, I'm in more than one enterprise with Neville, but as far as the kindergartens go, you're as much involved as I am, so don't turn up your academic nose at me.'

'Brian, I'm not, I wouldn't be so – '

'You see, as far as you and I are concerned, it's not simply the financial implications I'm worried about. A crash wouldn't do your reputation any good either.'

'What do you mean, a crash?'

'A collapse. A failure.' His normally reddish face looked blotchy as he thought of the unthinkable. 'I can't be associated with anything like that. If *Private Eye* got hold of it, or the Party – '

'Whatever makes you think there might be a crash?'

'I've got a feeling Neville's playing silly buggers. Don't forget, Buffy's the one who owns the bloody thing. Neville can't operate without her agreement – or at least her signature. All the property's in her name.'

'Oh my goodness.' Fidelis pressed the palms of her hands to her cheeks. 'So it is. Why ever didn't I think of that?'

'So you did know.'

'Well, yes, I must have been told ages ago, I'd completely for-gotten. I thought it was a tax dodge, or something of the kind, I never thought it actually meant anything. Neville's always been in charge and Buffy never behaved as though she had any say in the matter – or in any other matter, either.'

Brian Day moved to the front of the box and stood by the broad velvet balustrade, holding his drink precariously over the milling audience below. 'There's Mandy,' he murmured. Fidelis watched the girl's narrow figure, the gleam of teeth as she threw her head back laughing at some acquaintance's joke. He said more loudly, 'There's cheques unsigned. Suppliers kept waiting. I get around, I hear things.'

'Surely Neville doesn't – '

'He says Buffy's away on holiday somewhere.'

'I knew she'd gone away.'

'You see quite a lot of her, don't you? I thought you might know . . . We're in the same boat here, Fidelis, if the company goes down it's you and me carrying the can. If you had a word with Buffy, explain to her . . .'

'But I don't know where she's gone. Neville doesn't either.'

'Neville doesn't know where his wife is?'

'He's worried himself. He asked me to look round the house to see if I could pick up a clue about where Buffy might have taken herself off to.'

'That's just fine.' Brian Day plonked his glass down on to the red velvet so sharply that the champagne slopped over the edge. A few little drops fell on to a chattering couple in African tribal robes who, Fidelis was relieved to see, took no notice at all. 'That's really dandy. Buffy Cox disappears with the control of the company and cash and her bloody husband doesn't know where to find her. That's all we need. No wonder he can't pay the bills.'

'Let me think about this. Can we talk again later?'

'We'll have to, here's Mandy. Don't say anything in front of her.'

The orchestra was filing back and the reassembled audience stilled itself in anticipation of Brahms's first symphony.

It was a work Fidelis loved, and had heard in many interpretations, but she could not concentrate on following it or give herself to the sensuous pleasure it usually conveyed. Her thoughts kept returning to the Coxes. What would happen if the business was in trouble? What were her own liabilities and responsibilities? Would she be asked for money, be responsible for debts, was she even at risk of going bankrupt herself?

It had all seemed so easy back in the 1980s when people were making big money and unworldly university teachers like Fidelis, despised on account of their pitiful salaries and irrelevant preoccupations, were being exhorted to become entrepreneurial and money-orientated. In those days it seemed to be a brilliant coup for someone like her to become associated with an aggressively money-making, competitive business. Nobody warned, in those days, that what goes up must come down, where money is made, money is lost, and when she joined the real world of business she took on liabilities as well as assets.

What happened to a bankrupt retired academic? Would she have to leave her flat? Would she lose the valuable copyright of her own books and articles?

The second movement began. Fidelis shifted uneasily as she listened to its restless rhythms.

I've watched Buffy sign documents for Neville, Fidelis thought, remembering how he would put piles of papers before her and she would sign without reading, in her unsophisticated, round, even handwriting. Elizabeth Cox, Elizabeth Cox. 'What fun it would be to have a really glamorous name,' she said idly one day. 'Amaryllis, for instance, or Anastasia.' Fidelis laughed and said Buffy had been reading too many romantic novels, and Buffy immediately praised the book she had just finished on Fidelis's advice, a great, sad, shocking novel about the transportation of African slaves in the early nineteenth century.

She tried too hard to please me, Fidelis thought, reading the books I liked, adjusting what she wore. She lengthened her skirts, draping shawls round her shoulders as she'd seen me do though she never looked comfortable in them. When Sophie and I looked in her wardrobe the clothes were still mumsy.

You can't make yourself over in someone else's image. It goes against the grain. Remember the time she went on a cultural cruise . . . Neville had offered to lend the house to American colleagues for a fortnight while he was golfing in Australia.

'Go where you like, Buffy, I'll pay,' he'd offered. Buffy didn't like. The thought of going away all alone terrified her. One of the neighbours told Neville he should send Buffy to a health farm but she didn't dare face all the smart women who would be there. Neville suggested she should take herself off to a comfortable resort. 'Go to Bournemouth, say, or Sidmouth, you've never been to the West Country.'

Buffy said she could never stay alone in a hotel or rented apartment, what would she do all day? And anyway, she added with a perverse, masochistic triumph, 'nobody would ever speak to *me*.'

Fidelis had mentioned a recent trip, travelling between Petersburg and Moscow on a cruise ship. All escorted, in the company of others interested in Russian culture ancient and post-communist; the tour had been fascinating and illuminating – to Fidelis. Neville had seized on the idea as a solution and booked the trip for his wife, with a financial penalty for cancellation too large for Buffy's conscience to accept. She went, reluctantly, and returned claiming to have enjoyed herself, but another acquaintance of Fidelis had been on the same voyage and found herself sharing Buffy Cox's table for meals. 'The poor woman hated every moment of it,' she had reported. 'She simply didn't have the get-up-and-go to do anything unless someone jollied her along and I gave up after a while – after all, it was meant to be my holiday.'

Holidays. There had been holiday brochures in the Cox house. Was it junk mail, sent because their name was on a mail-order list?

The music approached its triumphant ending.

I do think she must have gone away of her own volition, Fidelis thought, remembering those two black lines ruled across the page of the engagement diary, as though in finality, marking the end, the closure of an era. Yes, Buffy decided to get up and go. But where?

The last flourish boomed through the great space, its resonance drowned by the roar of applause. Fidelis turned to Brian Day and said, 'I understand what you're worried about, and why you needed to talk to me. What I don't know is what you think can be done.'

'Run Buffy Cox to earth for a start. That's the most urgent, get hold of her in a hurry. It's her signature that's needed, don't you see? Without that nobody can do anything. We're stymied.'

19

Barbara stood in the bow window of Robert Stanley's sitting-room. The view and the frame through which she saw it were disconcertingly familiar from the painting Colin had given her. She looked down on the lichen-yellowed roofs and the grey stone of the little town.

'It's funny,' she said, 'when you're walking round down there, it looks as though nearly all the houses are whitewashed and appealing, with all those pink climbing geraniums and window boxes and carved name plates. It's only when you look down on it you see the bones of the place under its superficial prettiness. What St Ives really is, is tough and dour and weatherproof. The old inhabitants planned for hard winters.'

'Yes, you're right. This town does seem schizophrenic, at one moment it looks as though it exists for nothing but balmy summer holidays and the next you're reminded how hard the fishermen's lives were and that it's a bastion of Nonconformity.'

'The artists' colony can't have been very popular with the local Methodists at first.'

'No, and it still isn't. When they built the Tate, most local people said they'd rather have a sports centre.'

'But Robert, you're local.'

'By birth. You could say I straddle the two cultures. I'm a trustee of the chapel as well as of the Penwith Gallery.'

'You're obviously a patron of painters,' Barbara said, gesturing at the crowded walls.

'I certainly spend more than I should on art, though grateful clients have been very generous. Have a look, if it interests you.'

It would have interested Barbara, in other circumstances, if she were not making superficial conversation as a self-control mechanism. Robert too was using the impersonal subject as a buffer, or bridge, between real life and the surreality into which Barbara felt she had been plunged. Side by side they moved round the walls. The hall and the downstairs rooms were crammed with pictures. Robert introduced them to Barbara almost as though each was a living entity, varying first names and surnames just as he would between people he knew well and less well. 'This is a Wallis, here's a Lanyon, d'you know Rose's work? This is by Terry, this is one of Perdita's, this little drawing's an early Nicolson, Tony gave me this one, look, I love this one by Margo, don't you? And these are Willie's.'

It was a good technique for soothing a frantic client down. When Robert had driven Barbara away from Camborne she had been shaking and sweating, with the infuriating, erratic tug at her eyelid, which, ever since Toby fell ill, had twitched at moments of stress or tiredness.

They drove without speaking until the western end of the Hayle bypass. High white clouds scudded at speed across a blue sky. The daffodils on the verges were bent and tattered in the strong wind. The tide was high, and the water in the estuary whipped into turbulence. When Robert turned off the main road towards St Ives he said, 'We'd better not go down to Barnaloft now, Barbara, it'll still be buzzing with photographers and reporters. I'm afraid it got out, that you were "helping the police with their inquiries".'

'Oh Lord, did it? If they hear that in Bristol I'll get the sack.'

'You might be suspended for a while, but they can't dismiss you.'

'What would happen to the work in progress?'

'You'd have a better idea than I would. The workings of the planning inspectorate are a mystery to me – speaking as one who's appeared before it as an advocate more than once.'

As they drove through Carbis Bay she caught glimpses of the sea, dark and light blue with white-capped waves, and beyond it the lighthouse gleaming white on its distant island. That view had delighted her and Colin when they first saw it on their honeymoon. Now she looked at it with detachment. It seemed admirable but no longer filled with delight and promise.

When they reached the road fork where one road led left, down into the town centre, and the other up, behind it, towards the huge hillside car-parks, Robert turned away from the town. Barbara said, 'Aren't we going to your office then?'

'Better not, it's quite a walk from my parking space and you might prefer to keep a low profile for a while. I thought I'd take you back to my place, if that's all right. We can ring Colin from there.'

But when they sat down, Robert with a yellow pad and pen, Barbara with her third cup of espresso coffee, she said, 'Actually, there's something I think I should ask your advice on, Robert, if you won't tell anyone.'

'Everything you say to me is in strict confidence, naturally.'

'You won't even tell Colin?'

'Nobody.' He looked at her with a severe, professional face, its expression very different from the jovial friendliness she had seen on the occasions they had met socially. He looked reliable but formidable.

'I'm not sure how much you know about my work.'

123

'Is that what you want to talk about?' he said, obviously surprised.

'Yes, I – Oh. I see.' Chilled again, discouraged, she said, 'You thought I was about to confess to killing Clarissa Trelawny.'

'Are you?'

'No. No, Robert, I didn't have anything to do with it, I don't know anything about it.'

'Nothing?'

'Nothing. Trust me. I only know what I've deduced from the questions the police asked me.'

'Tell me.'

'It was all, where was I, can I prove it . . . that sort of thing. They asked if anyone saw me last week when I was staying in a motel in Taunton but I can't prove I stayed put all night. I could easily have driven down here and back up to Somerset without anyone noticing. Then they asked if I had a wet suit, God knows why.'

'Interesting. They must think someone dressed up in one as a disguise and went into the sea to wash the blood off afterwards.'

'Oh, I see. You're probably right. How disgusting.'

'What else did they say?'

'They asked if I knew Clarissa had left money to Toby. I didn't, actually, but I can't prove that either, though now I come to think of it I did overhear her talking about it on the phone. I'd no idea that was what she meant.'

'She didn't sign the will,' Robert said. 'I oughtn't to tell you even that much, by rights, but since the police gave so much away I might as well. She instructed me to make a will leaving everything to your son. She was going to come in and sign it next week.'

'Good heavens,' Barbara said faintly. 'Did she have a lot to leave?'

'I hadn't gone into details, but she seemed to be very comfortably off, yes.'

'But then you must know something about her background. The police were asking me.'

'She didn't say anything about it and I didn't ask.'

'But Robert, there must have been a residuary legatee, or legacies to some other people, surely you can tell something from the will?'

'Nothing at all. The whole lot to your Toby with me as executor. But you do understand he won't be getting it, the will was unsigned and has no legal consequence of any kind.'

'I hadn't got as far as even wondering. But who will inherit in that case?'

Robert said, 'It all depends on whether she had made a previous will and whether it can be found. Otherwise the rules of intestacy apply. If she was married her husband will inherit.'

'Honestly, Robert, do you mean to say you don't even know whether she was married or divorced or a widow? And you her solicitor! That sounds completely peculiar and extraordinary to me. Didn't it strike you as fishy?'

'It's not my business to probe into my clients' affairs beyond what I need to know and they want to tell me. Such as, Barbara, what it is that's on your mind, if it isn't this murder inquiry?'

'Well, it is of course, don't think I liked spending the day in a police station. And I was certainly scared enough at first when the police came. But I do realise now that nothing could ever be proved because there really isn't anything to prove. I simply had nothing to do with it, that's all, even if I was a bit jealous of Clarissa.'

'Did you tell the police that?'

'I didn't need to, they asked.'

'Did you have cause for jealousy, Barbara?'

'It was just that Toby and Colin both went on about Clarissa so much, I got fed up. But the idea that I hated her enough to kill her, it's simply too silly to discuss.'

'You may have to discuss it further,' Robert warned.

'I'll wait till you're there too, in that case. I am allowed my solicitor present, aren't I?'

Suddenly she felt the delayed relief of getting out of the police station, away from that stuffy, intimidating little room. She went to the window again, and said, 'It's the most beautiful day. This weather! The view! It's even better than ours, so wide and complicated, with the whole bay. We just look out on the sea.'

'Yes, but you get the evening sun. I'm usually home too late for that.'

'Let's swap.'

Robert looked at her briefly, his face suddenly softer and vulnerable. He was a ruddy man, with short-cropped black hair and brown eyes which almost disappeared into folds of skin when he smiled. Tall and burly, he looked more like a farmer or fisherman than a lawyer. She saw him switch back to professional mode, an obvious transition. He said, 'If you're retaining me to represent you, there's a standard agreement.' His tan leather briefcase was by the table and from it he took a printed form, wrote his name twice and passed it across for Barbara's signature. As she gave it back, he said, 'But you wanted advice on another matter too, didn't you?'

So she told him about the telephone call in the hotel in Reading and the second one to her home. Putting the threat into words for the first time made it at once more real and frightening, and more manageable. At least she had emerged from the paralysis of terror.

'Of course High Court judges on circuit are protected from that kind of pressure,' Robert said thoughtfully. 'Secluded in their expensive lodgings with security guards and marshals . . . I wonder why people doing your job are left on their own. Given the amount of money to be made or lost as a result of your sole say-so . . .'

'Yes, and there's often a lot of money riding on a decision. There must have been on that one. But I was justified in giving permission, honestly, I might have done anyway, there were strong planning arguments, if it had been a completely impossible appeal I wouldn't have . . .' She rehearsed the arguments which she had used to her boss and, many many times, to herself. They were weak. They did not convince.

Robert listened with non-judgemental courtesy.

Barbara felt unutterably ashamed. She said, 'I've always loved that job. Do you think I can go on now, Robert? What do you think, as a lawyer?'

'You will do as you think best, of course.'

'But what really matters, is what do I do about it now, at this moment?'

'In my view,' Robert said, 'there is little choice in the matter. It's necessary to tell both the planning inspectorate and the police.'

'But Robert, then Toby won't be safe. What if they – '

'He'll need protection,' Robert said soberly.

'No. I can't. I won't. Protection for the rest of his life? As though he hadn't gone through enough! That's exactly why I haven't already discussed it with anybody else, I didn't want – '

'You haven't told Colin?' He sounded shocked and Barbara suddenly realised how shocking it was. Colin was the child's father, her own husband. Of course he had the right to know. Was it a sign of their growing further apart, that she had not dared or even wanted to tell him what had happened? Did it have something to do with their non-existent sex life, did she respect his judgement less than she used?

No, it's that I'm becoming arrogant, Barbara thought. Sitting alone on that dais, making my decisions alone, I'm getting into the habit of thinking everything is up to me. Have I become a castrating woman? Perhaps that's the reason Colin doesn't want me any more. She said, 'I didn't dare tell Colin, I was so afraid of how he'd react. But you're quite right, I ought to have told him straight away and now I will.'

'Toby will have to be protected until the perpetrator is identified.'

'But suppose that isn't enough? Suppose – '

'Look at it this way. The planners, your bosses, need to be warned this kind of threat can be made, if they don't already know, but this kind of thing may have happened often before. It wouldn't have been advertised or talked about, but I shouldn't be surprised to find there's a routine reaction, oiled wheels will start turning. And naturally the police must be informed when a crime has been committed, especially when you are involved, however innocently, with a different one.'

'But there can't be any connection.'

'Who knows? It has to be investigated. And Colin needs to know that Toby's got to be watched over more closely for a while.'

'He'll be so angry. He has to be treated carefully as it is, about my having the job and being so busy and away all the time – it doesn't come easy to a man of his generation to have his wife as the only breadwinner.'

'I suppose not.'

'How old are you, Robert?'

'I'm thirty-nine.'

'Only three years younger than me. Colin's twenty years older.'

Robert backed off from this too. 'Come on, I'll walk you down the hill. If you go in from the back the press might not see you. We'll go down past the Tate and along Porthmeor Beach.'

It was windy enough for the concealing hood and scarf Barbara wore to be a welcome protection as well as a disguise. Stinging sand was blown against her cheeks and, with a tiny clicking sound, against the reading glasses she wore to hide her eyes. Plodding towards her home along the beach, she pulled the scarf over her nose and mouth, and, empty-handed as she was, felt burdened as though she were an exhausted fisherwoman of the last century, trudging in the dusk towards the fish cellars with a basket full of mackerel strapped to her back.

The fish cellars had been converted into an art gallery. The remains of the fishing fleet were threatened by risks and regulations. But the modern equivalent of the gossips and fishwives still turned out in flocks to hiss rumours from mouth to avid ear.

Barbara trudged up the heavy sand to the tunnel under Barnaloft, through which residents reached the beach if they did not want to walk round by the road or jump from their balconies; and through the tunnel she saw that a group of people was waiting in the courtyard. She hesitated in her safe obscurity, and then walked quietly on, hoping nobody would notice her arrival from that unexpected direction. She sidled out, and along towards the stairs.

'There she is!' Halted by the triumphant cry, Barbara turned to look at the women – they were nearly all women. She did not recognise any of them. These were not the artistic incomers who turned up at exhibitions or invited Toby to their children's parties. These were the descendants of much older residents. This was an incipient mob.

Barbara tried to seem as impassive as the Mrs B. Pomeroy BA, MRTPI who swept past protesters on her way into a planning inquiry. There was a moment's pause, as a battery of eyes focused on the woman who had been 'helping the police with their inquiries'. The women seemed to be merely curious, not angry or revengeful. No rotten tomatoes, she thought, with a burst of hysteria, quickly suppressed. At that moment the thunder of shouting and lightning of flash bulbs burst over her.

'Mrs Pomeroy. Barbara. Babs. Did you do it? What happened? What did you tell the police? Look this way, Barbara. Over here.'

Some people were standing on the steps, barring her way. She looked up. The door of her flat had opened and Colin had come out. He was running along the walkway and down the stairs, he was pushing a photographer and a woman holding up a tape recorder. He came between them towards her and put his arm round her shoulder and battered a way for them, forward and up, with questioners moving backwards, in front and on their heels.

At least none of them tried to come into the flat. Colin pushed Barbara ahead of him, and followed her in, banging the door, and then double locking and chaining it. He rattled the blind down over the frosted glass panel, and switched off the hall light.

Barbara went forward into the living-room. Toby was standing in the middle of the floor, his cheeks so pale the freckles stood out against them. He said, 'Mum. What have you done?'

'I haven't done anything, darling, it's all a misunderstanding. Come to me.' She held her arms wide, but he did not move towards her.

'Everyone says you killed Auntie Clarissa,' he said. 'How could you do it? Why did you? I hate you for it. I really absolutely hate you.'

20

The card showed the new Tate Gallery in St Ives, a sparkling white, asymmetrical building with a cylindrical centre and huge windows which reflected the sea and sky. Fidelis looked at the picture for a while, humming a tune from Dvorak's New World Symphony and remembering that she had promised herself a trip to Cornwall to see it, before folding the card open to read the message.

'With all good wishes for a happy Christmas and New Year 1994,' it said, the words printed in red capitals. Under them was a signature, written in blue biro. It said, 'Buffy.'

'Sophie.'

'Coming.'

'This card, can you find the envelope it came in?'

'I'll have a look.' Sophie emptied out the overflowing waste-paper basket and scrabbled energetically through a heap of torn paper and indestructible padded envelopes. 'Might be this one.' She held up a square white envelope with a typed name – Dr F. Berlin – and the address without the post code.

'Can you see the date on the postmark?'

'No, it's smudged. Quite unreadable, I'm afraid. Why? Oh, I see, it's a Christmas card. It must have got caught up in the machinery or been lying at the bottom of a pillar box or something. I can complain to the post office for you if you like.'

Fidelis had said not to bother and they went on to a more pressing matter. Now, a few days later, Sophie had stayed at home catching up with her dissertation work, and Fidelis was trying to clear her desk and in-tray, before the two of them got down to a concerted attack on some new findings from Denmark on the effect of what the translator called 'multiple carers in infancy and early childhood, a pan-European perspective'. One of the places the research had been done was a Cox kindergarten. Stacking the papers into a different wire basket for later consideration, Fidelis exposed the forgotten Christmas card and was reminded that she had not spoken to Neville since her visit to his house.

Not surprisingly, there was no answer at that number. Fidelis rang the Docklands office, and eventually winkled his present address out of a temporary secretary who knew she wasn't supposed to but couldn't see any reason to keep it secret from someone whose name was printed on the company masthead. It was in the Barbican, and as Fidelis had been invited to a book launch in the Museum of London she decided to look in on the way.

Fidelis climbed and descended hundreds of stairs, retraced her steps several times and thought, for a claustrophobic moment, that she was stuck in a lift. Eventually, cross and panting, she found herself in the right building. The porter did not think her friend lived there.

'Mr N. Cox, you said, madam.'

'Neville Cox, that's right.'

He sucked his teeth and shook his head. 'Nobody by that name, I'm afraid, madam. Are you sure it wasn't one of the other buildings?'

'This is the address I've got written down. If you wouldn't mind just looking down your list again. I know you have quite a turnover of residents here, you might not have come across him yet, or perhaps you've got it spelt differently. Might it be under Cocks?'

The cursor travelled down the flickering screen. 'We have to be very careful, madam, you see, not to muddle the names. There's three Johnsons and two Joneses and a Johns just to complicate it further. I've got an E. Cox.'

'That must be it.'

'Well, madam, if the name isn't right . . .'

'A man in his fifties, with silver hair, quite tall and solidly built, very blue eyes.'

'That sounds like our Mr Cox. In that case, madam, it's the fourth floor. Shall I telephone ahead?'

'Don't bother, I'll just go on up. Thank you so much.'

More trudging along long corridors, though at least this lot had carpets. Fidelis's feet hurt. She stopped at a narrow window embrasure which overlooked the jammed traffic, and in which she was reflected, and took off a shoe to massage her instep. How I loathe the sight of myself these days, she thought. The loss of her breasts had jumped her immediately and completely from the state of a woman still able to seem in the prime of her life, to one who recognised that everything was being closed off: opportunities, changes, adventures, all diminishing in number, in interest and excitement. If her flat chest did not remind her, then her aching feet or deteriorating eyesight did, or a tricky shoulder muscle, or two new gaps between her back teeth.

Fidelis had had to fight to keep her own teeth as a teenager in Wales. Her foster mother could not understand Fiddle's adamant refusal to co-operate. Why have those nasty painful fillings when one could have convenient and painless artificial substitutes? Eirlys and Dilys were having the lot out on their sixteenth birthday, a rite of passage whose primitive parallels Fidelis had recognised even then. 'I'd just as soon have a tribal nose ring!' she had insisted. Even now, when European adolescents did commonly place metal rings in pierced noses or nipples, Fidelis was repelled by the idea of false teeth and endured the dentist's struggles to save her own; he did not always succeed.

Teeth. Feet. Muscles. Wrinkles. What next – a dowager's hump? But the hormone replacement therapy should keep that at bay. Not knowing whether she had inherited a tendency to the thinning of her bones, Fidelis took every precaution her doctor would prescribe.

Pull yourself together, she adjured, forcing her shoes on and glancing again in the darkened window. Shoulders back, chin up. You haven't been neutered, you're still an attractive woman. Neville still flirts with you – see if he doesn't now. She rang the bell, waited and rang again, but did not hear footsteps before the door opened.

Sophie Teague stood there. She had been in the bath or shower. Her wet hair straggled across her forehead and shoulders, drops of water glistened on her warm pink skin. She was holding a white towel round her body, just above her full breasts and below her round bottom. Fidelis noticed her toes, long, knobbly, with scarlet nails, and the short black stubble on her legs.

'Hullo, Fidelis.' She sounded pleased, unsurprised, above all entirely unembarrassed.

'I wasn't expecting to see you here,' Fidelis said, trying to sound equally light and uncritical. Not that it mattered. Sophie was not of a generation which saw any shame in a young woman having a sexual relationship – any sexual relationship – with an older or any man.

'Come on in. Neville's not here, but it's nice to see you.'

'I didn't even know you knew Neville.'

'You introduced us last summer in Dorchester, remember?'

Fidelis followed Sophie into a living-room furnished with such anonymity that it was immediately obvious this had been let as a fully furnished flat. 'I'll be right back,' Sophie said, going into a dishevelled bedroom.

Fidelis looked round. Two sofas and a coffee table, all from Habitat; the only colours beige and off-white; Sophie's familiar bag, a battered leather rucksack; some papers lying on a white laminate surface. Bills for gas, electricity, water, telephone, all in red. Fidelis pushed them aside with her finger and saw that some cheques were with them, waiting to be put into envelopes. They were Buffy's. The typed name was Mrs Elizabeth Cox, and each was neatly signed in Buffy's familiar schoolgirl's cursive. E. Cox. E. Cox. E. Cox. Was she back then? If so, not here, with Sophie.

'Where's Neville?'

Sophie, dressed now in her usual black tights and long sweater, was tugging at her hair with a plastic brush. 'He's gone back to the States.'

'Back?'

'Yes, he's been there a lot recently, he always seems to be away.'

'Are you . . .'

'We're going out together.'

'You mean, staying in?'

'Well, Fidelis, I can't afford to pay rent, you know.' Sophie grinned as she flicked her hair into a wide elastic band.

'Why didn't you say?'

'Never seemed relevant, really. It's only a temporary arrangement, till I've finished at the college. Tea, Fidelis?'

While Sophie was clattering cups in the kitchen, Fidelis poked around more on the desk. There was a year-planner, the entries in Sophie's familiar italic handwriting. Neville was travelling a lot.

He'd been in America last week too, according to this. The week before it had been Sophie who was away. S to Cambridge with F. That had been a conference at Newnham. Fidelis had introduced Sophie to several people eminent in her field and now found herself wondering whether she would shack up with them too. Stop it, she thought, what's wrong with you? Why do you care?

'Fidelis, you don't mind my living with Neville, do you? Because if it's – '

Fidelis took the steaming mug. 'Of course not, why ever should I? It's nothing to do with me.' But her hands were trembling. Selfish cow, she admonished herself silently, bitch in the manger. You don't want Neville yourself.

No, but even if Fidelis had wanted him, she couldn't have him, or anyone else either, not any more. That was what she was minding, not Sophie's relationship with Neville Cox but that she had a lifetime of relationships ahead of her, and Fidelis's was finished.

I wish she were my daughter, Fidelis thought suddenly, and was at once surprised at herself. She had never wanted children, never for one moment thought of committing herself to any other human being, man, woman or child. Sometimes a man or even a woman friend had told her she was 'cold'. It was true, for her affairs with men and friendships with women had never given more than superficial warmth, like a radiant fire scorching one's legs while the rest of the body shivered. Now, at last, she could have done with central heating: the steady, reliable warmth of a permanent person in her life, whether lover, husband, child or sibling.

'Fidelis? Is something wrong?'

Fidelis astonished herself by replying without premeditation, in a low, husky voice, 'I envy you, Sophie.' The unspeakable, never before spoken by Fidelis, words having been released from her unconscious, imprisoned, inner self, she immediately felt a rush of emotion. Only make yourself say things and they will become thinkable, as she had often told her patients, and now, standing in this impersonal habitation, on an ordinary day in the midst of ordinary preoccupations, Fidelis found herself changed.

I don't envy other people, she told herself fiercely, I don't want a family, I'm the cat who walks by herself.

Fidelis was successful. She was good at everything she turned her hand to. She was well known, respected in her profession. She had made money. In her own world, hers was a name to wield influence with. Anyone, whether friend or antagonist, whether admiring or awed, who was asked to describe her, would have spoken of her intelligence and understanding, her industry, her self-sufficiency. She had lists of ex-lovers. She had professional and social friends. She had what she called intimate friends, Ruth and Tina, but with them too she shared intimacies about sex not love, mechanics not feelings. To whom could Fidelis ever have admitted her loneliness? When, before today, had she ever even recognised it herself?

'*You* are envious of *me*, Fidelis? What do you mean?'

But Fidelis was already overcome by embarrassment, furious with herself for letting out words she had never said or even been aware of thinking. Now Sophie would be sorry for her!

'Oh, I just mean living in the Barbican, so modern, the concert hall, all the buzz and excitement . . .' Her heart was pounding. She sat down on the oatmeal-coloured sofa, its back at the wrong height and angle, its arms uncomfortably chrome, and added, 'The heating's a bit fierce though.'

'I'll open the window.'

Sophie had opened the windows when they arrived at the Coxes' house in Knighton Rise too, walking confidently around it as though she lived there. But now –

'Has Buffy come home, then?'

'Not that I know of.'

'I wish I knew what had happened to her.'

'I could make a guess where she went, actually,' Sophie said. 'Do you remember there was that funny postcard we saw at the house, and then your delayed Christmas card – they both came from Cornwall. St Ives. I was wondering whether she might have gone there.'

'She certainly always had a hankering to be an artist. But why keep it secret? You'd know if she'd been in touch with Neville after all?'

'I'm pretty sure she hasn't, Fidelis, he's really worried, I can tell. I think he's afraid she might have . . . done something stupid.'

'Committed suicide, you mean.'

'Well, yes.'

Fidelis said in a professional tone, 'I would not consider Buffy to be a suicidal type, Sophie, and if she had reached the stage of wanting to take her own life, she would, in my view, have done so in such a way that her husband and friends knew of it.'

'*Now they'll be sorry*, you mean,' Sophie said, describing a well-known impulse.

'I would think she had that kind of personality, yes.'

'Well, you'd know. Neville hardly mentions her to me, though he did tell me once that she lost interest in him after their son died and wouldn't care about me at all. He says she doesn't want him for herself any more in – in any intimate way. He says she's neurotic. She broods about what happened to Andrew.'

'If you call grieving for your only child neurotic.'

'Are you saying coming to terms with it indicates some lack of feeling then?' Sophie asked.

'All I know is I wish I'd ever loved anyone like that,' Fidelis said sadly, and added, 'And I've never told anyone that before. You're going to be a damn good psychologist, Sophie. People say things to you they don't tell other people.'

'You may not have learnt how to love yourself,' Sophie said. 'But you know more about it than most people, even if it's not from your own experience.'

'Yes. I can define what parental love is and I think I know what children need. That's the best I can do, though.'

'Do you remember anything about what happened before you were sent to England? You must have been – what? Five?'

'Four. Consciously, no; and I've never tried to uncover what's buried. There are, evidently, suppressed memories, but they wouldn't be verifiable – my family all vanished without trace more than half a century ago – and I haven't ever wished to disturb my own ignorance. Being a soul doctor I should heal my own first. But I could never bring myself to.'

'Why not, do you think?' Sophie asked gently.

'I daren't.' To her horror, Fidelis felt her face crumple and tears well in her own eyes. 'This is ridiculous. I don't cry, I never never cry. What have you done to me, Sophie?'

'Why don't you dare?' Sophie persisted.

Fidelis angrily knocked the water off her cheeks. 'Because I don't want to know it was my own fault,' she whispered. 'It's the classic syndrome, Sophie, I'm sure you've learnt all about it. The child thinks she brought the disaster of parental separation upon herself by her own behaviour. Rationally, I am aware the likelihood of that is minimal. I am sure, intellectually, that I was sent to safety by loving parents who did it for my own good and to their own sorrow. But just suppose that isn't true!' She wiped her eyes again. 'I don't want to risk finding that out.' Sophie came close to Fidelis and put her arms round her. Both women were tall, both thin. Their heads were on a level, Sophie's jutting, soft bosom filled the space where Fidelis was now flat and empty. Fidelis had often lectured on the value of physical contact, on a child's need for hugging and kissing although (or perhaps because) she had never had much of it herself; her foster mother thought that sort of thing was 'soft'. Now Fidelis rested, like a child, in the comforting embrace of a woman young enough to be her own daughter, and Sophie swayed gently to and fro, rhythmically rocking like a mother with her babe in arms.

21

Everything had gone wrong.

Barbara Pomeroy should have been relieved to be back home again. The second time they took her in for questioning she was held in the police station for the maximum period the rules permitted. Then they had let her leave. The clear implication was that she was the prime suspect, and they were just looking for enough evidence to satisfy the Crown Prosecution Service it was worth charging her. Neither the press, the public nor Barbara's own family had failed to draw the inference.

Printed comment managed to avoid contempt of court by writing profiles of Barbara as though she were merely being shown as a successful career woman, one who had managed to combine work and motherhood; they didn't add, until she flipped and murdered a rival. They just wrote about planning and planners. Cold, inadequate human beings, ran the sub-text, interested in bricks and mortar not flesh and blood. A brief lover from Leicester days surfaced to say Barbara had been competitive and ambitious – code words for ruthless and selfish. Formidable, an unnamed observer at a planning inquiry was quoted as saying. That could be interpreted as domineering and determined to get her own way, by violence if necessary. On the same page, but separated by an irrelevant column about water bills, was an account of the murder investigation in St Ives. 'A woman has been helping the police with their inquiries,' it said. She had had the motive and opportunity; the means had been handy by. All that was missing was real evidence.

Sent home to await developments Barbara was stupefied, in an incredulous daze. How could this be happening to her?

She stood with her body pressed against the plate glass of her study window. Her eyes were open upon a grey, choppy sea merging into a grey ragged sky and the cheerless green cliffs of Carrick Du which marked the end of the beach and the town.

Even in this weather the place was lovely, she thought angrily and hit the side of her fist against the glass hard enough to hurt. What was the good of it all? She'd been happier back in the slums of her childhood; less beset, or at least less lonely, when Toby was lying in the renal ward.

Here she was in the kind of home other people dreamed of, she'd brought her husband and child here to comfort and safety and maintained them by her own hard labour and what damned use was it all?

Colin distrusted and Toby hated her.

The invincible certainty of her own innocence really didn't help at all, Barbara thought and wondered whether she would soon be driven to doubt it herself. Had she killed Clarissa and forgotten it, suppressed the memory, was she in denial? At this moment, beleaguered by worse anxieties than Toby's wandering affections, Barbara could not imagine how anyone could believe jealousy of a neighbour sufficient reason for her to have taken such un-likely action. I can't even squash a fly, she muttered. I'm not the type to take direct action, can't they see that, doesn't Colin know it?

Couldn't they see how impossible it was? Even to put Barbara Pomeroy and murder together in the same sentence – of all people! She'd never even seen a corpse. Colin had seen corpses. She deduced from what he never said that he'd killed – enemies, admit-tedly, but human beings, living people.

Barbara had never struck anyone in her life, not even Toby at his most provoking. I don't have the get-up-and-go. I can think and argue and even make decisions, but I don't *do* things.

Except, it seemed, the wrong things. She'd been suspended from her job. Oh, they hadn't put it so bluntly, she was still being paid, but all the work in her diary for the foreseeable future had been redistributed to other colleagues while Barbara was given time 'to catch up'. But she nearly always was 'caught up'. She had never, until this spring, fallen behind with her work, never received telephone calls asking for overdue decisions. She was meticulous about meeting deadlines and keeping appointments and had never been so much as a fraction of a second late for a site meeting or inquiry, careful to follow the advice given to trainee inspectors and arrive early enough to lurk out of sight until it was time to make an entrance on the dot.

And now, it had all turned to dust and ashes in her hands. It's not my fault someone tried to blackmail me, she protested silently, the refrain familiar after the last weeks. What could I do? What would they have done? What did they expect me to do?

But she knew exactly what they thought she should have done. She had been told in no uncertain terms when she went to Bristol the previous day. She should have told her boss immediately, been taken off the inquiry. And put Toby at risk.

Barbara had gone by train, wondering which, if any, other passenger was following her to make sure she really did get out at Bristol Temple Meads, to stop her making a run for it, to watch her go straight to the ugly, windswept civil service building in which the planning inspectorate was housed. A young man in a green anorak got into the small train at St Ives with her, changed with her into the InterCity at St Erth, stayed on board, as she did, for four hours. He didn't look like the sort of person who would normally travel first class. Was that a ticket he showed the conductor, or a warrant? Was he watching her into the lavatory and out of it again, trailing her as far as the buffet car and back?

Could he, could they, really believe Barbara had killed Clarissa Trelawny and might do a runner?

Her boss said nothing about the murder. Perhaps he did not even know about it. But he, and his superior, and the Chief Planning Inspector himself, said plenty about the threat which had been made at the Reading inquiry. Under their sympathetic words was a disagreeable implication. This sort of thing had never been known to happen before. In some way Barbara must have brought it upon herself – upon them. She had attracted blackmail by virtue of being a woman and a mother.

Not so long ago a senior inspector had announced his belief that to do the job properly an inspector needed a wife to answer his telephone and iron his shirts. Despite his prejudice, the small proportion of inspectors who were female did their jobs happily and successfully for most of the year, but come the annual general meeting they were reminded of their own peculiarity. Last year the gathering took place in a vast, high room which had once been part of Isambard Kingdom Brunel's railway station. Three hundred men in similar dark suits, however professionally unobtrusive, overpowered the thirty women among them. Barbara had thought carefully about her clothes that day. Should she be subfusc too? Or should she do as women members of another male club, the House of Commons did, and wear a bright colour? She compromised, in the end, in an unthreatening lavender, and after the formal proceedings spent much of the day with the other women. They talked about how to look after their children when they had measles and an inquiry had overrun. One woman said she'd granted an appeal for a kindergarten following the precedent of Barbara's decision at Sherbury. The conversation spread more widely, as other colleagues joined in a discussion of consistency in decisions, and overbearing barristers and weeping witnesses. One man asked if the others often found the same appellants reappearing in new cases. A suspicion was voiced that the clerks were doing it on purpose, but squashed. It was pure coincidence. 'There aren't enough of us. If one firm makes lots of appeals we're statistically bound to get the same lot twice. Or even more.'

Barbara remembered who had said that, a long-serving, experienced man, and quoted him when she was, as it seemed, on the carpet. For they had looked into the Reading case, and (though they didn't say so) compared it with all Barbara's previous decisions, to see whether she might have made any of them on *improper grounds*. It transpired that some names in the Reading papers were similar to those in the Sherbury kindergarten case.

They showed Barbara the letter headings.

Allday Properties: Directors, Mr Brian Day, Mr Neville Cox and three other names.

Cox Kindergartens: Directors, Mr Neville Cox, Mr Brian Day, Dr Fidelis Berlin.

Barbara said, shaking, 'Listen. The voice on the telephone those two times can't have been Day or Cox. It was a woman. And I've heard Dr Berlin, she gave evidence at Sherbury and her voice was

139

completely different, she sounds slightly Welsh. It couldn't possibly have been the same person.'

'Nevertheless, there's a connection.'

'So will you tell the police? Will they check up and make sure nobody goes near my son? Will they keep Toby safe?'

There was, there could be, no assurance.

Barbara remembered Neville Cox, who had given evidence at the Sherbury though not at the Reading inquiry. She remembered Fidelis Berlin too, an impressive, authoritative witness Barbara had liked the look of. Surely that well-dressed woman, with her string of academic honours and qualifications and her sympathetic manner, could not be involved in corruption – still less in making threats against a child?

But Barbara knew she was no judge of character. She knew about such things as land use and conservation. When it came to knowing whether someone was good or bad, or even nice or nasty, she had come to rely on Colin, who could always tell.

Going back in the slow train, Barbara read and reread the cutting from *Private Eye*. '. . . a decent and characteristic suburban road in Reading, designed in a modernist classical style by Andrew Macmillan of the important Oxford practice of Macmillan, Foster and Grant. Built of brick and stone the façades have striking decorative panels in the art deco manner. The houses are listed grade two and stand in a conservation area, but unfortunately number fifteen was acquired by the developers, Allday and Co., who wished to clear the whole site and redevelop it . . .' The article went on to talk about the virtuous local planning committee which had refused permission and the officiously vile planning inspector who had overruled it. A case for an appeal to the High Court? it asked.

Barbara wondered what the reporter would have written if he had known about the pressure she was under. What else could she, as a mother, have done? What a mess she was in, both at work and at home. The finding of Clarissa Trelawny's body had signalled a new and miserable state of affairs.

But back home that evening Barbara realised she had been excluded from the whole business. Colin could not suspect, or at least did not show it if he suspected, his wife of killing Clarissa, but when Toby accused her Colin's rebukes were not, Barbara felt, wholehearted. He was not being supportive. He was not on her side.

Behaving like a very correct, well-trained houseman, Colin deferred to Barbara when she chose to cook or clean, as though she were entitled to displace him; but even as she filled in her time in that way, she felt a usurper. And Toby wouldn't eat what she cooked. He wouldn't meet her eyes. He wouldn't let her protect him. 'Dad will take me to school, thank you,' he said, and 'Dad said I could go and get a hamburger.'

'Toby, you don't really believe Mummy could do anything to your Auntie Clarissa, do you? I'm not capable of it. I never wished her any harm.'

Colin said smoothly, 'I'm sure Toby doesn't, Barbara, he didn't mean it, but he's upset. Aren't you, Tobe? Leave him alone, it'll be all right in a while.'

'But Toby, you know me, darling, you know I couldn't . . .'

'So why does everyone think you did?'

It was true, everyone did think it. Barbara had the strength to confront a critical crowd when she was in her official capacity and merely the personification of the state's involvement in environmental protection. But she could not bring herself to go out as a suspect in her own home town.

Imprisoned by her own cowardice she watched the surfers, who even on this dank day were out obsessively riding the breakers on to the shore and at once wading out as far as they could to do so again. One wonderfully agile black figure twisted and bent with graceful elegance. Perhaps it was him, she thought, him in his wet suit washed in the waves, or him, or him. Perhaps it was Colin. All she knew was that she was not guilty herself. Why did anyone think she was?

22

Staying the Friday night with Sophie's mother Fidelis had found Sophie creeping into her bed in the small hours to warm them both up. They lay in soothing embrace, arms round each other but their hands still and unstraying. Sophie smelt of sweet, young skin, of clean hair, of – Fidelis found herself thinking – innocence. That physical consolation – and it had been no more, though what the coming weekend would bring was another matter – made it embarrassing to thank Jean Teague the next day. Fidelis sounded insincere to her own ears as she praised the food, interior decorations and the bread Jean Teague had baked.

The house was sizeable but shabby and not very comfortable. The decorations might have been smart when first designed, but they were of the kind which need replacement and repair, and there evidently hadn't been the money to do so. The showy chrysanthemum chintz of the curtains and loose covers had long lost its glaze, the metallic, seventies-style pattern on some of the wallpapers was tarnished and there were threadbare patches in the fitted carpets. The mattress of the spare bed sagged and the duvet was made of and covered in sweaty artificial fabrics which made Fidelis itch. She knew that Sophie's mother had been determined to stay in the matrimonial home while her children were growing up, and Sophie did not pretend to have liked it, or that she didn't bitterly resent the absentee father who had left his first family to struggle. Sophie seemed to view her mother with a mixture of pity and irritation. Nobody likes to be the beneficiary of someone else's self-sacrifice, not even that of her own mother.

Jean Teague looked as though she had been tired for years. Tall and dark, like Sophie, she had deep, black channels under her eyes where Sophie had elegant shadows. She wore her hair in a straggling bun and was dressed in jeans and training shoes. Fidelis felt uncomfortable with her, partly because Jean Teague seemed so unnecessarily grateful to her. 'You know,' she said more than once, 'I'm more grateful than we can say for your kindness to Sophie.'

Was it proper for her to be grateful to anyone who employed her daughter? Perhaps this was yet another illogical aspect of 'motherhood' which Fidelis needed to understand.

'Not at all, it's very kind of you to put me up,' Fidelis countered.

Jean said she envied them. She'd been longing for ages to go down to St Ives herself and see the new Tate Gallery. For a nervous moment, Fidelis feared she would suggest coming too. 'I'm surprised Sophie doesn't insist on taking you on her motor bike, now the weather's turned so nice.'

Sophie's brother Dominic, who still lived at home, came into the kitchen with a trug full of muddy vegetables, which he put on the wooden draining board beside the deep white porcelain sink. He said, 'I can't tell you what a relief uncomplicated carrots are after a week of conveyancing.'

'Oh, why did I have the idea you were a criminal lawyer?'

'I don't know, Dr Berlin, I haven't ever had much to do with the sharp end. Not my line at all.' He had the family height, but was mousy in general colour and seemed pliable and unsure of himself. 'Mum, d'you want these scrubbed?' He began to wash the root vegetables under running water.

'I was just saying to Dr Berlin how grateful we are to her,' Jean Teague said.

'No need, really, she's a great help to me,' Fidelis said.

'It's such a relief after all her troubles,' Jean said.

Dominic met his mother's eyes for a moment, and then said, 'She's talking about Sophie's illness.'

'I used to wonder if she'd ever – '

'That's a long while ago, Mum, no need to bring it up now.'

'Sophie's put it all behind her and so, thank the Lord, have we,' Jean Teague agreed. 'You wouldn't think she was the same girl as – '

'Mum, you know Sophie doesn't like it to be talked about.'

'Of course not, it's just that it's so good to know she's settled. Things are so difficult for the young nowadays, what with graduate unemployment and everything so expensive.'

'Sophie's always had expensive tastes,' Dominic said with a grin.

His mother went on, 'And they all want so much of everything, don't they? Records, clothes, cigarettes. In our young day there wasn't any need to have things like cars and videos – we made do, didn't we, Dr Berlin? I remember, when Dominic was a baby – '

'Don't start on all that old history, Mum.'

'I only meant, seeing all the things their contemporaries have got, it's no wonder if young people don't want to have to wait.'

Jean Teague twittered. A nice, silly, well-meaning woman who must drive her children crazy, Fidelis thought.

Sophie had gone out to say hullo and goodbye to the veteran pony grazing in the field beside the drive. Fidelis could just see her through the kitchen window, her dark head resting beside the grey muzzle, a picture of pastoral peace framed in pink flower-sprigged curtain material.

'Isn't that sweet?' Jean said.

Dominic said, 'We'll miss the train if we don't get on our way. I've put your bag in the car, Dr Berlin, it's out this way.'

He drove his sister and Fidelis into Bristol. Sophie sat in the back of the car without speaking and Fidelis sustained a conversation about law schools and solicitors' partnerships. When they were in the train Sophie said, 'Sorry you had to put up with all that, Fidelis. My family can drive you up the wall.'

'Not at all, they are charming.'

'Well, personally I'm glad that's over.'

Like Jean Teague, Fidelis had planned to visit the new Tate ever since it was built. She paid subscriptions to be 'a friend' of nearly all the London art galleries and although she was not as emotionally affected by painting as by music, she was still knowledgeable and appreciative. She told herself again, as she had already said several times to Sophie, that they were going to see pictures. If they came across any clue to where Buffy might be, or to her being in the area at all, they would simply tell Neville and not let it spoil their little holiday. 'Bearing in mind', Fidelis reminded herself, 'how unlikely it is. One woman in a big place – ludicrous to imagine we'd find her even if she's there, which I doubt.'

With rare self-deception, she did not admit even to herself how little she now cared. Suddenly this last week, in Sophie's loving company, she had shed most of her previous preoccupations.

So she looked with relaxed delight at the turquoise sea and the brilliant yellow of the sand, and caught charming glimpses of the lighthouse whose image she had seen so often because it illustrated every television discussion about Virginia Woolf. She could smell the quasi-culinary sweetness of daffodils and gorse on the cuttings through which the branch line ran, and when the little train pulled up in St Ives, she leapt enthusiastically out to take deep draughts of the fresh sea air.

Looking down towards the main part of the little town she saw a pattern of grey roofs patched with yellow lichen, a curved inner harbour, another stretch of sea over the top of other houses, and above all a soft, clear light which lent enchantment, she felt, to every view.

Sophie had rung a letting agency to book a holiday apartment with all mod. cons. It turned out to be a tiny whitewashed cottage, in a row of equally small properties. The taxi put them off nearby saying it was accessible only on foot. They walked along a cobbled alley on a small peninsula with the sea on three sides. Three high granite steps led to the yellow front door, above which a basket of bright flowers dangled beside a carved wooden sign reading Hyacinth Cottage; there was even a clump of grape hyacinths in a terracotta pot.

'Mind your head,' Sophie called, running up the little flight of stairs to the only bedroom. 'Oh Fidelis, it's perfect, the window's no bigger than a tea tray but I can just see the sea, and there's a pink camellia out in the garden.'

The sitting-room was dark, with wooden beams and another minuscule window, and its furniture looked more serviceable than elegant, but it and the lean-to kitchen provided everything one could need for a few days, even including some food, if only one were content to eat sliced white bread and drink instant coffee.

'Sophie, I want to go out and buy some proper coffee and things like that. I wonder whether we should have brought it with us? But no, there must be somewhere that sells them here.'

'Wait for me.' Sophie ran down to join her and together they turned round corners and down steps into Fore Street, where they entered the spirit of the place by wandering slowly down the hill, licking ice cream in cones and shop gazing. Some shops were still closed, with signs saying 'Open after Easter', and others were being prepared for the holiday season, with scaffolding, and work benches jutting through their open doors, but most were open. Displays of fruit and vegetables spilt out on to the pavement, washed in the pervasive smells of baking from the bread and pasty shops and artificial perfumes from the souvenir shops. A few people moved as though they lived here and were trying to conduct a normal life which had no connection with short-term visitors, but the street was busy with idlers, slowly sauntering along in bright coloured clothes as they looked from side to side with mild interest.

'What's that tune, Fidelis? The one you're humming?'

'Was I? I didn't notice.'

Sophie hummed a few notes, and said, 'It sounds such happy music.'

'Schubert's Trout Quintet. Yes, very happy, complete contentment.'

'So you don't feel like a fish out of water here then?'

Laughing, Fidelis took Sophie's arm and pressed close together. 'I feel relaxed, released – the holiday spirit.' As they walked on she hummed the baroque tune of 'Begone Dull Care'.

They went into all the galleries, those which displayed chocolate-boxy pictures of dreamy land- and seascapes, those with nothing but screaming abstracts, one which specialised in the art of the golden age in St Ives, another showing good contemporary paint-ing by artists whose work Fidelis had admired over the years. When they reached the new Tate Gallery, they stood back to admire its style and setting before going in. From the glass-walled terrace on the top floor they recognised the view represented in such variety on the walls below: the island with its small stone chapel, the low-built town, above all the sea and its shores.

'Perhaps we should move to live here,' Sophie said in a dreaming voice. 'Shall we, Fidelis? Why don't we?'

'I imagine lots of people have that idea when they come on holiday and live to regret it if they act on it.'

'Why should we regret it? It's so pretty and relaxed. I could get a job and you could write, and meet interesting people, think what fun it could be.'

Strolling back along a different road, chillier and less crowded now the spring dusk was setting in, they came to another gallery whose windows advertised a retrospective exhibition of Perdita Whitchurch's work, gaudy, vehement expressions of non-accept-ance.

'I'd like to look at those, I bought an early one of hers done years ago, before she moved to Cornwall,' Fidelis said. 'You know, Sophie, the bowl of cherries above the mantelpiece in my flat.'

'I love that. Can we go in?'

Light spilled out from the colourful space. A chattering crowd of people were drinking wine inside it.

'We'd better wait till tomorrow,' Fidelis said, turning away.

'Don't do that,' said a white-haired man who had followed them along the street. 'Come on in.'

'But we weren't invited.'

'Doesn't matter, believe me. It's an opening, not a private view.'

It was a friendly group, and the more so when Fidelis was recog-nised by an old acquaintance from her days of singing with the Bach Choir.

'I simply don't believe it, my old friend Fidelis – how long has it been? No, don't tell me, I can't bear to think. Of course you haven't changed at all, I recognised you at once across the crowded room, as they say.'

'And I recognised you, of course,' Fidelis lied. Evelyn, she recalled, was a typographer, whose gender had not been immediately obvious from his name or appearance, with brown hair cut in a page boy style, long, pink features, and always dressed in unisex trousers and sweaters. The voice had been a light tenor, not strong but remarkably pure and clear. But Evelyn could no longer be mistaken for a woman. His head was bald but for a semicircle of grey hair running from ear to ear, and broken veins mottled his wrinkled cheeks.

'This is Nat, my partner, Fidelis. I'll introduce you to the artist in a moment, look, that's her, in the red jacket, but come and meet some other friends. Over here, look.' He drew her into a group of people who were animatedly discussing a local sensation. A local woman artist had been battered to death in her studio apartment, another local woman had been undergoing questioning about the crime by the police.

Fidelis sipped the sour wine and listened with an outsider's detachment, as though the conversation were a radio play.

'She must have opened the door and let the killer in herself,' Evelyn said.

'Isn't it terrifying? I can't sleep for thinking about it.'

'But how would anyone have got away afterwards? They say there was so much blood – I know someone whose son works for the contract cleaners over in Redruth, it took them days to get it clean.'

'Ugh.'

'I know. But that means someone went through the town all bloodstained, I can't think how they got away with it. You'd have thought someone would have noticed.'

'I heard they think the murderer was wearing a wet suit.'

'It would still seem pretty funny, dripping gore off the rubber,' Nat said, shuddering histrionically at the idea.

'No, don't you see, she lived on Back Road West, one of the Piazza flats, so they could have nipped straight downstairs and into the sea to wash it off, it's very close and there aren't many people around there at night at this time of year, so she could easily do it without anyone noticing.'

'She? Who's she?' an elderly woman asked, her eyebrows raised and eyes wide, the very image of a member of a Greek chorus.

Evelyn looked over his shoulder before answering. 'Don't speak too loud, they might be here. You must have met her, the couple who moved to Barnaloft the year before last, a man about my age with a much younger wife and a son, pretty boy called Toby, about ten or eleven.'

'You don't mean the Pomeroys!'

'Yes, do you know them?'

'Well of course, they always turn up at the galleries, one sees them everywhere, they could be here now.' Everyone looked round with a mixture of guilt and curiosity, before the man went on, 'I don't see them. He's a charming man, positively courtly – an ex-officer, surely they don't suspect him of having anything to do with it.'

'It's Barbara they've been talking to, not him.'

Fidelis thought, I know that name. Barbara Pomeroy, where have I come across it? In a low voice she asked Sophie whether it rang a bell with her too.

'Do you know her, Fidelis, do tell us more,' Evelyn cried. 'My dears, this is my friend from the big city, Dr Fidelis Berlin the famous psychiatrist no less, if anyone can cast light on this human mystery she can.'

'I don't know anything about it. Really not, I don't know what Evelyn means,' she said to the others in the group, who had all moved a little closer to stand in a circle round her like eager art students waiting to be told about the works on display.

'No,' one said, 'but you might have some idea what could drive an ordinary woman, someone like us, middle-class and well educated with a good job – I forget what – '

'Well, that just makes it even more extraordinary to think she could have done something like that.'

Fidelis looked round at her audience, all, as one of them had said, middle-class people, all presumably cultured even if not educated, given their presence at this exhibition, and now all as excited by having been brushed by the hem of the skirt of violent death as if they were indeed the chorus to a classical tragedy. Fidelis had not given psychiatric evidence in a criminal case since the early years of her career, but she remembered enough about it to be disgusted by her interlocutors' heartlessness. At the very least a woman was

148

dreadfully dead; at worst, another woman whom they all knew had been driven to killing her. Fidelis said coldly, 'I'm afraid I don't know what you are all talking about.'

'No, it hardly hit the national papers,' Evelyn said. 'Too many murders these days for our little local difficulty to seem interesting. But it's our own home-grown drama.'

'Who was killed?'

'They are calling her the mystery woman now. Her name was Clarissa Trelawny, came down here last year. We all met her, a nice enough little person she seemed, used to turn up at any artistic do like this one, dabbled in art . . .' His voice, a professional artist speaking amongst other artists, was disdainful.

'And who's been charged?'

'Her name's Barbara Pomeroy, I think she's a planning officer.'

'No, she's not, she's one up, a planning inspector – '

'Oh, that's why I know the name!' Fidelis exclaimed.

'You know her?'

'No. No, I don't, but I have seen her once, last summer . . .' Fidelis was silent, thinking back. She remembered the planning inspector vividly. She remembered being pleased it was a woman, not only because she was more likely to give planning permission but also because she always took it as a tiny personal triumph when she saw women in positions of power and responsibility.

A burly, tall youngish man turned round and said loudly, 'Actually she hasn't been charged, she was asked some questions because she and her family knew the dead woman better than anyone else. I really don't think there's more to it than that – and I don't think you should be talking about it like this.' He looked from face to face with a quelling fierceness which caused most of them to slip casually into a different group, or move off to look at the exhibition. Turning towards the door himself, he added, 'It's the trouble with small communities, we gossip.'

'What's come over dear Robert?' Evelyn said with a giggle. 'Perhaps he's in love with the lovely temptress.'

'More likely he's her lawyer,' Nat said.

Fidelis suddenly thought she couldn't be bothered with all this. Gossip about and by strangers has an emetic quality, she told herself; and murder stories had never been to her taste either in mystery fiction, which in her professional view bore little relationship to real human beings and their motives, or in fact, which so often turned out to consist of repetitive tales of matrimonial discord. Ninety-nine per cent of killings are domestics, she remembered, and the rest are for money. It's only in stories people kill for pleasure or revenge.

She turned with relief to the pictures on the walls, and moved round slowly, concentrating on the progression from innocent, violent emotion to control. She heard someone say, 'Perdita's calmed down a lot, these last couple of years,' and thought it was true. Her own painting of cherries was so energetic and flamboyant it was as though the fruit were shouting from the wall, 'Look, feel, taste.' But there was a depth of perception in this recent, less representational work, which made it not only impressive, but, she suddenly decided, irresistible. I'm going to buy this one for Sophie, she thought, a memento of this trip. While Sophie was choosing some picture postcards, Fidelis whispered her decision to the gallery owner and said she would slip in the next day to pay and collect. As she and Sophie left the noisy room, the red label was being stuck on to the picture frame.

There was pasta and Chianti for supper, with marrons glacés which Sophie had lifted from her mother's dining-room. Then Fidelis sat by the little, spitting wood fire while Sophie pottered in the kitchen.

'I say, Fidelis, this is funny.'

'What's that?'

'I'll show you.' Sophie came into the sitting-room holding a scrap of newsprint. 'The lettuce was wrapped in it.'

Fidelis looked at the page. 'The *St Ives Times and Echo*. What about it?'

'Look at the back.'

On the other side was a photograph of a painting, showing the portrait of a woman. Above it were the words, 'Mrs Clarissa Trelawny, mystery victim of studio slaying.' Fidelis looked up at Sophie in silent question.

'Does it look like anyone you know?'

'I don't think so. But then it doesn't look like a very good picture.'

'I know, it's rotten, but the funny thing is, it reminds me of that photo of your friend Buffy, the one I saw in Knighton Rise, do you remember?'

'Honestly Sophie, I can't see any resemblance at all.'

'Maybe not to Buffy as she is now. But I never met her, all I've seen is that photo of her when she was much younger, and there's something about this – the eyes, the nose . . . Fidelis, I think the mystery woman could really be Buffy Cox!'

23

For nearly forty years Fidelis had worked with her patients' minds, not their bodies, but being a qualified physician she was naturally expected to be unmoved by cadavers. She could not admit to the wave of pity and horror which always swept over her at the sight of that discarded envelope of the soul. She steeled herself against the familiar but odious smell and walked into the morgue chatting to Chief Inspector Berriman about church music. He had heard her humming the very chorale he was rehearsing for a Good Friday concert in Truro Cathedral; and soon they discovered they had sung in more than one of the same performances when he was stationed in London. The knowledge seemed to free him to speak more candidly than otherwise or, perhaps, than he should.

When the body was wheeled before Fidelis all but the head was discreetly shrouded. On it, the damage was visible but had been cleaned up as far as possible, which was not very far, and Fidelis felt a revival of the queasiness by which she had been overcome at her first dissection, back at medical school when she was nineteen. Unconsciously humming the Handel tune whose words promise this corruptible must put on incorruption, she stared at the horrible wreck of a woman's face and head.

The immediate cause of death was loss of blood. 'You know how scalp wounds bleed,' the attendant added with morbid accuracy. 'What with that and the cuts on her neck . . . the jugular was almost severed.'

'What was the instrument?' Fidelis asked.

'A wine bottle,' said the attendant.

Jack Berriman expanded. 'A full bottle of Rioja, Cosecha 1985 to be precise. She'd bought it herself in Penzance three weeks before. We believe the killer held it in a cloth and hit her with it on the head once, sufficiently hard to render her unconscious, and then again, both with the full bottle and then again with the broken base. A woman could have done it easily. The wine had soaked in, of course, and the jagged shards of bottle glass – '

'I can imagine,' Fidelis said hastily, who had noted with horror the hatching of scars on the disintegrated, decomposed flesh exposed to her gaze. A civilian undertaker would have disguised the scars and painted the cheeks for a family viewing, but this was a meeting of professionals in a forensic mortuary. What Fidelis saw was hideously shrunken and irregularly brown, marked with darker stripes. It was the sight of what could happen to bodies which had confirmed Fidelis's early choice to be a doctor of souls.

At last she said, 'The hair – is the hair dyed?'

'Yes, it would have been pepper and salt underneath.'

'Even so. Her eyes – they were deeper set, she looked older. She had more wrinkles and lines . . . and the nose.' She crouched down to see the nose in profile. 'That's different too.'

'This woman has had plastic surgery, it looks like a nose job plus eyelid tuck and face-lift, all done at the same time, from the scars.'

'In that case, I suppose it could be. But surely you could find the clinic where it was done? They'd have before and after pictures. Going on what I'm seeing here and now I guess it is her, but put me in a witness box and I'd be hesitant. I couldn't swear this is the body of Elizabeth Cox.'

Back in the interview room – a rather superior little cubby hole, with three red armchairs and a picture of the Duke of Cornwall getting out of a red helicopter – the chief inspector said, 'Have you advised the police before in an investigation?'

'Once or twice.'

'So you'll know the terms we can talk on? Confidentiality, all that.' Fidelis nodded, and he went on, 'Had to get that out of the way.'

'Of course.'

'We're trying to find where the plastic surgery was done, which should be possible so long as she didn't go abroad for it. But assuming for the moment that it is your friend, tell me a bit more about her. You know her husband, I assume?'

'I do, yes.' Fidelis realised Neville would be the prime suspect if this were indeed Buffy's body. If she had ducked out of his life into hiding, taking his property or money with her, then he would have had good reason to feel vengeful. But with his wife dead presumably he would get it all back.

'Did she leave a will?' Fidelis asked.

'A local solicitor made one but she hadn't signed it yet.'

So Neville would inherit on her intestacy, or, if Buffy had made any previous will, almost certainly it would have been done under his eyes and in his favour.

He had a good motive, she thought sadly, and wished she could put it past Neville to do such a thing. But she could imagine it only too easily: Neville, a physical man, fit from ski-runs and golf courses, losing his temper, his face taut and scarlet as it was at moments of sexual passion, his strong hands grabbing a weapon, driven by uncontrolled fury. It was that determined demon which made money. He was not burdened with compunction. Fidelis had always known that.

'Surely it must have been an intruder? Wasn't the motive just robbery? There's no need to think about her personal life, really, is there?'

'We thought it was at first,' Jack Berriman said. 'An unpremeditated crime done on impulse. But nothing seems to have been stolen. A neighbour who knew the flat says everything he remembers is on the list we showed him, and the estate agent says his inventory matches it.'

'That means it's more likely to have been something to do with her, herself, as a person. I understand why you think so.'

'If this is Elizabeth Cox why would she be calling herself Clarissa Trelawny, do you suppose?' Inspector Berriman asked.

'It does sound impossibly romantic, doesn't it? But if you're choosing a brand new identity it might as well be a glamorous one, I suppose. Buffy used to read a lot of slushy novels whose heroines were called names like Clarissa or Arabella or Petronella.'

Fidelis thought about Buffy losing herself in sentimental schlock, imagining sheiks or princes, dreaming of living with a hero who bothered to make her earth move. How different her outer persona had seemed, practical but passive, sensible and subdued. Could she have made so dramatic, so decisive a revolution in her life? What would it have been necessary for her to do?

Find a plastic surgeon, check into his clinic and have the operations, convalesce where nobody knew her – where would she have gone to do that? 'Why don't you see whether she was at a health farm while the scars were healing?' Fidelis suggested, and watched Jack Berriman write it on his pad. 'And then she'd need some sort of identification, wouldn't she?'

'Hard cash is quite a good passport,' he said drily.

'But to get cash she'd need a bank account. You'd have to get a cheque made out to you, or just money I suppose . . .'

'Bank managers don't quibble if there's enough of it.'

'Don't they always want references at least?'

'They are supposed to, and of course you'd have to for overdrafts or other services, but if all you need is a place to keep the cash there's always some bank or building society that'll take it. But did your friend have much money?'

Another difficult question. Buffy Cox must have had lots of it on paper, by law. Neville had ensured that all their property – the house, the shares, everything traceable – was in his wife's name in case he ever went bankrupt, as from time to time in his chancy career he must have seemed likely to do. As far as Fidelis knew, it had never made any difference. Buffy signed her name where he told her to, without question, and spent only what he said she might spend to the extent, Fidelis recalled, that Buffy once admitted she had never cashed a cheque in her life. Neville had always handed her such spending money as she needed.

But there can't actually have been anything except her own supinity to stop Buffy from deciding one day to do it all herself instead. She could have gone to the bank and withdrawn the money. She could have instructed a stockbroker to sell the shares. She could have taken all the fortune Neville had built up. He would have been left to discover with mounting dismay that he had – what was the expression Brian Day had used? – a cash flow problem. He wouldn't have been able to pay his bills.

'I think', Fidelis said slowly, 'that she actually had access to a good deal of money. She always signed the cheques.'

Or someone else signed them in her handwriting. Had Neville forged the signature E. Cox on those cheques in his flat? Fidelis wouldn't put it past him.

But by that time, most of the money would be elsewhere, rebanked in a new name, by a woman with a new look. No wonder it was so urgent for Neville to find where she had gone.

'He must have been desperate for ready money,' Jack Berriman said. 'And desperation drives men to desperate deeds.'

'Drives *people* to desperate deeds.'

'If Clarissa Trelawny was your friend Buffy Cox, what would

154

have made her decide to come here? Would it have been desperation?' Inspector Berriman wondered.

'I don't know. What sort of life was there for her in St Ives? Did she become part of the community there?'

'She painted a bit, and she made friends with some neighbours. The Pomeroys – he's a retired soldier, she's a civil servant and they've got a boy – nice little chap, seems perfectly healthy now even though he had a kidney transplant.'

'He had a . . .' Fidelis's voice trailed into silence. From the back of her throat came an almost strangled sound. She was unconsciously humming Pergolesi's music of a mother's lament. '*Stabat mater dolorosa* . . . the mother stood in sorrow . . .'

A kidney transplant. That was it.

Andrew Cox was on a life-support machine. Buffy was on the far side of the world and it had taken urgent hours to locate her and for her to start the long journey home. In Buffy's absence Neville had given permission for Andrew's healthy organs to be used for transplants. Three other people were now alive or sighted, thanks to him. But Buffy had arrived to find it a *fait accompli*. She had been inconsolable for losing her son and incandescent with rage and resentment at his body's mutilation.

'He was mine, flesh of my flesh, every tiny molecule had been part of me, he came from my body. His skin, his hair, everything I touched and cherished and cared for all those years.' And then, later, much later, she said more calmly that she could have come to terms with losing her son. What she could not ever accept was that part of him was still there without her knowing where. Who was it, in whom Andrew's very self was living to that day? Somewhere there was someone in whom she had a share, of whose life, or death, she had a right to know. 'I've got to be told when he dies, where they bury the parts of Andrew they stole. Or if he lives and has children one day – my tissue, my blood, my grandchildren.'

Nobody would tell her anything. It was not policy to divulge such information, the hospital said, it was better for her not to know, better for the recipient, better all round. 'Who are they to say what's better for me?' she raged. 'Little Hitlers. Interfering brutes. They've stolen my son.'

After a few weeks she spoke about it less, but that didn't mean she'd changed her mind, she said once, adding that the matter was not closed. Fidelis began to see her less often though, and did not know whether Buffy had been able to keep her resentment on the boil.

Now she knew. Buffy never got over it, Fidelis realised and blamed herself for not doing so before. What sort of shrink am I? She remembered young patients she had treated who were traumatised by the notion of living from someone else's death, and thought, I should have known.

'Find out', Fidelis said, 'whether the boy's parents ever wrote to thank the donor. Can you do that? Could you ring them up now?'

'I could, but why?'

'Because Buffy's son was killed in a car crash, and Buffy never forgave Neville for donating his organs for transplanting. That's what brought her here, that's what she came for. I can see it all.'

Fidelis clasped her hands and stared unfocused into space. Buffy had been a chameleon, a woman who spent her life fitting in; she pretended to do with enthusiasm whatever the people she knew were doing and talking about. She had even acquired and pretended to read the books Fidelis was reading.

She wasn't good-looking, she'd never been pretty or clever, but she knew how to fit in. She must have planned it for weeks after she got the letter. The transfer of assets into a new account in a strange place where nobody would think twice about a middle-aged woman coming to start a new life. The plastic surgery – a straight nose, a smoother skin, a different coloured hair, a whole new wardrobe. And there she is, Clarissa Trelawny, a widow or divorcee, well off, nice-looking, moving to a flat near the child's family and ready to join in with their interests no matter what they were.

'She'd have been good with the boy, she was with her own. Muscling in. Making herself indispensable. I wonder whether his mother was jealous. I wonder just how jealous she was.'

'We thought she might be jealous for another reason.'

'Both, perhaps. Buffy knew how to make men comfortable.' Fidelis heard the acid in her own voice. She could not fail to recognise her own discomfiture. A fine psychologist I am, she thought, to have been so thoroughly taken in. Fancy letting myself believe Buffy was a truly simple person, candid, incapable of deceit or disguise. And to think that's what I liked about her, damned patronising, snobbish bitch that I am. 'I have been a fool,' she said aloud, and left soon afterwards in search of cleaner, clearer company. She was driven back to St Ives in a small panda car by a cheerful young woman police constable who called her madam and did not know the difference between a psychologist, psychiatrist and psychotherapist. Fidelis found her company pleasantly restful.

24

Before the next fortnightly edition of *Private Eye* could appear, the story of the Reading planning scandal was taken up by another journal even less cautious of the law of defamation.

Fidelis Berlin was tracked down in St Ives by Brian Day in person, who, with Neville Cox, was the other person vilified. He had rung, left messages and eventually gone round to her flat in Hampstead, where after a good deal of self-identification and justification he managed to persuade Fidelis's neighbours to divulge at least what part of the world she was in and that she'd gone to look at pictures. His secretary spent most of a day telephoning every hotel and letting agency in the area; none had heard of a Dr Berlin, since her booking had been made by Sophie. The secretary then rang every single art gallery in West Cornwall and struck lucky when one owner, in saying aloud he'd never heard of Fidelis Berlin, did so in the presence of her friend Evelyn, who had.

When Brian Day at last got Fidelis at the end of a telephone he told her she had to do something about it. His voice grew louder and higher until he was almost screaming.

Get hold of Neville. Find out what was going on. Do something about it. 'This is completely intolerable. I've had Central Office asking questions. It's a disaster.'

Barbara Pomeroy received a copy of the article by fax. It was the last straw. Without asking Colin, she wrote out her resignation from the planning inspectorate and faxed it back immediately, not giving herself a chance to change her mind. She didn't tell Colin, but he saw the letter on her table and, addressing her directly for the first time in days, asked her what it was.

'I've got to give it up, Colin, I can't go on. You don't know how difficult it's been, I'm treated like a pariah, they all think I'm beyond the pale. And I did do wrong. I've admitted it. I should have told someone what had happened. I should have told you. I can set up as a planning consultant. I could work from home. Wouldn't that make things better?' She was speaking without hope or conviction. As they stood there, the fax machine began to spit out a sheet of paper. The planning inspectorate had immediately accepted her resignation.

Colin looked at his wife with chilly distaste. 'If you've given up your job you could clean up a bit in here,' he said, gesturing at the heaps of papers and disordered files. She met his gaze sideways, fearful and deferential. His grievance, if not his suspicion, was justified. 'We can manage on your pension for a while, can't we?' she said meekly.

That night Colin wanted to have intercourse. It was not love-making, not even sleeping with – rather, a demonstration that he was master and paymaster in his own house again. Barbara accepted his joyless, unenjoyable embraces with gratitude.

Neville Cox arrived in St Ives that evening. He had not yet been warned about the planning scandal, having come back from the United States, changed terminals at Heathrow and continued his journey to Cornwall by air; if he had had a chance to buy the London *Evening Standard* he could have read a report of what he was supposed, by innuendo, to have done in obtaining planning permission for a profitable development by fraud or worse; but the little plane only carried the *Plymouth Evening Herald*, whose readers were not expected to care what went on in Berkshire suburbs.

Sophie had booked a room for Neville in a hotel in Penzance, having looked surprised and shaken her head when Fidelis asked whether she wouldn't prefer to stay there herself too, and then Fidelis realised it wouldn't have been appropriate for Neville and his girlfriend to stay together, given that Neville was coming for the specific purpose of viewing his wife's putative body.

He came to Hyacinth Cottage from the mortuary. It had indeed been his wife, changed but identifiable. Buffy Cox had been living in St Ives as Clarissa Trelawny. She had an unmistakable pattern of small raised moles just beside her Caesarean scar.

'They wanted to know where I was in the first week of April,' Neville said, yawning hugely and stretching his limbs as far as he could in a room whose beamed ceiling his head was scraping. 'God, I'm tired.' Silently Sophie handed him a whisky and soda.

'And where were you?' Fidelis asked.

'South Carolina, where I've just come from now. Luckily I can prove it. I flew on the second and spent the whole time living with Chuck Velinowski like Siamese twins, talking about golf courses. I think we've got a deal going. God knows I might have wanted to strangle Buffy for leaving me in the lurch like that, but at least nobody can possibly suspect me of doing it.'

'I thought the body was too – ' Fidelis stopped to express herself more delicately. 'I thought they couldn't fix the date of death so exactly.'

'Don't ask me the details! All I know is she bought a newspaper and some milk and bread on the third, but by that time I was out of the way. Lucky for me. It could have been awkward.'

'Did they give you any other details?' Sophie asked. 'Was there evidence – fingerprints or anything? Sorry, is it ghoulish to ask?'

'Killers wear gloves these days, they learn to on TV.'

Sophie had bought mackerel direct from a fishing boat, and went out to the kitchen to grill them. The strong smell oozed through the little house.

Fidelis said, 'Neville, when you asked me to find where Buffy was . . .'

'To be perfectly honest with you, I had a cash flow problem without her. You know everything's always been in her name, just in case . . . It's been difficult, these last few months, you can imagine.'

'When you told me about it, over lunch at the Savoy, just after I got back from the States myself, you were on the way there yourself the next day.'

'I shouldn't have left it so long to look for her, frankly I blame myself for that. But after what happened to Andy she wasn't herself, you saw that, Fidelis. I suppose I just thought she must have gone off to sort herself out on her own, get her head together again.'

'Neville, had you seen the letter from the parents of the child who received a transplant?'

Before saying no, he hesitated, very briefly, almost imperceptibly calculating. And Fidelis, who had once learnt him intimately, understood at once, the shock registering on her mind before she even analysed what had caused it.

Neville was lying. Neville had seen the letter. He must have recognised the inspector's name at the Sherbury inquiry.

They had talked about her, pleased to have a woman deciding the issue. Fidelis, always such a careful watcher, also remembered most of what she had observed.

' "She's got a kid of her own",' she quoted softly. 'That's what you said, Neville. I remember I wondered how you knew, and then we got talking about something else and I forgot all about it. But you really did know she had a kid of her own, you had seen her letter. Didn't you guess Buffy would come here?'

'To tell you the honest truth it never crossed my mind. Why on earth should she come here? It's a pretty sick notion, Fidelis, I must say – and Buffy'd be the last person the other parents would want to see, or me for that matter. Put yourself in their shoes.'

'That's just it. I think that's exactly what Buffy was trying to do.'

Fidelis walked up and down the room, humming one of Mahler's Kindertotenlieder as she empathised with and visualised what Buffy Cox had done and thought.

It must have seemed as though her son was returned to life again when she heard about the other boy in whom his very essence had survived. She took a holiday flat nearby that summer. Had she come to look round even earlier, before deciding what to do? Probably; and then she would have made her plan.

Turn the assets which were legally hers but actually Neville's into money and bank it in another name, a heroine's name. Book the surgery, arrange to convalesce at a health farm; transform herself into a heroine. She had drawn a line under Buffy Cox's life – two lines, actually, thick black stripes marking the last day in her engagement diary – and left her home to become a person the Pomeroys would wish to know.

The face-lift, an eye job. Arriving in St Ives with tell-tale bruises, she had mentioned a minor car accident to explain them; Buffy had been an over-age, eager Cinderella going out to find her own fairy godmother. Always a good copyist, an imitator, she would soon have found out what interests to seem to share with the Pomeroys, which books they chose to read, what topics they would enjoy discussing. Without her own original ideas or tastes, she could turn herself into whatever the Pomeroys would like; a family friend, a granny substitute, no threat but a useful neighbour only too pleased to help out, to take care of their child, to entertain him.

But how much had the boy's mother liked that? Working full time herself and away from home a lot of the time, it can't have been much fun for her to have a rich rival muscling in. Colin Pomeroy had painted Clarissa's portrait, badly but with signs of some schmalzy emotion showing through. Had she begun to think about entering more deeply into their lives, about Colin as a man who was more than Toby's father?

Fidelis remembered Barbara Pomeroy vividly, not the sort of person, she would have thought, to have violent emotional reactions; ruled by her head not her heart. But mother love was an anti-intellectual animal instinct. She could well have wished Clarissa Trelawny dead.

'She's in deep trouble, that woman,' Fidelis said. 'But so are we. It can't be a coincidence that this same woman knew Buffy and is involved with the . . . Neville. Look at me. Tell me. What happened at the Chambers Grove appeal?'

'Allday's Reading site? I didn't do that one myself, I thought it wasn't a runner, but we did get the permission much to my surprise – wait a minute, Fidelis, why are you asking me that? What do you know about Chambers Grove?'

'Only what every reader of *Scallywag* knows.'

'I haven't read *Scallywag*. What are you talking about?'

'Only that Barbara Pomeroy, the mother of the boy who received an organ from your son, the woman who lived close to Buffy, was also the planning inspector who's alleged to have broken the rules to give permission to your scheme.'

He looked surprised. 'I don't know about breaking rules,' he said slowly. 'Though I don't deny the fact of the matter is, we really needed that permission. Getting it has just about saved our bacon, we're selling the site for enough to keep us afloat for the next few months.'

'Was it a peculiar coincidence that she did both?'

'No, one often sees inspectors again, developers get to know them. But that she's tied up with Buffy . . .' He frowned, thinking; and watching him Fidelis remembered what she had found attractive in him when they first met all those years before, and what she had grown to take for granted or even dislike in the subsequent years. He thought with his whole body, his muscles tight as though

161

he were about to use them, hands clenched, shoulders rigid, jaw clenched. He was a totally physical being and she could read his body language.

'Food on the table,' Sophie called. She would not eat the mackerel herself, but had cooked it to please Fidelis.

Not a lover, not even a daughter substitute, Sophie was a loving, lovable girl, whose physical presence, by Fidelis's side during the day, snugly, sexlessly close at night, had brought pleasure, warmth – yes, Fidelis thought, the idea unfamiliar and reluctantly acknowledged, she's brought me happiness. But she was taken in by this mendacious, dangerous, but powerfully attractive man. Who am I to criticise? Fidelis asked herself; but realised she had to rescue her in time.

25

The last act of the drama began in another municipal building. The inquest on the woman known as Clarissa Trelawny and identified as Elizabeth Cox was held at the Guildhall in St Ives, on a wet, chill morning when all the participants scurried into its shelter bent double against a strong east wind and horizontal rain which left a salty taste on the lips.

Fidelis was not called as a witness herself. She paused outside the building to look at the strange Barbara Hepworth statue called *Dual Form* before climbing the steps behind a couple who had walked together but with a good yard between them, a tall, thin, upright man and a small, anxious woman. At one moment she put her hand on his arm, and Fidelis saw him shrug it away. When they stood taking off and shaking out their raincoats Fidelis realised the woman was Barbara Pomeroy, diminished since she had last seen her. Of course she was not occupying a position of presiding power today; but quite apart from that she looked older, tired and discouraged. Her skin was muddy, the curly hair had lost its gloss and her make-up was clumsily applied. Fidelis lip-read her whisper.

'Colin, must I really go in?'

Colin Pomeroy looked at her coldly and spoke perfectly audibly. 'Yes, go up. Go on up there now.' He was to give evidence of finding the body and went alone into the hall below.

Fidelis followed Barbara up to the public gallery, and saw the other people already there stare at her openly. In so small a space the observances of civilisation survived. Nobody made any more dramatic gesture than to draw away from Barbara and whisper. Their voices were loud enough for Barbara to hear but quiet enough for her to pretend not to have been able to.

'There she is, she's got a nerve, turning up here. She doesn't look like a murderer. My cousin Karenza says she neglects that boy of hers. Do you think she really . . .? Her husband must be a saint, putting up with . . . Fancy showing her face here today.'

The coroner had not yet arrived.

Fidelis said, 'You won't remember me, but I recognise you from an inquiry you held last year. Fidelis Berlin.'

'Oh. Yes, I think I . . . how do you do?' Barbara Pomeroy said in an anxious, congested voice, quite unlike the clear and authoritative tone Fidelis remembered.

'And here's my assistant, Sophie Teague. She's kept me a seat, why don't you sit with us? When are they starting, Sophie?'

'It says ten o'clock on the board downstairs.'

'Have we met before too? I seem to know your voice,' Barbara asked Sophie.

'I don't think so. I was at the Sherbury inquiry but just to observe, I didn't say anything.'

Colin had not glanced up at Barbara. He didn't talk to her; they lived together in silent, hostile separation, speaking only to and through their son. But Toby wasn't saying much to Barbara either. It broke her heart to see the set expression on his small face, to notice his eyes sliding away from hers, to feel him duck out of any physical contact with his mother. When she asked him a question, he looked at Colin first to see him nod before answering briefly and with undisguised hostility.

Robert Stanley came into the hall. Barbara wondered whether she should get herself a different solicitor. But she could not bring herself to believe Colin would carry on distrusting her much longer. Nor could she really credit that anyone still supected her of a murder she did not commit. Why wasn't it patently obvious to all that she could not possibly have done it? How could anyone think she was capable of it? Surely they would find the real killer soon. Surely Colin would realise she was innocent. Without his moral support she was lost; oppressed by the feeling that he hated her, she was becoming almost suicidal. Two days before she had gone down to the garage with the vacuum cleaner as though to clean the inside of the car and tried fitting the hose on to the exhaust pipe. And then she realised that there was almost no petrol in the tank and went up again, back to the flat, and Toby came in from the beach and she told herself she'd been crazy, of course she wasn't going to gas herself. Things would have to get better soon.

They hadn't yet.

Oh Colin, oh Toby.

What can I do, how can I prove to you that I'm the same Barbara, it's the world that's changed, not me. She thought, I don't care if Colin never makes love to me again so long as I live, if only he trusts me. And tells Toby to trust me too.

Perhaps, she thought, after today Colin would be able to let Clarissa rest. Was an inquest like a funeral, did it draw a line, beyond which participants could go back to their own lives and start again?

'All rise,' the usher called.

The coroner had an ashy white face and deep wrinkles and folds of hanging skin, as though he had once been stout and rubicund but was now dwindling from illness. He sat slowly, patting and stacking his papers, before raising his head to survey the room.

Robert was not officially representing either Colin or Barbara, since she had not been charged and was not a party to the proceedings. But Robert had decided to attend just in case. He turned to scan the crowded public seats, smiled at Barbara and sat down beside Colin.

Neville Cox sat on his own: a sober, responsible, grief-stricken man who had lost his son and then his wife, a man to be pitied.

This coroner was a lawyer, but he seemed to relish the medical and forensic details, especially those which described the horrific post-mortem changes to the battered, bleeding body of Clarissa/Buffy as it lay in a hot and airless room for unnumbered days. It was almost as though, Fidelis thought, the coroner were considering his own imminent end.

The proceedings were not long or revelatory. Evidence as to identity; uncertain time and date of death, undoubted cause of death. Verdict, murder by person or persons unknown.

It was afterwards, standing half-way down the stairs in a scrum of people, most of them women, who were waiting to leave the building, that Fidelis found herself half hearing, half lip-reading through the wrought-iron banisters a muttered conversation between the policeman she had already met, Jack Berriman, and a man who, from his friendly recognition of her earlier on, presumably represented Barbara Pomeroy. He was talking about something called the *terminus ante quem* – the time boundary before which the murder victim must have been alive. The police officer was saying something about milk and bread as the two men moved away in the scrum of people and Fidelis was swept on towards the door and out into what was by now a full-blown gale. As she reached the pavement, the press halted to let some traffic pass by: a group of black-leathered bikers. Distracted, Fidelis wondered why the word she first thought of, before making herself correct it, had been 'gang' and then she followed her own train of thought to the break-in at her flat the summer before, by what her neighbours had described as 'kids in bikers' gear'. The press of people was stuck in the narrow lane, and an image of her own violated rooms made Fidelis briefly shudder. The mess in the kitchen . . . she had thrown everything in the bin. Spiteful burglars could have left poisoned or contaminated food just as easily as taking it away.

Left food behind . . .

There was milk and bread and a newspaper in Buffy/Clarissa's flat. Her death was dated by them, a date before which she must have been alive. But what if someone had put them there to falsify the apparent date of death? What if someone had needed to show that the obvious suspect could not have done the murder because by then he or she had been out of reach?

The perfect alibi, she thought.

The hard wind drove against her face and Fidelis wiped water from her eyes. At that moment the sound of a siren soared above the other sounds of the town. The crowd was momentarily still and silenced, recognising the summons to the lifeboat crew; then nearly everybody turned together and bustled or ran down towards the harbour to see the boat launched.

Fidelis found herself alone with Sophie Teague. She faced her, two tall women, eye to eye, and Sophie stretched her lips in that tender, archaic, endearing smile which had melted Fidelis's heart, and put out her arm to encircle the older woman's shoulders in a gesture of protective affection.

'Sophie.'

'Mmm?'

'What were you doing at Bullwood Hall?'

'Where?'

'That day we first met in Dorchester, a man remembered you'd been there. It's a young persons' detention centre, isn't it, and a women's prison? Why were you there?'

'God, Fidelis, you're going back a bit. I had a job there once. Why d'you ask?'

'Had you been sent there? Is that what your mother meant when she mentioned all your troubles?'

'Fidelis, I really don't know what you're on about, but do come on, let's get back to the cottage, you're getting drenched. You'll catch your death.'

Solicitous, kind, loving, caring, helpful Sophie.

Fidelis said, 'I've got things to do, Sophie, you go back. I'll see you later.'

'But Neville's brought lunch to Hyacinth Cottage for us. Local prawns and smoked salmon, just what you like.'

'You go.' The girl did not move, and Fidelis said, 'I want to do something on my own.' It reminded her she had bought a picture the other day, intended to be a present for Sophie. She knew Sophie had watched her buying the Perdita Whitchurch painting. She said, 'It's a surprise.'

Sophie said, 'Goody, I love surprises.'

'I'll see you later.'

Alone, Fidelis walked slowly down to the harbour. She put her hood back and let the hard rain batter against her face, not knowing herself whether the water in her eyes was tears.

She moved again when the lifeboat returned safely from a false alarm, bouncing on the waves. A tall young man was saying into a hand-held microphone, 'The St Ives lifeboat was launched in a force nine gale this afternoon . . .'

She walked on, slipping on the cobbled pavement, along the harbour front, past the Sloop Inn, into which a crowd of sodden tourists was now pressing, past a row of shops which had not opened for the season yet.

There was a telephone box.

While Fidelis hesitated, a man went in and she thought, That's it, I won't. I don't have to.

But he came out immediately. Perhaps I haven't got the right change, she thought, but it was a card phone and she had her card. With hesitating fingers Fidelis dialled directory inquiries, and then tapped out the number she had been given.

There might still be a way out. If the psychologist she knew was not there at Bullwood any more, she'd give up. But he was. There was his familiar voice.

'Steven Pettifer.'

'Steven, it's Fidelis Berlin.'

'Hullo, stranger, long time no hear. How's you then?' She had forgotten his invincible facetiousness, an understandable defence mechanism against the jeering, hostile women with whom he spent most of his working life but exhausting in normal life. Fidelis explained that she wanted to ask about someone she believed to have been an inmate.

'Sophie Teague. I'm not sure she was an inmate but – '

'I can tell you about her without even checking the files, I was talking about her only the other day with Dermot Brown, who used to be on the staff. I remember Sophie perfectly.'

Indeed, alas, he did. Sophie had been sent to Bullwood Hall for theft. She had a long previous history of minor offences, dishonesty and drugs. 'It was a sad case, as it happens,' Steven said, jokiness banished when he got on to his professional expertise. 'Her father grassed on her. She'd forged some of his cheques. He must have been a very unforgiving character, I read the court transcript, he wanted the book thrown at the girl. She got fifteen months.'

'Why do you remember her so well?'

'She wasn't quite our usual run of customer, very bright indeed, very naughty – skilled forger, while she was here she nearly got away with . . . well, never mind. She was a natural leader, always knew how to convince all the girls to do just what she wanted. A very manipulative character, she made people believe she cared for them. Do you remember the occupational therapist, Fay Ashe, such a nice, well-meaning woman?'

'Yes, I knew her once.'

'Sophie Teague took her in properly, behaved like a daughter, all solicitous and affectionate – but it was all a con trick, of course, she was trying to – '

'I don't need to know it all, Steven,' Fidelis said hoarsely.

'No, it's all old history now, though poor Fay never came back to work again. That Sophie . . . Dermot was telling me about her now, she's doing a degree . . .'

Fidelis stood clutching the receiver. She ignored a boy who tapped insistently on the glass, mouthing, 'Hurry up.'

Then Steven said, 'Her father died not long after she got out, didn't he? There was some question about it, she was suspected of having something to do with – though I shouldn't gossip. But his brakes failed and people said she might have tampered with them.'

'Would she have known how?'

'She was top of the car maintenance class here, and I have to say I could quite believe it of her. A very smooth operator, but ruthless, I'd say. Why are you asking?'

'Steven, I'm running out of money. I'll call you back.' Fidelis put the telephone down and went out into the rain.

A police car was parked on double yellow lines beside a sandwich shop. Jack Berriman, wearing a trench coat and trilby like a detective in a pre-war movie, came out holding a package of food and a polystyrene mug. 'Dr Berlin.'

'Inspector Berriman.'

'Well, you can't say we aren't showing you Cornwall at its worst.'

'I've got something to tell you.'

'Get in out of the rain then.'

Fidelis looked at the luridly marked car and shrank back. Glancing at her ravaged face, the detective put his food on the passenger seat and shut the door. 'There's an umbrella in the boot.' He held it over her head and they walked side by side up among the cottages, round to the other beach, the one which faced west, where wet-suited surfers seized the torrential waves.

She didn't have very much to say to him. No suspicions or inferences, no hints or rumours. Only facts: the fact of Neville Cox's financial problems, the fact of his relationship with Sophie Teague. The fact of where to check up on Sophie herself.

It was after Berriman had left her, with grave, formal thanks, that she stood alone piecing together the little scraps of information and memory which made a picture to break her heart.

There before her eyes was Neville arriving home to an empty house. He wouldn't notice anything wrong at first. Buffy must be out with the girls, walking round the block, down at the hairdressers. And then he'd ring round the neighbours. 'Is Buffy with you? Have you seen Buffy?'

How long before he realised she had emptied the bank accounts? And even then, it would take him a while to understand what Buffy had done. He would never have thought she had it in her. He probably didn't expect her to have taken in that she was the legal owner of all the property he thought of as his own.

She'll be back soon, he'd tell himself, she's just trying it on.

How long before Neville was in real trouble? Fidelis wondered. How long before he was desperate enough to work it out?

The letter from Toby Pomeroy's mother.

Of course Neville must have seen that when it came. Buffy would never have kept it secret from him, Andrew's father. She might reasonably have expected him to feel about it as she did. Reasonably? Fidelis brushed the doubt aside. The morals of spare part surgery were not her concern today. All that mattered was that Neville would not have had much trouble in guessing where Buffy had gone, or in then tracking her down in this little town. Would he have telephoned first, or come in person straight away?

Easy to imagine his bullying, overbearing attitude. 'Come home at once, you're ill, obsessed, unbalanced . . .' He wouldn't have believed her when she told him she was going to stay on in St Ives. 'Come on, old girl, a joke's a joke but enough is enough.'

Perhaps he talked about money. Perhaps Buffy said it was all hers by law, she'd taken advice, she knew the position, Neville might think he had a right to it but Buffy had another idea and what's more she was going to leave it all to Toby Pomeroy.

All Neville's fortune to a completely strange little boy! One could almost pity him when he realised she meant it. Did that justify what he did? Or at least explain it?

Neville had to act quickly before Buffy could sign her new will. Neville stole a wet suit – easy enough to do here, as Fidelis had observed – used it as a coverall while he killed his wife and washed her blood away in the sea.

Had it been unpremeditated, the result of a fit of frustration and rage, Fidelis wondered and hoped, or had he planned it carefully?

Later on, he did plan. Almost at once he must have realised the money would be out of his reach for good if the body were never identified as his wife's. But as soon as Clarissa was identified as Buffy Cox, he'd be the first to be suspected.

And that, of course, was why he asked me, reliable, respectable

Dr Berlin, foolish, credulous, incurious Fidelis Berlin, to find her. Now I see it, Fidelis realised. Only an innocent man could have wanted to find her so badly, he knew I'd believe that, and tell the police so. And I did.

I believed him. I trusted him.

I trusted her.

And I loved her.

Sophie had been the first woman Fidelis could remember loving, since once before she had (or so, at least, she assumed) loved a woman and lost her. All her life she had doubted – emotionally, even if not intellectually – that her mother really loved her too.

'I've been kidding myself,' she said aloud. 'I so wanted to believe my love was returned. Funny, that. Love always made me more observant before. I've always loved men as a way of knowing them better. With Sophie I have been blind, right from the very first moment back in the Town Hall in Dorchester, when she met Neville Cox. I introduced them to each other myself.'

A right pair, they were. Made for each other.

No, don't, don't think that. He corrupted her.

Fidelis stopped herself, made herself think dispassionately that Sophie was already corrupt, the whole thing could have been his idea or hers.

Neville picked up the spare set of keys he'd found in the St Ives flat and gave them to Sophie. Either of them might have thought of her going there to plant evidence that she was alive after he had left for America.

Sophie roaring down on her powerful motor bike, three hours from London at her speed. Unidentifiable in leathers she bought milk and bread and a newspaper in a garage shop, entering the flat to put the clues in the hall kitchen.

Oh Sophie.

At least she needn't have seen the body. They said the door was closed. Perhaps she didn't go in. She might not have known exactly what he'd done. She didn't have to go in there.

Fidelis moved down towards the water's edge and stood with the furious, icy waves washing over her expensive leather shoes and flannel trousers, unconscious of the tide, unaware of the sodden strands of hair whipping across her cheeks. She felt so disappointed and mortified she could have walked out into the murderous sea and drowned her shame. Foolish, blind, bedazzled ...

Clever perceptive Fidelis, kidding myself I had the understanding to advise other people. The love may have been brief but the disillusion will be very long. As a soul doctor, I'm done for, Fidelis thought. I'll never work again.

Facts, facts. Remember what happened, not what you thought.

Sophie had realised Fidelis wasn't getting there. She pushed pre-prepared clues in front of her eyes so blatantly it was a wonder Fidelis hadn't realised it before. Manufactured postcards or Christmas cards to show that Buffy was in St Ives. The picture from the local paper of a portrait which really didn't look at all like Buffy and even less like the old snapshot of her at Knighton Rise Sophie had claimed it resembled. A holiday brochure from Cornwall.

She doesn't love or care for me at all. She used me.

26

Later – minutes? Hours? Long enough, in any case, for the sea to have retreated some distance from where Fidelis still stood – she felt a hand on her arm.

'Dr Berlin? Fidelis? I saw you from my window and thought perhaps . . .' It was Barbara Pomeroy. 'Are you all right?'

Fidelis was drawn back to the moment, and to a vestige of the saving, cynical realism which had been the bedrock of her life. She thought, this wasn't the first time a professional had been taken for a ride by a con-artist and it wouldn't be the last. The only miracle was that it hadn't ever happened to her, to Fidelis, before. A misreading, that was all.

She looked through eyes screwed up against wind and water at Barbara Pomeroy. The rain had turned Barbara's hair into slimy spirals and soaked through her proofed jacket and jeans, to whose darkened denim patches of sand uncomfortably clung. She looked cold and unhappy.

'I suppose I'd better . . .' Fidelis did not want to go back to the rented house where Sophie and Neville must be. She had a flash-vision of them as she entered: jumping guiltily apart, ready to perform their rehearsed untruths. 'Perhaps a cup of coffee first . . .' she murmured.

Barbara was in no hurry to return to the silent suspicion of her husband and son and to the heap of accusatory fax messages sent from the planning inspectorate.

'We could go in there,' she said, pointing towards the Tate's exotic glass and painted white curves. Side by side the two women battled against the wind towards the gallery. Its entrance consisted of an external rotunda with three tiers of benches used as a surf-board park. Several were propped against the walls, along with discarded wet suits and mammalian flippers.

Their sodden, sandy shoes grated against brick steps and white vinyl floors. In the cloakroom Fidelis rubbed a towel over her face, and then wiped the damp paper more carefully under her eyes to remove the trails of make-up. She tugged a comb through her dripping grey hair and passed it to Barbara, saying, 'Here you are, madam inspector.'

The reminder of that status brought Barbara back from the psychic wasteland in which she had been standing. Running hot water over her icy hands she said, 'That's all over.'

'No. It's going to be all right.' Fidelis used her professionally reassuring voice, a voice which had calmed down many more difficult subjects than Barbara. To use it was even soothing for herself, reminding her who and what she was. She leant across to turn off the tap and handed Barbara a towel.

They went up the stairs in a jostle of other damp visitors. The main galleries were closed to the public while the press had its preview of a new hanging of work by the St Ives painters, and several journalists from London had just arrived to see it. They chattered loudly with the self-confidence of those who are paid to express their opinions.

The journey – too far to come, too inconvenient, the wrong time of year. The weather. Out in the sticks, down in the boondocks. Daphne du Maurier country – history, mystery, twistery. Where were the gorgeous brutes of fiction? one woman squeaked. Roll on Seth or Max.

Names, dropped and brandished: Ben, Barbara, Peter, Naum. The conversation of insiders.

Fidelis, who would normally have understood it if not joined in, at home herself in this transplanted world of metropolitan, intellectual fashions and artistic movements, slid her eyes without interest over and past the huge, wild oil paintings by the abstract artists and the more accessible little landscapes. If great art consoles, she thought, this can't be great art; or I'm inconsolable.

'The café's up another floor,' Barbara said.

A large room at the top of the building, white and chrome, grey and black, with a view of the whole town and its surrounding sea, a scene from which colour had been leached. Rain lashed relentlessly against the glass. Barbara moved to the other window.

'Are you staying here?'

'On the island, near Porthgwidden Beach,' Fidelis said, pointing in the direction of the island, so called, actually a grassy headland crowned by the fishermen's bleak chapel to St Nicholas which, in many works of art, seemed to symbolise St Ives.

'There's something going on over there today. Police cars. Toby went to have a look. Something to do with the lifeboat going out, I suppose,' Barbara said.

A young waitress brought a tray of steaming drinks over to them. 'They're saying the fuzz have blocked off the approaches to the island. Nobody knows if it's to do with that murder or drug smuggling, but I heard there's a criminal hiding out there. There's only three roads off the island, he's holed up like a squirrel. God, I hope they don't get him before the end of my shift. Half an hour to go.'

Fidelis moved to look out in the other direction, away from the action the waitress was trying to see.

It was so wet outside that the glass wall was like the side of a vast aquarium, and the black, leaping, twisting figures could have been marine monsters at the bottom of the sea rather than humans skimming its surface. Absorbed, skilled and infinitely graceful, they made her momentarily sad that her whole sedentary life had gone by without so purely physical or athletic a delight.

Like seals, the surfers lost their grace when they moved on to the land. Some of them were leaving the water now, half a dozen black bipeds waddling on their flapping flippers up the awkward sand. Two more hurried up behind them, from the north-east side of the beach, to catch up, and moved with the group towards the shelter of the gallery's circular entrance.

'You know about Allday Properties, don't you?' Barbara Pomeroy said.

Fidelis took a moment to understand the question before shaking her head. She said, 'Do you mean Brian Day?'

173

'His lot, yes. Brian Day and Neville Cox. Clarissa's husband. You must be involved with them, otherwise why are you here?'

'No, the only one of their concerns I have anything to do with is Cox Kindergartens, but of course I do know Brian Day through that. Allday must be named after his wife, Allie Day.'

'Could she be the one who threatened me?'

Fidelis did not know what Barbara was talking about, though realised the other woman did not quite believe her when she said so. All the same, Barbara did explain. Her words should have been practised for she had told numerous people the same story by this time, but every time she mentioned the threat to Toby she stumbled and her voice shook.

Fidelis Berlin was the first person to hear it who immediately grasped what had happened and how dreadful it was. Her face was already drawn and pale, the make-up dissolved to reveal the traces of every long day of her age. Now it seemed to grow even more long and gaunt. Her bloodless lips drew in upon themselves in an expression of pain and grief. 'How could she? How could any woman have done that, threatened your child – for any money?'

'Who? Do you know who rang me up?'

Yes. Fidelis knew.

Had Sophie always wanted money, ever since that juvenile crime which had sent her to Bullwood Hall? Or had she been a reformed character, studying, taking her degree, planning her research and career like a virtuous daughter of the professional classes?

No. Standing in the steamy chill of a late Cornish Spring, Fidelis remembered the heavy heat of London the previous June, when she had come home to find her apartment ransacked. The neighbours had seen a biker; and when Sophie wrote pleading for a job, she knew what ornaments Fidelis treasured. What had she said? The words returned, Fidelis's voice reading them aloud to the sceptical Tina. 'I could clean your copper and porcelain.' Yes, Sophie knew very well what she wanted, when she came up to Fidelis that day in Sherbury and introduced herself. The girl knew all about her already.

And then I introduced her to Neville Cox, Fidelis thought. Through me, she moved in with a man whose guiding motive was always money. And then it was back to old tricks and on to dreadful new ones. Forging Buffy's name on cheques. Becoming

Neville's accomplice in murder. Extorting an enriching planning permission out of a tortured mother.

'And I don't even know how they knew!' Barbara wailed, as she had so many times already. 'How did they know who I was, and about Toby? I still don't understand.'

'But you wrote to them, don't you remember?' Fidelis said. 'You wrote to thank the parents of the transplant donor.'

'You mean Clarissa – ? Her child? Toby's kidney? Is that why she came? Colin told me not to do it but I meant so well!' Barbara had not wept before. Now difficult tears began to roll out of her eyes.

Fidelis felt the hard surface of her lifelong public face closing over her wound. Listening as Barbara wept about her husband and son, taking it in and understanding the other woman's pain, she thought, I'll cope as I always have, I'll be the better and stronger for this, I'll know more about human nature.

She heard her own warm, reassuring voice say, 'It will be all right. I am sure of it. Your husband will be so sorry. I expect the police have told him already.'

As the two women turned towards the stairs, they saw that a man and a boy had come into the room and were standing there silently. Colin Pomeroy was very upright, like a soldier on parade, his eyes forward and lips rigid. He put his hand on his son's shoulders and gave a gentle push. Toby stepped forward towards Barbara, and when she opened her arms to him, he ran forward into her embrace. Colin came forward more slowly and Barbara took one hand from her son and held it out to her husband.

'Toby will be safe now,' he said. 'They can't get away, the police will catch them whichever road they take. A man and a woman, Clarissa's husband and his girlfriend. They killed her.'

That man won't ever apologise, Fidelis thought as she went alone down the stairs, but it will be implicit in his behaviour and Barbara will forgive him immediately and not say anything about it either. They are both so reserved and buttoned up, that's a relationship of deeds not words.

And what about me? she wondered. Pausing to consider her own reaction, Fidelis realised her familiar mind was already at work on the problem, an observant analyst at work on a human problem. Sophie had been an aberration; a learning experience. Catching sight of her reflection in a picture glass, Fidelis nodded as though to a friend who was at last herself.

Down below as the gale backed and lessened, while the police cars blocked the lanes leading to the narrow peninsula of the island, and lurked on all the roads which led away from St Ives, while criminal records computers chattered and whirred, a pair of wet-suited surfers, carrying flippers and masks and with their concealing goggles pushed only a little way above their eyes, padded quietly and unobserved up the hill and out of the little town.